Reunion

Published by:
Spirit Light Publishing
Amarillo, TX,
through lulu.com
www.spiritlightbooks.com

Printed in the United States of America

Cover Design, Ash Arceneaux
www.ashleyroland.com

Library of Congress Cataloging-in-Publication Data
is available upon request.

ISBN 978-0-615-24290-3

Reunion

Staci Stallings

To my loyal fans, those who ask how it's going,
those who ask when the next book's coming,
those who call to get more chapters,
and those who encourage, support, and love me.
You will never know the difference you make!

God BLESS you ALL!

Fearing that she would be knocked off either by them or by the jerking of the trailer, Camille grabbed onto the bale of hay behind her. It was in the next breath that she realized who was sitting right next to her, but the tractor was already going too fast to jump off and run.

"Oh, sorry," Jaylon said, regaining his balance. He ran two sets of fingers through his dark brown hair to push it out of his eyes. "You okay?"

No words would come as she nodded even though her body still clung to the bale. He was so close, the smell of his cologne made her head spin dangerously.

"Who's that?" Seth asked, bending down so he could get a look at Camille.

"Camille," Jaylon whispered when he stopped long enough to see her. The name was obviously supposed to be an introduction, but it hardly made it from his mouth to her ears. He looked stunned speechless.

Chapter 1

"Mail call," Liz Rivas said as she dropped a stack of various-sized envelopes into Camille Wright's in-box.

"Anything interesting?" Camille asked, winding a light brown strand of straight hair around one ear although she never looked up from the design that held her attention on her desk.

"A test printout on the carbon-alloy that they ran yesterday." Liz sorted through the letters. "The transcripts from your meeting with Baker, and this." She pulled a green postcard out of the stack and held it up.

Camille looked up and squinted behind her chic wire-rimmed glasses. "What's that?"

"An invitation to a reunion," Liz said with small smile and a raise of her eyebrows. "Ten years? Huh? Wow. I wouldn't have pegged you for a senior citizen already."

"Ha. Ha." Camille reached up and swiped the card out of Liz's hand. She leaned back in her chair and surveyed it. '*Ridgecrest High School is proud to invite you back...*' She glanced at the date but did little more before pitching it onto her desk.

"You're going, right?" Liz asked with interest.

As she bent back over her work, Camille shook her head, causing several strands of hair to fall around her face again. She quickly pushed them behind her ear and bent back over the sketches, wondering if there was a clip in her desk across the way. "Probably not."

Liz shifted her weight to her other shapely leg just below the professional black skirt. "What? You didn't like high school?"

It took little trouble to push the thought of high school away from her. "There's only a couple people I would even want to see again. Why put yourself through that for two people?"

"You never know it might be fun. Old friends, old stories...old boyfriends."

Without looking up, Camille reached for the pencil tucked behind her ear and made a small mark on the paper. "Could you get me the files on the dimensions for the cockpit controls again? This isn't fitting like it's supposed to."

"Sure." Liz stood at the door for a single second more. "By the way, Ben called earlier. He said they've got the conference date set. April 24th."

"Great," Camille said, her gaze and concentration glued to the markings on the large paper in front of her. "Pencil it in. I can't afford to miss this one."

And with that, Liz stepped out. Camille's pencil traced again over the line. More than a billion dollars rode on this one design—the NightViper, an aircraft that would take over where the F-19 Eagle left off, and for the business—not to mention the sake of her job, it had better be perfect. With that thought, she picked up the phone and punched speed dial 3 even as she continued making small marks on the plans. Two more marks and she leaned back in her chair, listening to the ringing of the phone.

A tap at a time she turned her pencil end-to-end as her gaze crossed her design table. Unconsciously she laid the pencil down and picked up the green postcard to skim it. '*April 12th. 6 p.m. The Grand Plaza Hotel, Ridgecrest, N.Y. Catered hors d'oeuvres and meal provided. RSVP by March 15th.*' At that moment the phone clicked in her ear, and she yanked her attention back to it.

"Rai." She leaned forward and flipped the invitation back onto her desk. "Have you gotten those trial cockpit designs finished yet? I need them."

"Michael! Hey, that's your line, man! Where'd you go?" Jaylon Quinn asked in frustration from his folding chair at the bottom of the stage. Script in hand he sat, listening to the first read-through without scripts. It was like fingernails scraping down a chalkboard.

"Sorry. What is it again?" the short, black-headed senior asked from the stage without even bothering to try to remember it.

"'We've got to get out of here before...'"

"Oh, yeah," Michael said, and then he turned back to his accomplice. "We've got to get out of here before they call the cops. Nobody with any sense will ever believe this story."

"She did," Clay Heish, Michael's blonde-headed, dim-witted accomplice, said.

"Like I said, 'Nobody with any sense will ever believe this!' Now, come on. Hand me that crowbar."

All motion on the stage stopped, and Jaylon waited a full thirty seconds before shaking his head. "Clay!"

Clay stared off the stage in concentration. "I forgot it."

"'Where is it? I thought it was right here,'" Jaylon supplied, losing patience with each word.

"Sorry." Clay nodded. "Where is it? I thought it was right here."

With two fingers, Jaylon rubbed the bridge of his nose, sighed, and then ran one set of fingers through his hair. Somehow when he'd decided on teaching, he had never envisioned this. Michael, his star student for the past three years had never once bothered to really memorize a script until two days before the performance, and with Clay as his accomplice this year, things were sure to deteriorate from there.

"Well, look around, it's got to be here somewhere," Michael hissed. "Crowbars don't just disappear. Hurry up. She'll be back any second."

Jaylon looked at his watch. Fifteen more minutes and he'd be sprung. He couldn't wait. The stage went quiet again as the two boys stood with no more lines to deliver waiting for the surprise entrance of their hostess who didn't appear.

"Karen!" Jaylon yelled a little too loudly. "That's your cue!"

In half-a-heartbeat, Karen, a young-looking sophomore, ran onto the stage. "Sorry, Mr. Quinn, I was talking to Bethany."

Jaylon scratched his cheek in frustration. "Don't apologize, just get on with it."

On stage the reading continued although Jaylon was only vaguely keeping up with it. How had he ever thought he could teach kids? To him, they were enigmas—like trying to nail pudding to a wall. His head was starting to pound.

Again too much silence enveloped the room, and this time even Jaylon didn't know how to fill it. "That's it." He stood, throwing both hands up in surrender. "We'll start there tomorrow. And Michael, could you please work on memorizing a little more?"

"Sure thing," Michael said with a smooth smile that Jaylon had long since learned meant, 'I'm not even going to think about what you just said between now and tomorrow.'

Jaylon shook his head and gathered his briefcase as the students filed off the stage.

"See ya tomorrow, Mr. Quinn," Karen said in her cotton candy sweet voice.

All he wanted to do was choke her, but he simply smiled and said, "Yeah, take care."

As slowly as humanly possible, Jaylon climbed the steps and stepped behind the curtain to snap off the lights. Behind the stage curtains, he made his way to the back door of the stage, which led to his office. Office? It would've been nice if it was an office. Actually it was more like a broom closet with a two-foot table and a small trail littered with boxes leading to the chair.

The room itself still smelled like ammonia from the janitor who had reluctantly agreed to relinquish the space to save Jaylon from having to drag the theatre material across campus from the main building to the auditorium, which doubled as a cafeteria.

When it was built, the auditorium was never really meant to be more than a small stage to hold talent shows and kids' choral performances. Brickhaven I.S.D. in upper New York State had never even had a drama program until Jaylon landed there three years before.

Drama, it had always been his first love, but two years of off-Broadway productions that closed before the first performance had pretty much killed his undying devotion to the stage as well as wiped out his bank account. So, when he saw the ad for an English teacher interested in starting up a drama program while scanning for jobs on the Internet, he had called about it immediately.

Somehow he should've known the rest of the story the second he drove into the tiny town with one flashing stop light and a grocery store the size of a small gas station. The fact that the superintendent interviewed him on the spot and called just two hours after he'd gotten home should also have set off the warning bells.

But they hadn't, and now here he was three years later, sucking down aspirin like candy and wondering how life had led him here.

Fighting off the depression, he yanked his briefcase stuffed with work off the floor and stalked out. He had papers to grade, but then again, he always had papers to grade.

He just hoped that tonight he could actually find a little time to get some of them done. The prospect of Nicole showing up with more wedding problems threatened to send him right off the edge as he climbed into the old, blue Camaro Z28 and turned the car for home.

If he could just make it to May the 3rd with a piece of his sanity left, life was sure to get better. It could get no worse. He turned off the pavement and veered over to the little mailbox standing in the ditch. With one hand he rolled down the window, pulled the latch open, and dug for the letters. He didn't even look at them, just flipped them into the passenger seat and continued down the dirt road to the little turn off.

How fortunate he'd felt when he found this place. A hundred years old and just the perfect size for him. What he hadn't counted on was one of the pipes breaking two months after he'd moved in, which led to re-plumbing the whole house, during which they found out the wiring was shot too. Of course it, too, had to be replaced for fear the entire structure might burn to the ground around him.

By the time those repairs were completed, the last thing he had money to do was to go house hunting again, and so he had stayed— despite the draft that wafted in through every window when the wind blew from the Northeast and the thick layer of dust that accumulated when he wasn't looking. And now, at least for the next five months, it was home.

When he turned the last corner to home, all hopes of getting any papers graded vanished. In the driveway sat the little white Mustang with the DDYS GRL vanity plates. Nicole.

A bag of groceries, briefcase, and a handful of various traveling paraphernalia in hand, Camille trudged up the three flights of stairs to her apartment. At the door, she wrestled with the things in her hands so that she could get her key into the lock. When the door swung open, she took one step inside and dropped everything to the floor.

"Well, hello, Max," she said to the giant orange tabby cat that scratched its back against the dividing wall in greeting to her. "Yes, I brought you some more food."

She locked the door behind her and picked up the bag from the floor.

"I know. I know. I told you I'd get Happy Cat, but they were out again." With the practice of a thousand performances, she pulled the cat bowl up to the sink, washed and dried it, and then filled one side with water and set it back on the floor. Quickly she picked up the bag of cat food, ripped it open, and dumped some into the bowl.

For one minute she sat on her heels, petting the animal at her feet as she laid her chin in her hand. "So, how was your day? Huh? Did Old Mr. Hathington behave himself, or did he yell all day again?"

The cat continued to eat as Camille stroked its soft fur. If only every moment could be this peaceful. Her thoughts traced back to the office, and as though the straightjacket had fallen over her again, she stood and walked back to the door to retrieve the briefcase.

She needed to have more than a few preliminary drawings completed before Ben's meeting in April. Funny how four months ago April had seemed like more than enough time. But that was before Ben left for the consulting job of a lifetime and dumped the leadership mantle onto her shoulders.

Who was she trying to kid anyway? She was barely 28. Who in their right mind puts a 28-year-old in charge of a major design like this one?

Ben. It was strange how she could never think of him without that by-now-familiar twang in her heart.

She had never so much as acted interested in him, but that didn't stop him. Oh, no. First it was coffee after work to talk about upcoming projects, then it was dinner with clients, then dinner with just the two of them. Always business, and yet always with an undercurrent of something else.

Without bothering to take off anything more than her heels, Camille threw a TV dinner into the microwave and punched the buttons. She knew what Ben had thought back in November when she'd called in sick for his first conference. Honestly, she wasn't avoiding him—it's not easy to give a speech when you're throwing your guts up.

But still, she knew he was hurt. She'd heard it in his voice when he'd called later in the week to tell her about the conference.

"I just wish I could've seen you," he'd said, and she heard the sadness. "I was looking forward to it."

"Yeah, so was I."

It was true. One part of her always looked forward to seeing him. It was just that the other parts constantly wondered what half-step forward they would take this time. He had never pushed. Never so much as asked her out point-blank. But the undercurrent when he was around was hard to deny. A hand on the small of her back to lead her to the table, a look a moment too long, laughing at all of her jokes—even the ones that weren't all that funny. It was all the little things that added up to something. Something she wasn't sure she was ready for. Something she wasn't sure she even wanted.

The microwave dinged, and she carefully pulled the dinner out and set it on the table next to her designs. Ben would be able to finish this in two seconds. He would be able to see the problem with the design in a breath. She could hear him even as she sat and looked over them, "It's your perspective, Camille. You're too close. Back up. Give it a breath, and your answer will be there."

Back up. If only she had the time to back up, that was exactly what she would've done. The only problem was, there was no time to back up anymore. Isaac needed these designs in two weeks, and it was becoming clear that even if she worked non-stop until then, that deadline would probably still be beyond her grasp.

In frustration, she forked a piece of dry Salisbury steak in her mouth before erasing a full inch of her design and starting over. "Who's dumb idea was this anyway? Ben, I swear you had to be out of your mind to recommend me for this."

Jaylon walked through his back door and found Nicole seated at his table with white envelopes and pink invitations stacked around her.

"I thought you were going to be here an hour ago." She flipped a lock of wavy platinum blonde hair over her shoulder testily although she never looked up from her work.

"We had first read-throughs today." He set his briefcase on the two inches of table not covered with invitations.

"Well, Mom's going to have an absolute conniption if we don't get these things addressed and out." With her pen she motioned across the disaster as he dutifully walked over and kissed the top of her head. "We've only got about two hundred more to do."

He stepped over to the cabinet to grab a glass. "That all?"

"Ha. Ha. You know, if we'd have gotten them done over the weekend like I wanted…"

"I was trying to catch up with everything else."

"Everything else?" she asked, an undercurrent of sarcasm yanking the words down. "Like what? Masterpiece Theatre?"

"I had all the contest applications to get in." He took a drink of water trying to swallow the annoyance. "And I had papers to grade and lesson plans to write…"

"Please." She put her hands on her ears. "No more teacher stuff. I'm begging you."

Jaylon considered explaining that teaching was his job and that it required a laundry list of other responsibilities, but he'd heard her comebacks to that so many times it was pointless to start down that road now.

He sat down at the table and grabbed a stack of envelopes and another stack of invitations. Maybe if they got the invitations out, then he could get on with his life.

"Did you call Cazenovia yet?" Nicole asked without looking up as she addressed an envelope in perfect calligraphy.

Knowing even as he did that she wouldn't be pleased, Jaylon shook his head as his hands slid an invitation into the envelope. "I didn't have time."

"Didn't have time?" She looked up as her shaped eyebrows came together. "This isn't some little unimportant detail, you know? This is our future we're talking about."

"I know. I know. I thought about it at lunch, but I had cafeteria duty."

Nicole clicked her tongue in exasperation as her gaze dropped back to the invitations. "I really can't wait until you get a real job. Cafeteria duty? Jeez. If I have to hear about that the rest of my life…"

What? he wanted to ask. *Would that really be so terrible?* Sure, he didn't like a lot of things about his job, but it was a job. It was respectable, and for the most part it wasn't so bad. For a few hours a day he got to do something he really loved, but Nicole always found a way to make that sound so trivial, so beneath him, so beneath her.

"I had lunch with Daddy today," she said as her voice sweetened like honey. "His offer's still open."

"I already told you I'm not management material."

She laughed, and the sarcasm was back. "What do you mean? That's what you do all day—except you manage barbarians and don't get paid for it."

Reining in his fatigue and growing frustration, Jaylon ran his fingers through his hair. "I'm happy teaching."

Again with the tongue-clicking thing. "You know, unless you get on with a college at least as big as Cazenovia, teaching's a dead-end street. You know that and so do I."

He set his jaw. "Well, I'm not managing."

"Well, then I suggest you don't keep *forgetting* to make that phone call."

Camille's mind wanted a break. It needed a break. It had been working nearly non-stop since six-thirty that morning, and it was beginning to show signs of totally shutting down. Slowly she stood from the table, padded down the short hallway to her room and then into her bathroom. Nothing about her apartment was spectacular. It wasn't that she didn't make more than enough money to have a great apartment. It was just that those kinds of things had never held much interest for her.

On autopilot she undressed and pulled the knob to start the water. She reached up and pulled the clip out of her hair, which immediately sent the shoulder-length locks tumbling down. When she looked in the mirror across the room, even she had to admit she looked tired. A nice, long, hot shower and then maybe she could stay awake long enough to finish the plane's nose. If she didn't, she could always fall into bed exhausted enough to fall asleep.

Her worn out feet stepped into the shower, and instantly the rest of her body began to shut down with her brain. It was the same story every night. She was so tired she could barely keep her eyes open—until her head actually hit the pillow. Then her overtired brain simply wouldn't turn off and go to sleep. The designs were usually first and foremost in her thoughts, but there were other things too—like her little sister Daria and how things were going for her in North Carolina.

Why the girl had to pick somewhere so far away to go to school was still beyond Camille's grasp. After all it wasn't like they didn't have computers in New York. The thought crossed her mind that she needed to be watching for the tuition bill in the next couple of days. It was sure to be crossing her desk soon.

Mail crossing her desk wound her thoughts back to the green postcard, and her hands rubbed the edges of her arms. It had been so long since Ridgecrest, since Lexie, and Nick, and the play, and... With a jerk she opened her eyes and pumped the shampoo nozzle twice. She wasn't going, so it was silly to even think about it.

Silly. But still her heart filled her whole chest as the memories of days long past surged through her.

The anger was still in Jaylon's chest hours later as he sat on the soft mattress of his bed running a red pen over the last of the three stacks of papers. Nicole or no Nicole he was determined not to shirk his duties to this school or to these kids. There were already enough people doing that to them.

For too many of them, school was their one and only stable place in the whole world. That was simply the sad fact of life. He slid the top paper off the stack and came face-to-face with Michael's. Slowly Jaylon shook his head. Three years with that kid, and as far as Jaylon could tell, nothing much had changed. He was as unfocused and flighty as he had been during their first meeting—and just as talented.

A sigh escaped Jaylon's throat as he wrote the grade on the top of the paper and continued on through the stack. Next year, Michael would be gone, off to live his own life somewhere far away from Brickhaven, and what good had Jaylon really done for him? Forced him to memorize a few lines for plays that had been long since forgotten? What was that in the whole scheme of life? What good could that ever do anyone?

A pang stung through the middle of the anger. Those words—so hated and yet so familiar. They were always with him. It was like he couldn't really get away from them for any length of time.

Some small piece of him whispered that his father was right all along, but quickly he slammed that door shut even as he put the graded stack into his briefcase and slammed the lid. It did make a difference. It had to. If it didn't, then what was the point of living in the first place?

With three kicks he pulled himself off the bed and stomped to the closet to lay out his clothes for the next morning. Tomorrow would be different. Tomorrow he wouldn't let the long hours and the nagging kids and the frustrated co-workers get to him. Tomorrow he would be the teacher they deserved—the one they would remember long after Brickhaven was just a spec in the distance.

Like Mrs. Allen had been for him. As he snapped off the light and climbed under the covers, a smile came to his face. Mrs. Allen. He hadn't really thought of her in a long time. He wondered for a moment if she was even still teaching, even still in Ridgecrest. She would never believe it if she could see him now.

Sleep began its advance over his eyelids. No, Mrs. Allen would never believe it. How could she? He didn't.

At two thirty in the morning, her hair in a tangled, matted mess, Camille stumbled out of her room and back to the kitchen table. It was a confirmed fact. She would never get any sleep until these stupid designs were finished. She sat down and looked for a long moment at the phone.

Calling Ben now could be the very signal he'd been waiting for, but she was in no state to argue with herself. Trying not to think about what she was doing, she dialed the number and listened to the phone ring. "Come on, Ben. Where are you?"

"Hello?" the groggy voice on the other end finally said.

"Hi, did I wake you?" she asked, already running her pencil over the designs.

"Camille? What time is it?"

"Two-thirty."

"And you ask if you woke me up? Uh—duh!"

"I'm having some problems with these designs. You think I could run them by you?"

There was a long pause on his end. "Sure. I'll go turn on my computer."

"Thanks, Ben. I don't know what I'd do without you."

Chapter 2

The only thing that took more time than grading papers was going through the week's mail. There was no sense in trying to keep up with it during the week—Jaylon had learned that much his first semester at Brickhaven. So his solution was to simply pile it all in one spot and deal with it on Saturdays.

Over a cup of coffee and half-a-bagel, he sat at his table Saturday morning sorting. Bill. Bill. Trash. Magazine—put it in the pile to read if he ever got time to read something he wanted to again. More trash. More bills. It was truly amazing how much paper went through his house on a weekly basis. Bill. Bill.

Then his fingers came to a small green postcard, which he almost flipped over into the trash pile, but at the last second something caught his attention. Slowly he pulled it back into his field of vision and surveyed it. *Ridgecrest.*

A million memories—some good, some heart wrenching—jumped to his mind with the mere mention of that word. His gaze skimmed the card once and then again as he fought to get enough brain space free from the memories to comprehend what the card was telling him.

It had been nearly five full years since he'd been back to Ridgecrest although he thought about the place every other minute. There was no reason to go back there anymore. His grandmother had passed on when he was in college, and his dad's heart attack and subsequent funeral had dissipated most of the rest of the reasons he had to ever go back.

The only friends he had left in the town were Nick and Lexie McGee, but he hadn't seen them in years, and he wasn't even truly sure that they would ever want to see him again.

Lexie and Nick. Just the thought of them brought a sad smile to his face. That seemed like such a long time ago. Decades. Eons. He hadn't made it to their wedding although he had wanted to go. That was two nights before the opening of what was supposed to be his big, breakthrough performance. As he thought about it now, he should've gone to the wedding. The curtain had never so much as gone up on his big, breakthrough performance.

He pushed that thought and the stinging in his heart away. It didn't matter anyway. They were just being nice. It wasn't like they really wanted him at their wedding. They'd just sent him the invitation because of...

With a jerk he snapped that thought in half and pitched the postcard into the trash pile. Going back made no sense at all. He had too many other things going on—not the least of which was his wedding three weeks later. At that thought, he looked at the clock and downed the rest of his coffee.

If he didn't get going, he was going to be late to meet Nicole and her parents. Quickly he stood and picked up the trash pile. The trash can lid snapped up, and he dumped the contents of his hands into the top of it and smashed them down. Take the trash out. That was one more thing he needed to do. One more. And one more. And one more. If they could somehow form a logical line, maybe there would be hope to find his way out of them.

However, with another glance at the clock, he knew that tackling anything more than lunch was too much to ask right now.

The phone at Camille's elbow jangled, and in annoyance she looked at it. That was the purpose of working on Saturdays—no distractions. She let it ring twice more before she decided that it might be Isaac.

"Baker and Marsden. This is Camille." Deftly she laid the receiver between her shoulder and her ear even as she continued to trace across the page.

"Boy am I good or what?" a female voice asked in amusement.

Instantly the tracing stopped. "Lex?"

"What? Do you just work all the time?" Lexie asked as a loud squealing noise erupted in the background.

Camille smiled. "What's up?"

"Oh, the kids are driving me crazy. You?"

"Trying to fit a needle over a hundred thousand haystacks."

Lexie sighed as another shriek sounded behind her. "Hey, Samantha. Stop teasing your broth... Just a second."

Leaning back in her chair, Camille flipped her pencil to the desk and listened to Lexie play diplomatic authoritarian. It was a nice change of pace from the banality of her own workstation. Twisting the cord with her, she spun her chair around to look out across the Pittsburgh skyline. The trees in the distance called to her as thoughts of upper New York State wound around her in a perfect coil.

The last time she'd been back was for Samantha's baptism, and before that it was for Lexie and Nick's wedding. But nothing in Ridgecrest had ever felt complete since she had left there ten years before to go to Princeton. At the time she was following her dream, but now that she was living that dream, she wondered why it had ever felt so important.

"I'm back." Lexie's voice snapped Camille out of her reverie. "I swear that Goddaughter of yours is going to be the death of me yet."

Camille laughed but barely made a sound. "She must take after Nick."

"Well, she takes after somebody, but I don't think Nick is even that bad."

"How's Ryann?" Camille asked as she went through the dates and realized it had been more than eight months since the little girl had been born, and although she kept making promises to come see her, that trip had yet to materialize. In fact, the trip for Austin's birth three years before hadn't even happened yet. It was a vicious cycle promising and then finding an excuse not to go until they had both given up even having that conversation.

"Growing," Lexie said with a small laugh. "She says mama now, but only for me. She won't say it for Nick. It drives him up the wall."

Nostalgia wrapped around Camille as she closed her eyes. "How is Nick?"

"Same as always. He's supposed to take the kids out to the circus today so I can get some cleaning done. Three kids and a husband, this place is a disaster 98 percent of the time."

Without wanting it to, Camille's mind traced over to her own sparse apartment, and the loneliness of it enfolded her. "I bet Austin can't wait for the circus."

"You got that right. Nick made the mistake of telling him about it last night, and that's all I've heard all day long, 'But how much *longer*?' You'd think the kid was going to go into cardiac arrest if he didn't see a lion or a tiger in the next two minutes. Samantha! I said, 'Quit it!'"

Another shriek and again Lexie apologized just before she dropped the phone. Camille didn't mind the interruption. It sounded too much like the home she'd always wanted but never had.

"You want a couple kids?" Lexie asked when she came back on the line. "I'll sell 'em to you real cheap."

Camille laughed. "Thanks, but I think they're much better off where they are."

"Well, okay, but if I kill one of them, I'm naming you as an accessory." Then she was gone again. "Okay! That's it! Both of you, go to your rooms until your dad gets home. I don't care who had it first. Go!" In seconds she was back. "Ahhh!"

"Sounds like you have your hands full."

"Nothing out of the ordinary. Let me tell you." After a deep breath, Lexie paused. "So, did you get your invite yet?"

The question slammed Camille back to reality as her chair dropped down off the spring. "Oh, uh, yeah." She swung the chair around, picked up the pencil, and pushed the edge of her glasses up with it. "You?"

"I'm on the invite committee," Lexie said as though that information should've been perfectly obvious. "That's why I sent it to your office."

"Huh?" Camille asked in confusion.

"I figured you'd never see it if we sent it to your place. I mean, you're never there."

"I'm there."

"Camille, what day is it?"

She glanced at her calendar. "Uh, the 25th of January."

"No, ding-dong, day of the week."

"Oh, uh, Saturday," Camille said as she pushed her glasses up again, nervous although she had absolutely no idea why.

"Precisely, and where are you?"

"At..."

"Work," Lexie finished for her, and Camille shrank under the chagrin in her friend's voice.

"So, I'm busy. Is that a crime?"

"It is if you're using work to avoid life," Lexie said from point-blank range.

Camille shifted the phone to the other shoulder and pulled out a stack of printouts from the in-box. She should've had them memorized by now, but still they looked like some unintelligible foreign language. "You know, Lex. It's been great talking to you and all..."

"But you have to go," Lexie finished for her.

"I'll call you sometime when I have a little more time to talk." She dug through the printouts searching for the one with the dimensions of the cockpit seats.

"Yeah."

The line went silent for a full thirty seconds.

"Well, I'd better let you go," Lexie finally said with a sigh.

"Uh-huh. Take care." Camille picked the phone off of her shoulder. "And, hey, thanks for calling. Give the kids a kiss for me, and Nick a kiss for you."

"I will."

"Talk to you later." And they signed off. It wasn't until the phone was back in its cradle that Camille allowed herself the luxury of thinking again. Lexie had always known her far too well. Of course she was in the office on Saturday—where else would she be?

The circus crossed her mind, and she laughed. It would be nice to go to the circus, but going to the circus alone was just this side of pathetic. Besides she'd probably start crying when the clowns came out in their little car anyway.

No, what she needed to do was concentrate on work—on something she could conceivably do. If she could just get the control panel angled right, maybe it would fit somehow. It seemed hopeless, but somehow she had to find a way. If for no other reason than to not have to think about the crushing loneliness of the rest of her life.

"Don't slouch," Nicole whispered to Jaylon as they stepped into the Woodland Country Club.

"Sorry." He stood up straighter although that hurt his pride as much as his back.

"Wait," she said before they had taken two more steps into the foyer. She turned to him and straightened his tie before pulling twice on his jacket. Then she looked at him and smiled. "Perfect."

The temptation to run his fingers through his hair was beaten down by the effort it took to follow her into the small restaurant with tiny round tables standing a perfect distance from the chairs set around them.

"Nicole." Her mother, a woman with the staunch look of years of having more than enough money, offered a hand to her youngest daughter. "You look positively glowing, dear."

"Sweetheart." Her father stood to greet her with a kiss. The man, just taller than Jaylon with silver-streaked blonde hair, extended his hand to his daughter's fiancé. "Jaylon, my boy."

"Mr. Byrne." Jaylon shook the man's hand, and then he nodded to Nicole's mother. "Mrs. Byrne."

"Jaylon," she said formally.

Praying it wouldn't go crashing to the floor, Jaylon pulled Nicole's chair out, and she sat. With the same care, he pulled his own chair between Nicole and her father out and sat down. What he really wanted was a long drink of water, but by now he knew that the concept of table manners around this family was extremely important, so he simply folded his hands in his lap and waited to be addressed.

"Dear," Nicole's mother began, "here's my updated list. I added the Garnets and the Monroes..."

"Oh, please," her father said in instant annoyance, "can't we have one full meal without wedding talk? It gives me indigestion."

"Daddy," Nicole said, her bottom lip protruding.

"I know. I know," he said with a shake of his head. "It's just that I'd like to hear about how the rest of your life is going, too."

"Oh." Her face brightened. "I'm going to New York with Ms. Soren in May to finalize the fall line."

"Darling, that's marvelous," her mother said in obvious awe. "Imagine that. My daughter, the clothing mogul."

"Ms. Soren said I've really got an eye for fashion. I think if everything goes well, I might have a shot at becoming her assistant full-time by the fall."

"Now that's more like it," her father said, lifting his glass to his daughter.

Jaylon reached for his own wondering if Nicole had told him this wonderful news before this moment. He couldn't clearly remember. Maybe in the middle of telling him how useless his life was she had mentioned it. He pushed the questions away from his mind as he gratefully took a sip of the driest white wine he'd ever tasted. Choking it down, he smiled at the other occupants of the table although he could tell with little problem that they hardly noticed his presence.

"So, how's house-hunting in Syracuse going?" her father asked Nicole more than anyone.

"Oh, we found this great place on Hatherly. It's so perfect. Two stories, four bedrooms. I'm trying to talk him into it." Nicole took Jaylon's arm and leaned in to him. "But you know how men are. He thinks it's too expensive."

"Well, Jaylon, my boy. If you're having trouble providing for Nicki, I've still got that position opened."

"Oh, thanks," Jaylon said quickly. "But I've already called some colleges about a job."

A frown descended across Mr. Byrne's entire face. "I don't know why you would want to go to that much trouble. I've got a perfectly good position, open and ready—and it pays six times what they'll ever be able to pay you at some college."

"Now, I'm getting indigestion," Mrs. Byrne said in annoyance. "Can't you see the boy wants to make his own way in the world, Steven? Just leave him alone. Quit pestering him about that silly job."

"Well, he's got to start thinking about more than just himself now. Nicki here isn't accustomed to provincial living."

"I'm sure we'll manage," Nicole said with a confidence Jaylon wasn't wholly sure she actually felt.

"Yeah," Jaylon said, feeling at least six inches shorter than he had when he'd walked in. "I'm sure we'll manage."

Two e-mails and a bill from North Carolina State were waiting for Camille when she got home. At her table with Max rubbing her leg, she tore the bill open and pulled her checkbook out of her briefcase.

No one had to tell her that the cost of an education had increased exponentially since her own graduation. There was proof positive every time she opened the bills. As she wrote out the check, she tried to force gratefulness past the anger. Two years, and she had paid for everything that the scholarships and grants hadn't covered.

Of course, Daria was worth every penny, but the resentment that her mother would never recognize that ate one piece of Camille's gut every time she thought about it. Finally free of the cumbersome responsibility of raising two daughters, her mother had latched onto the first male moving west and kept driving.

As far as Camille was concerned, her mother could just keep going until she fell right off the edge of the earth. With defiance, she licked the envelope and sealed it. She didn't need her mother. She didn't need anyone.

The anger threatened to overwhelm her as she stood and stepped over to the computer sitting on the little desk in the corner. Her finger on the mouse button clicked twice, and there was the email—Ben and Lexie. She smiled and shook her head. They never let her down.

First she clicked on Ben's and scanned it quickly. Just a message to say he hoped all was going well and that if she ever needed anything, she knew where he was. Yes, she knew where he was, and for that, she was grateful. Her finger clicked on the other one.

"Camille,

I know you're going to come up with a thousand excuses not to come to the reunion—just like you always do. So, I'm going to erase as many of them as I can. You can stay with us. No hotel. No extra money. I'm sure Liz can make your travel arrangements so you won't have to lift a finger. And I wanted to tell you, Nick and I are thinking about having a pre-reunion party at our place the night before the big celebration. So if you don't want to come for the big one, please at least think about coming to ours.

The kids want to see you. Nick wants to see you. And the truth is so do I. I miss you, Cami. Please. Please. I'm asking. I'm begging. Don't turn us down out right. We'd really love to see you again.

Think about it.
Lex."

Guilt and sadness poured over her. Lexie was right. The unwritten words that they both knew were there said it all. She was avoiding them. It was just so hard to see them together—living the life she wished she hadn't thrown away years before.

Reluctantly she read back through the missive, but the one name that neither of them dared mention stared back at her even as she did. Jaylon Quinn. The one unmentionable in her life.

Camille hadn't seen or heard from him in years. She didn't even know what had ever happened to him. For the first couple of months in college they had written faithfully. He had even come to see her twice at Princeton that first year. But as the weeks became months and the months, years, keeping in touch seemed harder and harder to make work with her studies and his friends. He was always out, doing plays, going to parties, living the "true college experience."

After sophomore year, it just got too hard to hear about all the fun he was having, and she knew she was boring him with all the fun she wasn't having. Studying. It was all she'd ever done. When she got to college, it was no different—save for her job in the dining hall, which helped her scrape enough spending money together to fill in the gaps that the scholarships and grants hadn't covered.

Strange how all that seemed like a million years ago, but with a simple thought she was right back there again. Working and studying. Studying and working until she walked across a stage with a diploma in her hand and no idea where to go from there.

Baker and Marsden had been her first job application. Pittsburgh. It wasn't home, but in reality she had no home, so it didn't make much difference where she went. At the time she was just glad to get out of New York State so she could start over. The only bad thing was, when she left, she forgot to leave herself behind. And so, here she was working and working with no stage to contend with, no diploma to work toward, and no end in sight.

Sure, the work was challenging and the people at work were nice, but outside of work, she had no life. She glanced back over the e-mail and pushed the edge of her glasses up. A small part of her wanted to go—to see Lexie and the kids. But a bigger piece of her knew she would come up with some excuse to get out of it. No matter where she ran, Camille always caught up with her, and Camille simply wanted to bury her head in the sand until the entire world just gave up and went away.

That's the way it had always been, and the way it always would be. That's just the way it was.

Manage. We'll manage. Jaylon tried to breathe as he lay in bed that night, his head resting on his hands. How was he ever going to be able to manage? Nicki and her four bedroom homes that reminded him too much of the one he grew up in. Him, bowing to their visions for his life.

It reminded him of another time in his life that he'd thought was long since gone. Back then, marriage was a long way in the future— too far away to think about. Ariana. He hadn't thought of her in forever, but with the click of her name, she was right there in his brain again—making her grand entrances with him the requisite two steps behind.

Somehow he'd thought that time in his life was over, but now it was back. This time with blonde hair and sporting an engagement ring he was sure he'd be paying for the rest of his life. His mind traced back over meeting Nicki that first day coming out of Macy's in Syracuse.

Everything about her had been perfect from the beginning. He'd noticed her long before they had stepped out of the store together and the alarms went off—literally. Jaylon smiled at the thought of her looking at him in astonished fear.

"Excuse me," the manager had said, running up to them as they stood in the middle of the theft detectors, mesmerized by each other and absolutely oblivious to the beeping of the alarm. "I'm going to have to ask you both to step back into the store for a moment."

The offending item was a tie in Jaylon's bag that had been paid for but not properly scan-proofed. But by the time they walked back out, going their separate ways was out of the question. They'd spent most of that day as well as most of the next month in each other's company. In the beginning, he couldn't get enough of her presence in his life.

It had been a long time since any girl had caused his heart to make those strange fluttering feelings that he had when Nicole was around. A long, long time. A face drifted through his mind, and a piercing pain jabbed right into the fluttering. Camille. The long, flowing light brown hair. The straight nose. The wire-rimmed glasses. No, Camille had never been what he'd thought of as perfect.

She was too into her books and her shell. And yet somehow... He shook his head in frustration. Camille was gone. A ghost from a different lifetime. In annoyance he swung his legs to the side of the bed and sat for one moment before running his fingers through his hair and standing.

He made his way down the little hallway without bothering to turn on the lights. It wasn't necessary. He knew this house like the paths in his own soul. In the kitchen he walked to the refrigerator and pulled out the remainder of his lunch. With Nicole's parents sitting inches away, he hadn't had much of an appetite then, but now, it was back with a vengeance.

The microwave door opened with a snap, and he punched the numbers, still batting Camille's face away from his thoughts. Why was he thinking about her now? He should be thinking about Nicole and how perfect their life would be in just a few months. Even the ding of the microwave didn't startle him out of his determined daydream of the future he was contemplating with Nicole.

If he took his savings and added what he could make if he sold the Ridgecrest land his grandmother had left him, he would have enough for the down payment on that Hatherly house. Then, maybe he could come up with a way to make enough to cover the payments. Nicole deserved that much.

He dug into the Shrimp Elegante and took a bite, tracing through the plan. The one and only problem in the whole thing was the Ridgecrest land. It had been in his family for five generations, and selling it felt like selling a piece of himself. But realistically, he hadn't been back there in years, so why was he holding onto it anyway?

It was then that he remembered the little green postcard, and he sighed, knowing that would be the perfect opportunity to put the place up for sale. As he stood and headed for the trash, he pulled the little light over the sink on. Sure enough, the green card was lying right on top.

Carefully he lifted it out and scanned it. April 12th. Yeah, it would be the perfect opportunity. He could put those memories behind him, and then he would be ready to move on to the next phase of his life. Life with Nicole.

Chapter 3

For the next two months the postcard stayed in Jaylon's briefcase. Every morning he would remember that he was supposed to call, and every night, he would vow that he was going to call the next morning. And still he hadn't so much as picked up the phone. In fact, he didn't even mention it to Nicole until one Friday evening in early March when they were knee-deep in glue guns and centerpieces.

"Oh, I was going to tell you," he said, searching for some topic to get his mind off of the lace twisted around his fingers, "my high school reunion is coming up. I was thinking maybe we could go together."

Nicole's face scrunched in annoyance. "Why would I want to do something like that?"

"Because," Jaylon said with a shrug, "I thought it would be fun for you to meet some of my old friends, see where I grew up—that kind of thing."

Her face scrunched more. "In Ridgefield?"

"Ridge*crest*."

"Whatever." She glued the lace carefully. "When is it?"

"The 12th of April."

She stopped gluing. "That's three weeks before the wedding. You want us to take a trip three weeks before the biggest day of our lives? By then I'll be having fittings and showers and we'll be meeting with the minister and I'll be doing my wedding pictures and having the final meetings with the caterers and the bakery and..."

"I guess I could go alone," he said, suddenly thinking that sounded like a very good idea.

"Without me?" she asked with a tone he wasn't sure how to read. "I don't think so."

"Why not?"

She narrowed both eyes at him. "Why not?"

He shrugged. "It's just a couple of nights. What? You don't think you can live that long without me?"

Anger was the first expression, but then it gave way to a smile. "Hey, I'm marrying you, remember? Of course I can't live without you." A flash sparked through her eyes as she advanced on him. "What kind of question is that anyway?" She swung one knee over his legs and sat down on his thighs.

The lace in his fingers dropped to the side as she leaned in to his lips.

"Does this answer your question?"

Another Saturday just like the myriad before it and the myriad Camille could see staring at her when she looked down the road. The plans were better. At least the cockpit controls now fit into the cockpit. In fact, they were now fine-tuning the computer models. That was a definite improvement. Lexie had managed to call ten times in the last two months, not to mention the endless stream of emails.

She just didn't give up, and Camille couldn't for the life of her figure out why her presence or non-presence was so important. They lived life every day without the benefit of seeing her—why would two days in April be any different?

If she could just come up with something solid, some conference or terribly important meeting that she just had to attend. Something. Anything to get out of going.

The phone at her elbow rang, and without thinking she picked it up. "Baker and Marsden. This is Camille."

"I thought I'd find you here," Lexie said, and Camille smiled. "What's up?"

"I've got a minute before I have to go clean, but I wanted to tell you I RSVP'd for you this morning."

The pencil crashed to the desk. "You *what*?"

"We had a meeting to discuss the plans, and I told them you'd said you were coming."

"I did no such thing."

"Yeah, well, now you did. So, let's talk about flight schedules."

"Lexie!"

"You can fly into Rochester on Thursday—that way you can help me get my house cleaned."

Camille sighed in frustration.

"I can get the tickets if you want—I don't mind, and I can send them to you."

"Hey! Before you go planning the rest of my life for me..."

"Well, somebody's got to."

"What about me?"

"You. Ha! All you do is work, and that's not life, Camille."

"I like work."

"And I'm sure it likes you right back. Now, Nick and I talked about it, and you can have Austin's room. That way you'll have some privacy. Besides he loves to sleep on the couch anyway."

"Don't I get any say in this?"

Lexie stopped. "Okay, what do you want to say?"

"I want to say—maybe I'm busy."

"Of course you are, and if you're not, you'll convince yourself you are anyway. Big deal. So, what time do you want to fly out?"

"You're not hearing me. I've got this NightViper project..."

"Morning or afternoon?"

"And I've got a conference I need to prepare for."

"Morning or afternoon?"

"I can't just up and leave like that."

"Okay, morning," Lexie said, making the decision for her friend. "Cool. That'll give us more time on the house."

"Lexie."

"And I'll make them non-refundable—that way you can't just cancel them."

"Lexie!"

"What?"

"Have you heard a word I've said?"

"Yeah, you want to come, but you're afraid to."

The honesty in that statement slammed Camille back into her chair. "I'm not afraid."

"Cami, this is Lex. Remember?"

"But..."

"No buts. Now, you're coming, and that's all there is to it."

One thing Camille absolutely detested was being put into a spot she hadn't chosen for herself and one she didn't feel she could get out of without hurting scores of people—or at least the ones that mattered the most. Lexie's "offer" had firmly placed her in just such a box. She didn't want to go. The very last thing on the earth that she wanted to do was stand around with people she'd hated for most of her life, eating hors d'oeuvres and making small talk.

"So, how many kids do you have by now?" "Oh, you're in banking, how fascinating." Who cared? They had never cared about her in high school, why should she care about them now?

Over the preliminary blueprints spread across her office desk Thursday night, her thoughts skipped back in time to the Ridgecrest hallways. Everyone laughing, talking, enjoying life while she slid as close to the walls as she could, books firmly pressed to her chest, praying no one would take notice of her. And by and large they hadn't. Unless she called attention to herself.

Stage lights and a blue dress floated through her mind. Of course, she had thought about them since that night, but once it was over, nothing had really changed. Then her thoughts crashed into a pink lace and crinoline gown—shredded and grease stained, and a sinister face shot through her mind. Ariana.

A shiver crawled down Camille's spine at the very thought of that witch. Unconsciously her shoulders fell closer to the desk as her spirit curled within her. Anything she had accomplished during her ten years away would never make a dent in what Ariana had done, of that she was positive.

Ariana—the high school drama queen, the one person who could make Camille feel no more than two inches high and did so with glee on a regular basis. No, Camille definitely did not want to see her. The others were similar although not nearly so cruel, but she didn't want to see them either. She just wanted to stay home, with her designs and her cat and forget that Ridgecrest and everything about it had ever existed.

The phone jangled at her elbow, and Camille looked at it with trepidation. Someone tracking her down in the office at 8:30 at night was never good news. Without wanting to, she lifted the receiver all-but prepared to hang it up if it was Lexie. "Hello?"

"Well, hello, Sunshine," Ben said happily, and instantly Camille's spirit relaxed.

"Hello, to you. What's up?"

"Haven't heard from you in awhile. So, I figured that meant either you didn't need me anymore or you got fired. Neither of which would be very good news."

Camille laughed. "No, I didn't get fired, and I thought I already said thanks for the help you gave me."

"You did, but I thought you might want to say thanks a little more."

"Huh?"

"I'm coming into town tomorrow night, what do you say you take a break for a change and let me take you out?"

"Tomorrow?" her mouth asked as her mind crashed back into the office.

"Yes, tomorrow." He laughed softly. "You know, the day after today, two days after yesterday, and don't say you've got work to do. This is work. I need to go over some things for the conference with you."

Frantically Camille's brain searched for a way out. "Umm, you know, I'd really love to, b..."

"Great," he said before she could finish. "I'll pick you up about six. You want me to come by the office or your place."

The office? Uh-oh. "No, no, my place would be fine."

"Great," he said again as happiness and relief flooded through his voice. "Well, I've got some arrangements to get made, so I guess I'll see you tomorrow."

"Yeah, tomorrow," she said in trancelike fashion as she signed off and hung up. For several minutes she sat looking at the phone. Why couldn't everyone just leave her alone? Let her curl up in her little cocoon and forget about her.

With an annoyed shake of her head, she pushed her glasses up and leaned forward over the designs again. Work made far more sense than people ever had.

"I need to call the reunion committee," Jaylon said over their candlelight dinner. He didn't have time for candlelight dinners. The play was in six days and nobody was ready, but Nicole wouldn't be dissuaded, so he had given in.

Nicole's fork clattered on her plate. "You can't be serious about this."

"The deadline is tomorrow," he said slowly with only a single glance up. "I want to go, and I want you to go with me."

"To a class reunion? I don't even want to go to my own class reunion."

Jaylon sighed as he squared his shoulders. "Well, I'm going, and you can come if you want. Besides I thought it would give us a chance to go out to that land I told you about."

"Your grandmother's?" Nicole asked, looking more disturbed the farther into the conversation they went.

"Yeah. I was thinking about putting it up for sale, but I'd at least like you to see it first."

As she shook her head, wavy blonde curls danced around her like a halo. "Why don't you just call a real estate agent and have them get moving on it now? What's another month going to help?"

My nerves, he thought sullenly, but he shrugged. "I just want you to see it before I put it on the market." Truth be told, he wanted to see it again before he put it on the market. If for no other reason than to convince himself it wasn't the heaven his memory said it was. "We can go on Friday, meet with the real estate agent, go to the reunion on Saturday, and be back home by Sunday afternoon."

"And then what?" Nicole asked, obviously fishing for the pay-off she figured to get by going along with this plan.

Jaylon's soul arched away from the question, but he pushed the answer out of his mouth just the same. "And then we can go to Syracuse and put a down payment on the Hatherly house."

Nicole's face spread into a smile. "Are you serious?"

"Yeah," he said sadly. "I'm serious."

Over two plates of filet of catfish and with Ben sitting only two feet from her, Camille forced her nerves to stand down. It was just Ben—no big deal. Just dinner with a friend she hadn't seen in five months. But if that was the truth, why was this so impossibly hard?

"So, I guess the convention business is going well," she asked to make conversation.

"Too well," he said in exasperation as he set his glass down. The pure gold senior ring from Yale flashed in the light.

She looked at him with the dark jacket and the paisley tie set just over the squared shoulders and just under the nice but not fabulous face. "And that's a bad thing?"

His fork clinked against the plate. "No, it's just a lot of traveling and running and consecutive sixteen, seventeen, eighteen hour days. It gets old not really having a home sometimes."

Her gaze softened as she looked at him. He did look more tired than he had the last time she had seen those dark eyes, and his always-there tan seemed a little less there. "I can see where that would be a problem."

"But the work's great. I mean I get to line up all these speakers—people I would never even get to meet otherwise. And I get to help come up with the conference themes and consult with some of the top CEO's of companies and military brass—it's hectic, but it's pretty cool most of the time."

"So, how many do you have at a time?"

"Conferences?" he asked, and she nodded. "Well, let's see. I've got one in Cinci in two weeks. That one's on structural—bridges and stuff. Then one in Boston in early April. Then there's ours at the end of April. There's one in May on... umm... Oh, yeah, technical design of computer elements. I have a couple more throughout the summer. And I'm working on getting this one in Pittsburgh lined up for September or October. I've got two companies that want to collaborate on it, so it's kind of an interesting challenge."

"Sounds fascinating," Camille said as she reached for her glass. "And you've got a team that helps you with all of this?"

"Two of them. One that helps with the scheduling and the bookings, and the other one helps at the actual conventions—setting everything up, working with the hotels to make sure everything goes the way we want it to."

"And you?"

"Me? Oh, I just walk around and try to act important." He flashed her his game-winning smile.

"Huh," she said with the barest of laughs. "So not much different than before then."

"Hey," he said, mockingly wounded.

She laughed. "You know I'm teasing." Slowly she shook her head. "Man, we've been lost without you. This whole NightViper thing's got Isaac in perpetual brain bleed. I think he was fried two days after you left."

Ben's smile fell into seriousness as he spun the wine in his glass. "And you?"

Dodging the question, she smiled. "I was fried long before then."

Silence descended on the table between them as Camille fought to get her gaze to lift off the table. When he talked like this, it was intimidating.

"Well, I'm looking forward to working with you again," he said softly.

"Yeah." She glanced up only once. "So am I."

Chapter 4

Lexie, in her infinite wisdom, had gone so far as to ask Liz to personally escort Camille to the airport. How she had talked Liz into actually waiting until Camille was on the plane was beyond Camille's comprehension as she had difficulty getting her secretary to just get her a cup of coffee.

Nonetheless, when Camille glanced back over her shoulder as she walked up the jet bridge, Liz waved at her happily, and with a frustrated sigh Camille waved back. Maybe if this had been a stopover flight, she would've had the opportunity to get off, turn around and go home. But Lexie had taken care of even that escape route.

Once on the plane Camille found her seat four rows from the back next to the window. However, the first thing she did when she sat was to pull the window shade down. She didn't want to look, didn't want to watch herself getting closer to Rochester and inexorably to Ridgecrest.

Too many memories. Too many moments, forgotten and yet somehow not, traced through her overtired mind. By now her entire body was tired. Tired of fighting to get the memories to go away. Tired of struggling to come up with an excuse not to go. Tired of pounding back the images of ghosts that just would not leave her alone.

Her heart turned over at the thought of one ghost in particular. Jaylon. The thought of seeing him again sent her right to the edge of sanity and then dangled her there precariously. How many hours had they spent together that last semester of senior year? How many times had she known it would never work out between them? And still she had hoped.

She could still see his car as it drove away from her house that last time, the summer after her freshman year in college. Already then, things had been different. Already he was no longer the Jaylon she remembered, the Jaylon she saw in her dreams every night.

No, he had changed, and the reality was so had she. Being with Jaylon, even in high school, had never exactly been easy. They were simply too different, wanted different things from life, had different paths set before them.

As the plane taxied down the runway, she wrapped her hands around her arms as her mind went back to the one moment in time that she had forced herself to forget for nearly ten years. But with one breath it was back. The feeling of his arms around her. The feeling of being surrounded by the perfection of the night air and the stars and most of all the feeling of his lips on hers. It all came back in a rush.

Those feelings were right there, just under the surface, waiting for a weak moment. Angrily she forced her eyes open, and she reached for a magazine from the small pouch in front of her. As much as she had wanted to ask Lexie if he was coming, her heart simply couldn't take the answer. No matter what, she was doomed. If he was coming, she would get her hopes up and inevitably get them smashed just like always. If he wasn't coming, that meant that the possibility she would never see him again which was much more final.

Somehow that would be worse. Worse than seeing him again and knowing it was over. Or would that be worse? In frustration she flipped through the pages of the magazine without seeing a single one of them. Everything about the whole situation was worse.

Her fingers pushed her glasses up as she tried to focus on the words in the magazine, but it was useless. Her brain was focused on one thing, and it had nothing at all to do with the words on that page.

It was abundantly clear when she stepped off the plane that Lexie had no intention of giving her one iota of a chance to back out. Camille caught sight of her friend before she was even off of the jet bridge, and despite all the feelings of dread surrounding this visit, the smile that came to her face and heart were genuine.

"Cami!" Lexie enfolded her friend into her arms the second Camille stepped back onto solid concrete. "I can't believe you're here!"

Camille's face was buried in the deep ebony of her friend's embrace for a full, unbelievable minute before she managed to pull back slightly. "That makes two of us."

"Let me look at you." Lexie pushed Camille back to arm's length. "Man! You look so..."

"Jet-lagged? Brain-dead?"

"Sophisticated," Lexie said slowly.

In embarrassment Camille looked down at the silk suit she hadn't bothered to change out of from the office. "I didn't have time to change."

"No," Lexie said with a soft smile that made it all the way to her deep brown eyes. "It's a good thing."

The compliment and her awkwardness at handling it snapped Camille back to herself. "Well, look at you, Miss I've had three babies and still look like a model."

Lexie looked at her friend skeptically. "You have definitely been on that plane too long."

For one more second they stood, simply reveling in the thought of being together again. Then Camille looked past Lexie's shoulder remembering the other members of her family. "Where're the kids?"

"Three kids in an airport?" Lexie shook her head. "I don't think so. Come on." She linked her arm through Camille's, and together they walked away from the terminal. "So, how is everything?" Lexie asked as they walked past the floor to ceiling windows, which opened out onto the tarmac.

"Daria may make the President's list this semester," Camille said, expertly deflecting the question.

"Cool. Taking after her big sister, huh?"

"I'm just glad she finally found something she likes. Many more years of undecided majoring and I would've been broke."

After several more steps, their arms dropped from each other's even though the feeling of being together again didn't.

"How's your mom?" Lexie asked, trying to sound off-handed but failing miserably.

Happiness fell away from Camille. "Who knows? I think she's still out west somewhere—Kansas? Nebraska?" Camille shrugged. "Something like that."

They walked several more paces.

"So, how about you?" Camille asked, trying to steer the conversation in a different direction. "Are you about ready for this whole reunion thing to be over?"

"I don't know," Lexie said with a small laugh. "It's been kind of nice to have an excuse to get out of the house once in awhile."

"I'm sure Nick doesn't want you out of the house," Camille said, smiling at the implication.

"I wouldn't know. He's been gone a lot lately. They've had inventory coming in, and he's been pretty snowed under."

Camille nodded. "But he's going to be there...tonight I mean."

"For you," Lexie said with a slight smile, "he'd be anywhere. In fact, he took the rest of the week off supposedly to help me clean, but I don't buy that for a minute. He was as excited about seeing you as I was."

At the baggage claim they stood in front of the return, arms crossed, slowly dissolving back into their own worlds.

"So, the kids are good?" Camille asked, reaching for a topic that felt safe.

"Samantha starts school next year," Lexie said with exasperation just around the edges of the statement, "I can't wait."

"And Austin?"

"He's a sweet kid when his big sister's not pestering him to death. I'm looking forward to some one-on-one time with him. But the thought of being one of those moms who's constantly in her car driving kids everywhere is freaking me out a little."

Gently Camille looked at her friend. "I'm sure you'll be great."

The baggage return chugged on, and Camille stepped forward to watch for her bag. In six years no one had gotten this close to her. It was stifling. When her jet-black bag slipped out of the top and slid down to the rotating plates, Camille stepped farther away from Lexie to grab it. She set it down, right at her ankle and waited for the hanging bag. In seconds it, too, appeared, and suddenly she found herself standing in a place she had done everything to avoid for the last six years.

"That it?" Lexie asked, and Camille picked up both bags and nodded. Lexie smiled. "Then let's go home."

The trees flashing by the window brought up feelings from the middle of the bottom of Camille's soul. She hadn't thought she missed this place—until now. As she watched the landscape stream by, she wondered how she could've stayed away so long.

"We told everybody to come tomorrow night if they want," Lexie said, continuing what was proving to be a non-stop conversation with herself. Camille was barely listening. "Nick's going to cook out. We figured if it snowed or rained, we could always have it in town somewhere, but it looks like the weather's going to hold out long enough so we can have it at our place. Too bad I can't just put a Do Not Enter sign on my door and keep everybody outside though. Then we wouldn't have to clean."

Camille never said a word. The memories were too thick around her.

Lexie looked over at her friend for a long moment before she spoke again. "I got the official list today. You know, the one saying who's coming."

"Oh, yeah?" Camille asked, not really hearing what her friend had said.

"J's coming," Lexie said slowly, "and he's bringing a guest."

The weight of a 70-ton wrecking ball crashed right into the middle of Camille's heart as she looked over at Lexie, willing her face not to show any emotion. "He's coming?"

"Yeah."

The news settled between them like the proverbial elephant no one wants to mention. Fighting the searing pain in her heart, Camille squeezed her eyes closed in self-defense. But instantly his eyes were there—intense pools of blue so close they shocked her eyes open. This was always a possibility, and yet...

"I don't know when he's coming in though," Lexie said, trying to soften the blow. "I tried to find out, but nobody really knew."

Camille nodded although she never felt it. Her spirit had somehow detached from her body and was floating out over a long winding gash in the earth and a stately tree standing guard next to it. Tears stung her eyes as she felt his arms come around her. The memories wrapped around her with them.

Jaylon. No one had ever gotten as close as she had let him get to her soul. No one. Not even Lexie, who stood in a pretty solid second.

"So, who's the guest?" Camille asked, forcing the words out.

As she drove, Lexie looked over at her friend. "I don't know."

I don't know. I don't know could mean anything—a wife, a girlfriend, anything. Every piece of her spirit crushed her back into the seat, trying to make the car go backward. Every inch, every spin of the tires brought her closer to finding out the answer to I don't know, and yet not one piece of her wanted the answer to that question.

"Nick's so excited you're coming," Lexie said, routing the conversation in a different direction. "That's all he's talked about for a month now." She looked over at Camille. "He's not even going to know you anymore."

Confusion dropped in over the need for escape. "Why not?"

"Why not? Look at you—you look like the CEO of a fortune five hundred company."

Camille looked down at her black and navy suit without really seeing it. "Dress code. What can I do?"

"If I were you," Lexie said, glancing at her wistfully, "I wouldn't change a single thing."

The off-brown SUV pulled up through the winding grove of trees, which finally parted to reveal a small single story house. Lexie pulled the vehicle under the carport and killed the engine. "Home."

Pangs of envy and sadness stung Camille's heart as she pushed her door open and crawled out. "Lex, it's beautiful."

"Beautiful?" Lexie asked as she yanked Camille's luggage out of the back. "You've been in Pittsburgh too long."

At that moment the front door creaked open, and two small children—with blonde hair and beautifully tanned skin rushed out and down the front steps. "Mama! Mama!"

Lexie caught one on each leg as the children cowered behind her and gazed up at Camille in awe. Slowly Lexie dropped the luggage as she bent next to her children. "Sam, this is Camille. She's your Godmother. Remember?"

Camille was sure the child had no memory of her, and the misgiving in Sam's eyes confirmed that. Carefully she reached out to the child and touched her arm. "Hey, Sam. How are you?"

"And this," Lexie said, looking up to Camille as she placed her hands on the boy's shoulders, "is Austin Nicholas."

"Hello, Austin." Camille extended her hand and a smile. "You know, you're even more handsome than your mom said you were."

"Hey," a voice said from the still-open doorway, and when Camille glanced back, ten years evaporated.

"Nick." In a breath she left the children and her best friend to walk up the steps into his arms. "I can't believe it."

His presence and his arms wrapped around her like a warm blanket on a cold night. "Well, I guess Lexie finally convinced you," he said as he held her. "I'm glad."

When Camille stepped away from him, she had to wipe the tears off of her cheeks, but her smile was genuine. "So am I."

"Let me reiterate this," Jaylon said sternly as he stood in front of the class on Thursday. "If you so much as blink wrong for your sub, you will wish Shakespeare had never been born on Monday. You got that?"

Seventeen seniors nodded solemnly, and he joined them. "Good. Then have a good weekend."

On perfect cue the bell rang, and the seniors stood and filed out. Slowly he exhaled and set about stuffing the papers from the week into his briefcase. Maybe he would have some time in Ridgecrest to get them graded. It seemed that the further into the semester they went, the more difficult it became to keep up.

The seniors weren't really his biggest concern about leaving—it was the drama class. Once the play was over, their already tenuous attention span snapped in two. Since the Monday after the final performance, he had been pulling exercises out of the woodwork to keep them busy, but he was losing control of them by the day, and he knew it.

Maybe when he was in Ridgecrest, he could stop by and talk to Mrs. Allen. He was sure she would have some other suggestions for him. With two clicks he closed his briefcase and stepped out into the hallway. With only drama to teach after lunch, he had managed to wiggle an early release out of the principal.

On normal days he was the last one to clock out—generally working until even after the coaches went home from practice. There was always something more he could do. Another lesson plan to write, another test to write out.

Always something, and yet today that 'always something' had no hold on him. He was free—for three whole days, he was free. And in the smallest place in his heart where he was truly honest with himself, he knew when he walked back through those doors on Monday morning, he wouldn't have the papers or anything else done.

But for now, for this one moment, he didn't want to think about that. All he wanted to do was go home and get ready for tomorrow morning when he would finally have an excuse to go back to the place that had haunted the corners of his mind for weeks, for months, for years.

For the first time since he'd left Ridgecrest for NYU, he felt like he was actually going somewhere that he wanted to go. Somewhere that his soul wanted to go. Leaving right now would make perfection even more perfect, but between now and then, he had a ton of things to get done. Not the least of which was finding the deed to his grandmother's property. A twang plinked through his spirit, but he pushed that away from his mind.

He was determined. Nothing was going to destroy this trip. Nothing.

"You'll have to share the bathroom with the kids," Lexie said, leading Camille through the house to the back bedrooms, "but besides that, you should have enough privacy."

"I'm sure it'll be fine." Camille followed her friend to the bedroom at the far end of the hallway and stepped into it. Wallpaper decorated with baseballs and bats graced the walls about eye level and in one corner was a mountain of little boy toys.

"The bathroom's through here," Lexie said as she set Camille's luggage by the closet door. "Towels are in the cabinets." She walked back into the room and looked at Camille. "Just make yourself at home."

Camille nodded, wholly unable to get any words past the lump in her throat.

Lexie caught the look and smiled. "I'm glad you're here." Closing the gap on the expanse of time between them, Lexie stepped over to her friend and gave her a quick hug. "I'll have lunch ready in an hour. Take your time getting settled."

Again Camille nodded, and then she watched her friend walk out and close the door softly behind her. In a daze of certainty that this was some dream she had stumbled into, she looked around the room. The shelves were lined with small boy things—tiny horses, balls, dump trucks. Pulled to them, Camille touched each one gently. So many memories she had missed.

A picture frame sitting on the dresser caught her eye, and she picked it up and smiled sadly. Nick, Lexie and a tiny darkly colored baby in all blue gazed back at her. They looked so happy, so familial. The pangs in her heart were back, and pushing the feelings away from her, she set the frame back down and walked to the closet quickly.

The less she thought, the better off she would be this weekend. That fact was already abundantly clear. Another thought drifted through her mind, but she cracked it in two. No, she wasn't going to think. She was just going to get through this, and then she could go back to her apartment, and her work, and her cat. And there, she could be happy again.

Never in his life had Jaylon had this much trouble packing. It wasn't so much that he had nothing to wear. It was more that nothing seemed just right. Jeans too casual. A suit, maybe, unless everyone else would be just in casual dress. With half his closet arrayed across his bed he went over his options again.

Finally in frustration he picked up the seven different choices and stuffed them all into the hanging bag. He could decide when he got there. As soon as the clothing problem was conquered, he knew he had no excuse left not to look for the deed.

With a sigh, he sat down in front of the dresser's bottom drawer and pulled it open. Papers, all official-looking and lying in disarray, were strewn across the drawer. Slowly he reached in and pulled a handful out. His father's will. A receipt from the funeral home for his grandmother's burial expenses. Newspaper clippings, long since yellowed with age. Three lives compressed to 150 words each. The clippings slid away, leaving him holding a photo of a young woman, sitting on a porch, her arms around a young boy who was squinting into the sunshine.

The side of Jaylon's finger traced down her face gently. The woman, his mother, a ghost he remembered only concretely in pictures. The familiar lump formed in his throat as thoughts of her filled his mind. Knowing it was pointless to go there, he dropped the picture to the floor with the clippings, and he reached back into the drawer for another handful.

More memories he didn't want to relive. More ghosts from past lifetimes. One at a time he sorted through them—some bringing smiles, most bringing twangs of pain. Loss, so much loss surrounded his life. It was the fabric that the rest of his experiences were woven into.

Then as though it had lain there for just this moment, his hand pulled one picture from the others. A young girl in a sea blue dress, her soft face framed by wisps of straight brown-blonde hair. Beautiful hands, soft shoulders, and in a breath he was back, standing on a stage, her spirit calling to his in ways he had never been able to explain or even fully comprehend.

And now she was calling to him again. With a frustrated brush through his hair, he laid that picture aside and dug back into the drawer. Six more memories slid across time before he found the creamy-white red-edged paper. The deed.

Haze wrapped over him as he opened it and ran his gaze down it. Although his gaze was firmly planted on the paper, his mind saw only stars laid out on a midnight blue sky and her, resting in his arms, gazing up at him in perfect trust. In his mind he reached out and ran his finger down the side of her face, following her hair down the roundness of her shoulder.

His eyes fell closed on the feelings that the memory unleashed across his heart. Reliving a moment in time that he had convinced himself was the only perfect one he would ever have again, he let his head fall back against the bed frame. He could feel her in his arms as if she was there right now, and for the first time in nine years he let himself wonder what had happened to her.

Had she ever finished Princeton? He laughed at that thought. Of course, she had. She would've knocked the place down before she would've quit, and since as far as he knew it was still standing, it followed that she had graduated.

He traced back over the letters and the emails he had received from her when they had left high school. At first they came two and three times a day, and he had responded to every one—needing her presence to hold onto even if it was only in some words printed on ether.

Then as the days turned into months and then into years, the messages came fewer and farther in between until they had stopped altogether. At first he didn't really notice, and by the time he did, her email account was closed. He couldn't count the number of Returned Mail messages he'd gotten on his computer before he'd finally given up, and the four letters he'd sent to Ridgecrest had all been returned—Addressee Unknown.

She was gone, but in his heart she had never really left. She would sneak up on him with no warning—suddenly be standing on the stage in the guise of one of the girls in college or in someone sitting in the library studying. And when she did, he would smile and for one moment he would remember. But she had gone on with her life, and he had been forced to go on with his, and that's just how things happen when high school sweethearts go their separate ways.

With a shove he pushed the memories of her away from him and opened his eyes. He reached down and grabbed the stack of papers lying next to him. If she was there this weekend, he would simply smile and ask how she was, say how great that was, and that would be the end of it.

It had to be. He had gone on with his life. The drawer banged closed, and he stood with the cream-colored envelope in hand. After this weekend, Ridgecrest would be just a passing memory. Of that, and only that, he was completely sure.

Lexie had called it a night an hour before when she left to put Sam and Austin in bed. They each came over to Camille for a kiss before they skipped off back to Sam's bedroom, haggling over what story they were going to read tonight. Ryann had already been down for an hour before that, and so that left only Camille and Nick, sitting in the small living room.

"So, I guess Lex told you Jaylon's coming," Nick said, his voice saying he knew how explosive that simple statement might be.

"Yeah, after I got here today," Camille said with a slight tinge of anger lacing the words.

Nick smiled softly. "She didn't think you'd come otherwise."

"Smart woman."

For a long moment Nick sat in the recliner without saying anything. Then he glanced over at her. "Did she tell you he's bringing his fiancée?"

In one swipe the wrecking ball crushed the last of her carefully constructed denial tower. "His...fiancée? She said a friend... a guest."

"I figured she'd find a way around it." Nick's hands joined in front of him as he gazed across the expanse at her. "She really wanted you to come."

Camille nodded although his words brushed past her ears without ever bothering to go in. "How do you know it's his...fiancée?"

"He told Kara when he called." The soft blonde hair across Nick's head slid through the dim light as he put his head down. "I just thought you should be ready for that. I mean I didn't want you to get blind-sided tomorrow night."

Instantly Camille's heart pounded down the track. "He's coming tomorrow night?"

"I don't know." Nick shrugged. "We invited everybody who's coming for the weekend, so he might."

Suddenly Camille felt sick at her stomach, and air jammed the top of her chest.

"I just thought you should know," Nick said, obviously questioning the wisdom of telling her, but it was too late to take it back now.

Camille stood and walked over to the television, which had a large framed picture of Nick and Lexie, he in black, she in white, sitting on top of it. Their happiness had eluded her from the moment they had first laid eyes on each other, and now that happiness seemed to slip further from her grasp. "Would you mind if I take your car for awhile?"

"Now?" Nick asked with instant concern.

"I just want to have a little time by myself."

He nodded as he stood and reached for the keys on the little hook by the door. "I'm sure you're overwhelmed by all the insanity around here. Three kids will make you want to leave as fast as you can. Believe me. I know." With a sad smile, he handed her the keys. "Take care of yourself. Okay?"

Her smile barely broke the surface. "I will."

It was silly—wanting to get away, to drive and drive and never have to go back to anything—to her life in Pittsburgh, to Lexie's house, to anything resembling the reality she now found herself a part of. But that was exactly what she wanted to do. There, in their house, surrounded by them and the kids, Camille had never felt so alone. She was an outsider, looking in, and that hurt more than simply staying away. They didn't do it on purpose. It was just that her heart couldn't take watching everything she had given up.

Her hands guided the vehicle around the outskirts of town and down a road that had been etched in her heart for what seemed like forever. She didn't know if it was even still there—the tree, the old house, the opening in the earth, but for reasons she didn't want to contemplate, her soul wanted to be there again. To feel it as though nothing had changed. To make the clock run backward and grab hold of that moment, and then to do it all differently. So, so differently.

In the darkness the headlights snagged on the small reflector off to the left. She slowed and gazed out through the window to the darkness beyond. Carefully she turned into the yellowed weeds, hoping she wouldn't run over something she couldn't see and hoping against hope that it would all still be there just like it had been before.

The weeds were a perfect sea of yellow, no tracks, no sign that any life form had trekked across it in years. A smile broke through the misgivings in her heart when the headlights drifted over the old broken-down house and then across the tree. For a moment, she questioned the possibility that this really was a dream. However, her heart knew as it took in this scene again that this was far too good to be a dream.

Without instructions, her hand put the vehicle in park, shut it off, and then pushed out of the door. A night-chilled breeze brushed past her as her feet slipped through the weeds, but with only a few steps, her soul released all caution and her feet were running, carrying her back to the past.

In a breath she was at the tree, the rough bark sharp on her hand, the tears stinging her eyes. Above her the sky wrapped in a perfect rendition of every memory she had ever had about this place. The sobs wrenched her soul in a vice-grip. This couldn't be happening. She couldn't be standing here in the only place she had ever wanted to be again—without him. Her knees released their hold on her stability, and slowly she slid down the tree into the protective arches of its roots.

Regret, bitter and vicious, attacked her. How had she ever convinced herself that letting him go would be all right? That things would work out—that somehow they would find their way back to each other? That letting go wouldn't be for forever? How had her brain persuaded her that any dream was worth giving him up?

"I didn't mean it, J," she said to the wind. "Please. I didn't mean it. I take it back. Please, God. I thought Princeton was what I wanted, but it wasn't. What I really wanted was him. Please, God, I want to take it back. Can I choose again?"

Her hands wrapped around her arms as her head fell onto her wrists. "Please, God. Don't take him away from me forever. Please. He's the dream I want. He's all I've ever wanted." The pain stabbed into her heart like a thousand knives. "Why couldn't I see that then? Why?"

Then in the darkness she picked her head up and gazed at the stars that now seemed so far away. As the tears coursed down her cheeks, she gave voice to the words she had been running from for a full decade. "I love you, J. I always have...and I always will."

Chapter 5

"Are you coming?" Jaylon yelled as he picked up the three suitcases sitting at Nicole's apartment door.

"Would you relax?" she asked in annoyance, still putting her earring in as she walked out of the bathroom. "It's eight o'clock in the morning. I don't know what you're in such a big hurry about."

"We've got a two o'clock appointment with the real estate agent, and I want to go out and see the land before we go in." Two suitcases in one hand and the third in the other, he looked at her expectantly. "You ready?"

She sighed in obvious exasperation. "I guess so. Oh, wait! My make-up." Immediately she turned back for the bathroom.

Mystified, Jaylon looked down at the suitcases he held. "There's more?"

"Just one," she said, traipsing back out. With a sweet smile she handed him the small carry-on. "Ready?"

He pushed the irritation under the tugging of his soul. "Let's go."

"You were out pretty late last night," Lexie said as she stood at her sink cutting up vegetables. "Big party?"

"Oh, yeah. I'm such a party animal." Camille's head was still pounding from the tears of the night before, but she was doing everything she could to look absolutely normal. Her hands worked, shredding the lettuce until three heads were relocated into the Tupperware bowl. "What else you got?"

"There's a bag of tomatoes in the frig." Lexie scratched the edge of her nose with the back of her wrist as Camille pulled the bag out and looked at it skeptically.

"How many people are you expecting anyway?"

"Forty or fifty. They're figuring on two hundred tomorrow night."

"Two hundred? I thought we only had like a hundred twenty in the whole class."

"Guests," Lexie said off-handedly. "Can you hand me that shredder?"

"Oh, sure," Camille said, fighting to forget the first word Lexie had said. "So, you never told me. What's the plan for tomorrow night anyway?"

"Hors d'oeuvres at six, meal at seven-thirty, dance after that."

"Dance?" Camille asked in instant fear.

"Yes, dance. It was on the invitation, silly."

"Huh. I must've missed that part."

"We got a D.J. from Rochester—nobody around here plays our kind of music anymore."

"Oh, yeah," Camille said like a deflated balloon. "I can see where that would be a problem."

At that moment the front door squeaked open, and Nick and the three children made their noisy entrance. "Hey, you'll never guess who I ran into at the store."

Camille's shields flew up in anticipation of the name as he set Ryann's car seat on the cabinet top.

"Keane Dinsmore."

Air. It was a nice feeling for the moment, and Camille looked over at Ryann just so she could look at someone safe.

"He and Yvonne are coming tonight."

"Cool," Lexie said, accepting the kiss he gave her on the cheek. "You get enough hamburger?"

"Seventeen pounds. You think that'll be enough?"

"It better be." Lexie laughed. "I feel like I'm feeding the whole darn town."

"Hey, this was your idea," Nick said, running a gentle hand around her waist.

"I beg your pardon," Lexie said as she looked back at him teasingly.

"Okay, our idea. Same difference." He reached around her and pulled the grill brush out of the drawer. "I'll take the kids outside with me."

"Don't take Ry, I'm going to put her down for awhile."

"Your choice." Nick turned away from Lexie and slid up behind Camille before reaching around her and shagging a tomato slice from the bowl.

"Hey. Watch it," she said in mock anger.

"Oh, yeah? What're you going to do about it?" he asked, arching his eyebrows as he chewed mischievously.

She took the knife and stabbed it at him. "This."

"Oh! My fault." He put his hands in the air. "I know when I'm not wanted." He stepped around her and called down the hall. "Who wants to go outside with me?"

The two children came racing down the hall. "Me. Me."

He smiled at the two women still cutting up vegetables. "We'll be back in awhile."

"We'll be waiting with bated breath," Camille said dramatically.

"Yeah, if only I could get so lucky," he said, and then he shepherded the kids out ahead of him.

"You want me to do all of these?" Camille asked, looking into the nearly full bowl and then at the still half-full sack.

"Yeah, probably better. The last thing we want to be doing is cutting up more tomatoes when everybody else is out on the hayride."

In a breath Camille's brainwaves stopped. "The hayride?"

"Nick's dad has a friend that has this long trailer. We're going to take it out on this road that goes right by our house. We're about the only ones that ever use it anyway. It dead ends just north of here."

"Nobody said anything about a hayride."

"Well, it can't be any worse than that dance nobody told you about. Come on, Cami, this is supposed to be fun. Remember?"

She was trying, but it was difficult.

The metallic blue Z28 didn't bother to so much as slow down until Ridgecrest was in the rearview mirror and open land was spread before them. In his excitement, Jaylon reached across the console and took Nicole's hand. "You're going to love this place."

She never said anything although the annoyed look on her face told him exactly what she would've said had she put it into actual words. At the cusp of the last turn, his feet instinctively slowed the car, and he smiled when off to the left the old, brown house appeared. It looked older and sadder than the last time he had seen it, and immediately his heart twanged at the sight. Several shutters were now missing from the windows that were either cracked and broken or missing altogether. There were holes in the roof that hadn't been there the last time he'd seen the structure. They felt like holes in his very soul.

With the practice of a million times, he slowed at the turn and spun the wheel.

"Looks like we're not the only ones wanting to take a look at it," Nicole said, nodding at the two perfectly spaced tracks leading down the driveway.

Jaylon's eyes narrowed. Someone had been here—recently. As he drove across the tracks, he tried to push that thought away, but a feeling of intrusion sank into his core. Nobody was supposed to know about this place. This was *his* place, and he wanted it to stay that way.

"So, how many acres are we talking?" Nicole asked, gazing up and down the tract as though this was some business transaction that she wanted to complete as quickly as possible.

"About 20," he said never really hearing the question. His spirit was too busy filling with the unbelievable emotions of being in this place again. When he parked, he slid out of the car without taking his gaze off the amazing scene stretching before him.

"How much does land go for out here?" she asked, folding her arms in front of her when they met in front of the car.

Answering was pointless, he didn't know the answer, but more than that he didn't care. He reached over and wrenched her hand away from her chest. "Come on."

If she could've followed him anymore reluctantly, he didn't know how. It was like pulling a wagon with one missing wheel. He could feel her dragging the wings on his feet back to the ground all the way across the grass until they stopped at the edge of the slope, and he breathed in the familiar air. It had been too long.

"If we could get 600 an acre for it, we could make that down payment with no problem," she said, scanning the land around them as though doing so could tell her if it was worth that much.

Jaylon ran his free hand down the rough tree bark as he dropped Nicole's hand, feeling more than the land wrap around him. In a breath he was back, and even his memories couldn't compare with the feeling of standing here again.

Her presence in this spot was nearly palpable, her laughter as she ran away from his pursuit rang in his ears, her quiet company as she sat at the base of this tree studying, in the very spot he now stood. Her. Camille. He looked down and could almost see her sitting at his feet, book open and head bowed. Grief over one of the greatest losses of his life twisted around him.

"I don't think we'll be able to get anything for the house," Nicole said, gazing at the drooping front porch. She laughed derisively. "We'll probably have to pay them to take it."

His gaze followed hers back to the house as loss and grief gripped his soul. So much pain, so much loss... so much hurt entwined with this place, too much for him to bear. The sound of the bubbling creek below blended with the voice in his head saying the only way to be whole again was to just walk away from this place—just walk away and never come back.

Fighting the ache in his heart, he looked over at Nicole. The sadness pierced through him like a carving knife. "You ready?"

"Let's do it," she said, smiling at him happily, and with those three words, his heart cracked wide open.

"I hope you have more tables than this," Camille said, pushing her hair behind her shoulder as she lifted the edge opposite Lexie.

"We told everybody around here to bring tables, and we've got a few blankets if we get really desperate."

They hauled the table out into the yard and set it up.

"What time's everybody coming anyway?"

"Six-thirty, seven." Lexie shrugged. "Who knows? It was kind of an open invitation so people may still be showing up at three in the morning."

"Oh, good. That should make for a restful night."

Together they grabbed the next table and hauled it out of the back storage shed. They set it down on the ground, and once it was standing, Camille looked at her watch. Two o'clock.

"So, what else do we have to get done?" she asked as they trekked back for the last table.

"Well, I've got to finish that front bathroom and get the signs out so everybody can find us, then get the kids ready for Nana's house. I'll probably just take them over. Nick's going to be starting on the hamburgers about 5:30, so I don't want to stress him out having to run the kids around."

"Oh, yeah, he looks real stressed out," Camille said with a small laugh as she watched Nick chase the kids around the yard with the grill brush. Their squeals of joy sliced through her heart.

"Just wait, he'll be a basket case by six." Lexie helped position the table and then stood for a moment with her hands on her hips. "I guess chairs and we've got this one conquered."

"Fab. Let's get it." Camille's mind traced over the sparse clothing she had brought. A hayride and a cookout. Casual. Very casual. She picked up four chairs and made her way back out to the tables. Her gaze caught on the melee in the yard. "Hey, McGee! How about some help over here?"

Nick looked up and smiled. He pushed the children off of him and stood. "Come on, guys. Let's help."

Despite the tears in her heart, Camille smiled. What she wouldn't have given to be Lexie, living in the middle of this dream. What she wouldn't have given for this to be her backyard and her kids dragging chairs across the yard. The one and only thing she would change was the man who stepped out of the storage shed. Like he had never left her heart, Jaylon stood there for one brief instant, and in that moment everything in her world was right again.

Then reality bounced back as Nick approached her.

"What, I come to help and you quit?" he asked jovially as he snapped the chairs out.

She came back from the dream with a jerk as the tears threatened. "No. I didn't quit. I was just taking a break."

"From what? Reality?" he asked as laughter enveloped his words.

"Yeah," she said softly as she started back for the storage shed. "Something like that."

The bell over the real estate office jingled when Jaylon pushed it open for Nicole to enter. Inside, the little place had a musty smell that seemed to permeate everything including the off-orange carpeting at their feet.

"May I help you?" the lady who sat at the front desk asked.

"Umm, yes, we're here to see Ms. Tremain," Jaylon said, clutching Nicole's hand for fear that he might actually follow his heart and turn around and run.

"Ms. Tremain had a family emergency. Are you her two o'clock?"

"Yes, we are," Jaylon said, feeling the doom lift momentarily.

The lady nodded. "She asked Mr. Dinsmore to take that one. Just a moment, I'll let him know you're here."

They stepped back and watched the lady page the agent. After a few minutes she looked up and smiled. "He'll be with you shortly. Please, have a seat."

Together, they stepped back to the brown sofa and sat down. Trepidation wrapped around Jaylon as he reached into the inner pocket of his jacket to make sure the deed was still there. It was, but how much longer it would be in his possession, he couldn't tell.

Motion at the door caught his attention, and he and Nicole stood to greet a face from the past—different hair, older somehow, but familiar all the same. Jaylon extended his hand and a quizzical look. "Keane?"

"Jaylon?" Keane asked in disbelief. "Hey, how are you doin', man?"

"Great. Great. How about yourself?"

"Can't complain," Keane said and then glanced past Jaylon's shoulder.

"Oh, Keane, I'd like you to meet Nicole Byrne, my fiancée."

Keane's smile widened. "Well, somebody finally snagged him, huh? Congratulations."

"Thanks," Nicole said, shaking his hand solidly.

Keane looked back to Jaylon. "So, what can I do for the two of you?"

"Well, we were thinking about selling some land," Jaylon said, and then Keane seemed to realize that they were still standing in the middle of the foyer.

"Well, why don't we go back to my office? We'll see what we can do."

Jaylon nodded and waited for Nicole to step in front of him before he followed her to the back. The office wasn't new by any means. Dark brown paneling clothed the walls, and the ancient orange carpeting extended all the way back behind Keane's desk.

"So, I guess you're here for the reunion?" Keane asked when everyone had been seated.

Jaylon shifted uncomfortably in his seat. "Mostly."

Keane folded his hands on the desk between them and shook his head. "Man, this is just too weird."

"Too," Jaylon agreed with a small laugh.

"So what were you wanting us to do for you?" Keane asked.

"Well." Jaylon reached into his pocket for the deed. "I inherited this land when my grandma died, and we were thinking about selling it."

Keane accepted the paper from Jaylon and bent to examine it. "Is this out on 1575?"

"Just off of it," Jaylon said with a nod.

"That's pretty far out," Keane said, consulting a surveyor's map posted on his wall.

Nerves and hope attacked Jaylon at once. "You don't handle things out of town?"

"Oh, no, we handle it." Keane's eyebrows creased in concentration. "I just haven't been out that way in awhile."

"How much does land go for out there?" Nicole asked, her voice thick with excitement.

"Well, I'll be honest with you. We haven't sold anything out that direction in some time." Keane tapped on his computer. "I'm going to have to do a little research to even be able to answer that question." He consulted the deed and the surveyor's map again. Then with his fingers on the keyboard, he looked up at the clock. "I don't think I'm going to even be able to give you an answer this afternoon. I'm taking off a little early today."

"Oh," Nicole said and slumped back in her chair with a pout on her face.

"But I can get on it first thing Monday morning," Keane offered and then stopped typing. "If that will be soon enough for you."

"Yeah, that'll be plenty soon," Jaylon said.

Keane nodded and resumed typing. "So, you excited about the reunion?"

"As excited as somebody gets I guess," Jaylon said with a shrug.

"I can't believe Nick and Lexie. They must be crazy." Keane stopped typing. "Umm, where can I get in touch with you when I have something?"

Jaylon gave him the information even as the two names danced through his head. "Why are Nick and Lexie crazy?"

Keane stopped typing and looked across the desk. "You didn't hear? They've invited everybody out to their place for a cookout and hayride tonight."

"Oh, really?" Jaylon asked as ten thousand different emotions crashed into the center of his soul simultaneously.

Keane shrugged. "I figured everybody knew."

"No, but I'm surprised they found me to send an invitation in the first place," Jaylon said with a laugh. "I've kind of been out of the loop lately."

"Where is Brickhaven anyway?"

"Just North of nowhere," Jaylon said.

"It's right outside of Syracuse," Nicole said, and there was a slight tinge of anger in her voice.

"Syracuse, huh? I figured you'd be on Broadway or in Hollywood by now." Keane smiled at Jaylon as he finished the typing.

"No, I'm teaching now," Jaylon said, thinking that saying that out loud would feel like admitting failure, but when it came out, it felt more like pride.

"Teaching?" Keane asked taken aback. "Seriously?"

"English and drama."

Keane handed the paper back. "Well, I would've never guessed that one."

"Yeah, neither would've I." Jaylon looked down at the deed, now back in his hands, thinking that hadn't been nearly as hard as he'd imagined it would be.

"Well, I'll get on this first thing Monday and let you know something as soon as I can do a little work on it."

Jaylon extended his hand as they stood. "I'd appreciate that."

The three of them started for the door with Jaylon trailing just behind Nicole.

"So, we'll see you two tonight then?" Keane asked at the door.

"Oh," Jaylon said as his heart dropped to his shoes, "I don't know. Umm, we weren't really invited."

"Well, consider yourselves invited now," Keane said happily. "I can't wait for you to meet Yvonne. You're going to love her."

Jaylon looked at Nicole whose face looked as soft as stone. "We'll think about it."

"They live out on Highway 15. Nick says there will be all kinds of signs. You can't miss it."

"How many more do we have?" Lexie asked in frustration from the front window of the SUV.

Camille's foot turned slightly on a rock off the side of the road, but she regained her balance quickly as she set the sign in the ditch. "Six."

"We'll put one more here and then go down to the next corner," Lexie said. "I don't want anybody to get lost."

Wielding the hammer carefully, Camille pounded the sign into the earth and then ran to the side door. She looked at her watch with a sigh.

"What time is it?" Lexie asked.

"4:30," Camille said, feeling the advance of the clock clutch her throat in a stranglehold.

"I'm telling you I would never have made it without you today," Lexie said as the vehicle turned at the corner.

Without a response, Camille jumped out and grabbed another sign. By the time tomorrow night got here, she was sure she would be laid out cold somewhere. Her idea of work was sitting in an office, having her secretary run her errands for her, and the hammer was getting heavier with each sign. Forcing herself to concentrate on the task at hand, she pounded first one sign and then another in.

It took another fifteen minutes before they were on the road, headed back for the house.

"I hope Nick's got the kids ready when we get there, or I'm toast," Lexie said, pushing her foot against the accelerator.

"Hey, this is supposed to be fun. Remember?" Camille asked mischievously.

"Yeah. That's easy for you to say, you don't have half-a-hundred people coming to your house in an hour."

The thought of half-a-hundred people even fitting in her place caused Camille to choke back a laugh. "Hey, this was your idea."

Lexie pulled back into their yard. "Don't remind me! Ugh! What was I thinking?"

Camille smiled softly at her friend. "It's going to be fine. Okay? Don't stress out. Everything will work out."

As Lexie shut the vehicle off, she glanced over at Camille. "Well, you're here, so I guess my major goal has already been accomplished."

"See," Camille said as she extended her hands out with a shrug, "everything else is gravy."

With a sigh and a smile, Lexie nodded. "Gravy. Huh?"

"Yep. Gravy."

Chapter 6

Every hairstyle Camille tried looked far too over-the-top for a hayride and a cookout. The jeans were okay although she hadn't worn jeans in what seemed like forever. Most days she spent either in her suits or in her sweats. There was very little in between the two for her. Finally in frustration she just let her hair down, knowing she would regret it, but she was going absolutely squirrelly trying to find something different.

With a final check of her appearance in the mirror, she smirked at herself. She pushed up her glasses, a pair of thin, animal print ones that had replaced the stark wire-rimmed kind she had worn in high school. But besides that change, not much about her had really changed in ten years.

In a strange way, she felt no different than she had back then— geeky and inferior. Too bad ten years hadn't made her someone else. Then tonight might actually be fun. The way it was, however, she knew tonight would just be one long string of misery, leading only into tomorrow night's torture session.

Nonetheless, standing here feeling sorry for herself wasn't making the clock stop, so she opened the door and went to find Nick.

"Great, you're here," he said when she stepped out of the back door into the sunshine. "Could you find me the pepper? I think it's in that corner cabinet. And I need the spray bottle out of the cabinet by the microwave."

"You know, you really should get everything together before you start sending smoke signals."

A giant flame leaped from the grill. "Ha. Ha. Remind me to thank you for that advice later."

"I'll be sure to do that," she said and went back into the house to get the items.

It was too bad she hadn't hit it off with Nick. He was so much more her style. Being around him had never threatened to send her over sanity's edge, they could just laugh, joke, be friends, without the specter of dooming her life or his hanging over their heads.

She stepped back out to the backyard. "This what you're looking for?"

"You're a life saver," he said gratefully when she set the pepper on the grill and handed him the spray bottle.

Playfully she jabbed him in the ribs. "That's right, and don't you ever forget it either."

"So, you want to go, you don't want to go?" Jaylon asked, feathering his fingers through his hair as he paced across Nicole's hotel room in frustration.

"A hayride?" Nicole asked skeptically. "It sounds positively countrified."

"Well, I think it sounds like fun."

She regarded him with a harsh glance. "You would."

His feet stopped their pacing. "What's that supposed to mean?"

"It means: I'll never understand your love of nature and stuff. Give me concrete any day."

"It's just one night. One little night, and you don't even have to ride the hayride if you don't want."

She sat on the bed, saying nothing as the seconds passed. He wanted to say something else. 'You're killing me' came to mind, but he had enough sense not to let those words come out of his mouth.

"You really want to go?" she finally asked, gazing at him with undeniable doubt.

"Yeah, I really do," he said, fighting not to let how much find its way into his voice.

Finally she breathed a tired sigh. "Fine. I guess we can go."

He wanted to jump up and down, instead he just smiled and said, "Cool."

By six o'clock it wasn't Nick who was the basket case, it was Lexie.

"I forgot plastic ware!" she wailed just before her first guests arrived.

"Lex, it's hamburgers. You can eat them with your hands," Camille said in concern for her friend.

"But we've got potato salad! That requires *forks*!" Cabinets rattled as Lexie pillaged through them looking for fifty forks she had somehow forgotten that she had. "This is a disaster!"

"Hot meat coming through," Nick said, sliding the door open and stepping into the living room.

"What am I going to do?" Lexie asked in an all-out panic.

"What's wrong?" Nick asked as his face fell the second he looked at his frantic wife.

"Forks," Camille said simply. "Tell you what. Give me the keys. I'll just run into town and get some."

"You can't leave!" Lexie moaned.

"Well, you can't either," Camille said rationally. "Now, give me your keys."

Lexie looked at Nick for a better solution. At that moment a knock sounded on their front door, and all three gazes turned to it.

In fear, Lexie looked back at them. "They're here."

"Give me the keys," Camille said, taking charge. "I'll be gone twenty minutes—tops."

Nick stored the meat in the oven and turned it on as Lexie reluctantly handed over her keys. Quickly Nick retraced his steps to the door.

"Money," Lexie said, putting a hand to her forehead in confusion. "Where's my purse?"

"It's on me," Camille said with a laugh.

"You don't have to pay for them too," Lexie said.

"It's plastic forks. I think I can afford plastic forks." Camille took Lexie's shoulder and spun her toward the door as the first of a long line of people arrived. "Now, go. And remember, this is supposed to be fun. Okay?"

Lexie smirked at her but allowed herself to be pushed to the front door just the same. Without so much as waiting to hear the greetings, Camille tramped down the hallway to Austin's room. It was nice to have a reason to get out of here for a while anyway. A few moments respite from the torture session seemed like heaven on earth.

She grabbed her purse from the floor and pushed her hair over her ear. That hair was going to get really old, really fast. Her feet carried her back into the living room and past the growing party. By quick count there were already ten people—all looking very much paired off. "I'll be back."

"Camille," one of her former classmates that she couldn't quite put a name to said as she walked to the door. "You made it."

"Yeah," she said as she accepted the hug. "I made it." Then she glanced over at Lexie. "I'll be back."

Lexie nodded, and Camille took that opportunity to escape. The cool air outside felt good against her warm face. Just being outside away from people felt good. College was the last time she remembered being around this many people, and even then she had spent the majority of her time in her room studying.

With a bounce she climbed into the SUV, started the motor, and looked carefully behind her before backing out. Thank God for missing forks.

"You sure you got everything?" Jaylon asked as he surveyed Nicole's dress and heels—not exactly casual attire, but he wasn't about to say anything.

"Yes, I've got everything, could we please just get this over with?"

He followed her out the door, wishing that for once she could just be happy about something he was excited about. Besides Keane, it had been ten years since he'd seen any of these people, and meeting up with Keane had done nothing but boost his enthusiasm with the prospect of seeing them again.

The only real anxiety he felt had something to do with going to Nick and Lexie's house, but he wouldn't let that thought have a breath of a chance to take over. Tonight was supposed to be fun, and he was going to do everything in his power to have exactly that.

They climbed into the Camaro, and in seconds the engine was purring. Expertly he backed out and headed for Highway 15 with a quick glance at the clock—six-thirty. Good. They wouldn't be hopelessly early. His heart pushed the accelerator as they zoomed through the streets.

He was amazed how it all felt so familiar—almost as if he had never even left. A pang of sadness struck his heart as they passed the Hollybrook Care Center. How many times had he made that turn to pull in and see his grandmother? He wished now more than ever that he could just sit down and talk to her, tell her about his life.

But that time had passed, now he had Nicole to share his life. He glanced over at her, and pride swelled in his chest. She was beautiful. Gently he reached over and took her hand although that gesture did nothing to replace the frown on her face. That was all right. He was sure once they were at the party, she would loosen up.

Half a mile from the turn to Highway 15, he saw the first sign out in the ditch. "Party this way!"

Instantly the thought crossed his mind that he was glad there weren't many cars out here as the possibility of having more than class members show up would've been a distinct possibility. He dutifully followed the sign that said, "Turn here" and three more signs down the road until he caught his first glimpse of the festivities off to the left.

A smile he couldn't have stopped had he wanted to spread across his face. Nick and Lexie's place. It looked just like them. Simple yet picture-perfect. He turned into the driveway already lined with cars.

"Park somewhere so we can get out," Nicole instructed sullenly.

One piece of the smile fell from his heart as he followed her order. When the car was parked and they met at the back of it, he had the distinct feeling that the little wagon with the missing wheel was back. Heels were never meant to be worn on loose dirt and gravel, and he had the conspicuous impression that she was finding that out.

"Who's dumb idea was this anyway?" she hissed as she stumbled across the driveway next to him.

He looked at her with anger flashing through him. "Would it kill you to pretend to have a good time for like a minute?"

The look in her eyes matched the tone in his voice perfectly. "It might."

Hand-in-hand he led her up the front steps to the door where he knocked when he realized there was no doorbell. In an instant the door swung open.

"Jaylon!" three people said simultaneously, and he was pulled into the midst of them before he had a chance to think again.

"Hey! You made it." Keane stepped over with his hand tucked firmly in a small Puerto Rican lady's hand even as he extended the other to Jaylon. "This is Yvonne. Yvonne, this is Jaylon and Nicole—they're engaged."

Just as Jaylon went to shake the woman's hand, someone walked up right beside him.

"Engaged?" Seth Taylor, a guy who had been Jaylon's best friend throughout elementary school but who he had lost touch with the second they had graduated, said in disbelief. "You're engaged?"

Jaylon ducked his head as he felt the other gazes turn toward them. "Yeah."

"How cool is that?" Seth asked as he put an arm around his old friend's shoulders. "And this I presume is the lucky lady."

"This is Nicole," Jaylon introduced to the growing gathering of on-lookers.

"Well, Nicole." Seth leaned his corpulent frame in to hug her. "Congratulations."

"Th...thanks," she said, accepting the hug but plainly baffled by it.

Seth, who had gained at least 80 extra pounds in the ensuing years, looked back at his friend. "J.P., come on, man. There's somebody I want you to meet."

And thus began the long process of meeting everyone. Wives, fiancées, significant others. There were simply too many to keep track of.

"Hey!" Nick suddenly called above the crowd noise, and Jaylon turned and smiled at the sight of his old friend. "The food's ready in the backyard. Let's eat before it gets cold!"

"So, J.P.," Seth said, laying an arm over Jaylon's shoulders as Nick disappeared. "What have you been up to besides hanging out with gorgeous women?"

Seth's wife, Julie, a rather tall brunette and Nicole turned and followed them out, never saying so much as a word to each other as the guys carried on a non-stop conversation in front of them.

"Teaching, huh?" Seth asked to Jaylon's three-worded answer. "That's cool."

"Yeah, and we're getting married in May. I'm going to finish out the year in Brickhaven, and then we're moving to Syracuse."

"My sister lives in Syracuse."

"No kidding? Yeah, we're probably going to try to buy this place out on Hatherly. It's pretty nice."

"Hatherly?" Seth asked in shock. "I'd say that was pretty nice."

The four of them got into the line together as their conversation continued.

"So, what are you up to these days?" Jaylon asked as he worked on building his hamburger.

"I'm working on cars over in Brockport. Let me tell you, the computers they put on these things today would try the patience of Job."

Jaylon laughed. "You should've paid more attention in high school."

"I should've paid more attention in college, too," Seth said with a laugh, and then he looked back at Julie. "Isn't that right, honey?"

"Whatever you say, dear," she said not at all enthused about anything.

At the end of the table, plates in hand Jaylon turned to follow Seth but instead found himself face-to-face with Nick.

"Nick!" Jaylon set his cup down and juggled his plate so that he could get a hand out-stretched to his host. "Great party, man."

"Thanks," Nick said happily. "Glad you could make it."

"Yeah, I ran into Keane this afternoon. He told me about it," Jaylon said, getting lost in the conversation and forgetting about everything else. "Where's Lexie?"

"Probably freaking out in the house." Nick glanced toward the house with a laugh. "If more forks don't get here soon, she's going to have an all-out panic attack." Nick looked back at Jaylon. "In fact, I'd better go make sure she isn't having one right now." He stepped away. "I'll see you later."

"Okay, take care," Jaylon said with a raise of his plate. Then he turned only to find Nicole staring at him heatedly.

"You know you could've introduced me," she said as she stumbled across the lawn next to him.

"He was busy. There'll be more time later." Jaylon took a sip of his drink as they approached the table where Seth and Julie sat. "Hey, these seats taken?"

Seth looked up and laughed. "They are now."

Somehow twenty minutes had turned into forty, and Camille wasn't at all sure how that had happened. By the time she bounced back into Lexie's driveway, there were cars everywhere, and so, praying that her sense of measurements extended to parking cars, she weaved through the vehicles until she was safely under the carport again.

With a quick sigh to get her scrambling courage back under her command, she grabbed her purse and the forks, slid out, and slammed the door. She could hear the celebration already going on in the back, and for one fleeting moment she looked back at the SUV. What she wouldn't give to simply jump in it and drive. However, she couldn't do that to Lexie, and she knew it.

Four clumps up the steps and she opened the door without bothering to knock. Once inside, however, it seemed that the ensuing time had never elapsed as Nick and Lexie stood in the kitchen, cabinets banging around them.

"Sorry it took me so long," Camille said over the noise. "The first place I went was out."

"Cami!" Lexie shrieked in relief the second she saw her. "Thank goodness!" She grabbed the bag from her friend's hands and raced out the back door.

"Glad I could help," Camille called to Lexie's retreating back. She walked over and sat down at the bar as Nick watched her. "So, how's it going?"

He looked at her like he was about to tell her someone died. "J made it."

Her heart stopped with the news although every brain cell in her head was working to make that completely unnoticeable. "Oh, really?"

"He brought his fiancée."

The battle in her body intensified. "Oh, yeah? Is she nice?"

"I don't know. I haven't really met her yet." Nick looked at Camille with sad eyes. "I'm really sorry about this, Cam. When we came up with this idea, we didn't know he was getting married."

She smiled at him glumly. "Don't worry about it. I'll be fine. I'm sure he's forgotten all about us anyway."

Nick nodded as though he didn't believe a word she said but he understood how she felt all the same. "How about we go join the party?"

Camille looked at him, and for everything her brain was telling her about acting cool and this being no big deal, her heart simply couldn't withstand the pressure. "I'm just going to go put my purse away. I'll be there in a little bit."

Again he nodded, but the look of intense concern still permeated his eyes.

"Don't worry," she said with a soft smile. "I won't jump out the window and run."

"I wouldn't blame you if you did."

"Yeah." She laughed sadly. "I wouldn't either."

The whole concept of a reunion was going over so smoothly that Jaylon wondered why he had ever even considered not coming. In fact, the only thing not going perfectly was Nicole who looked like someone had forced her to eat lizards for breakfast. If he focused on her, he was sure the whole evening would be ruined, so he tried to think about her as little as possible. Instead he focused on reconnecting with people he hadn't even realized he remembered until now.

He had gotten a single look at Lexie as she fussed over the food table, but with Nicole glued to his side and Seth talking incessantly, he hadn't had the chance to even go say hi. With one arm resting lightly over the back of Nicole's chair, he was being entertained with Seth's boating stories when motion at the back door attracted his attention.

In a single breath the noise, the conversation, everything but the vision standing in the doorway vanished. Without him realizing it, his heart pulled him up to a sitting position as his arm dropped from Nicole's chair back. It was as though a flash of lightning had just struck his heart, and he was simply waiting for the thunderbolt that was sure to crack right over his head at any moment.

For most of the last nine years he had thought about her, remembered her in unguarded moments. The feel of her hair as his fingers traced down it, the depths of her eyes as she sat at the top of a set of stage steps, the softness of her face—they were as much a part of him as his own soul was, and yet somehow he had convinced himself that seeing her again wouldn't really affect him.

With one glimpse, however, that theory was as inconsequential as the one that said he was anything but kidding himself if he thought he could walk away from her again.

"Now that was a story, huh, J.P.?" Seth asked, yanking Jaylon's attention back to the table.

"Oh, yeah," he said softly. "That was a story."

The best one of his life, he thought as he looked back at the door and her. Pulling every rational piece of his brain to him, he forced his gaze back to the table although in truth, his attention was fixed directly on the beauty gliding across the lawn in jeans and a light flannel shirt.

How he could've ever thought she was anything but perfection was beyond his grasp at that moment. Wisps of her hair drifted around her face in the gentle breeze as the sound of a bubbling creek invaded his consciousness.

Across the yard Camille looked at Lexie and laughed as Jaylon's heart cracked down the middle. What he wouldn't give to simply walk over to her, take her in his arms, and never look back.

"May 3rd," Nicole said right in his ear, jolting him back to reality.

"Boy, you're brave," Julie said. "Vanishing three weeks before the wedding? My mother would've had a fit."

Seth reached for his glass. "When didn't she?"

"So, do you have everything ready?" Julie asked, totally ignoring her husband.

"I wish. We've got six million center aisle bows to get made. They messed up the first batch, and I haven't even taken my pictures yet."

"Well, you better get on that, girl," Julie said. "You've got to get them in to the papers."

"I know. I know. There's just so much to do, and somebody here hasn't exactly been helpful." She punched Jaylon in the ribs, a move he never so much as saw coming. "I'm just so ready to be walking down that aisle already. Mrs. Jaylon Quinn." She took his arm and wrapped it around her. "I can't wait."

It was the first time in two hours that Jaylon had seen an actual smile on her face, and the first time in as much time that there wasn't one on his.

With one look at the lovebirds across the yard, Camille knew her chances at anything resembling a reunion with Jaylon were nil. Ariana had always seemed perfect, but the woman now sitting next to Jaylon blew Ariana right out of the water. Gorgeous blond hair in gently flowing waves outlined an oval face, exquisitely set with arching eyebrows, drop earrings, delicate pink lips, and deep soulful eyes.

If she wasn't a model, she should've been.

Trying not to look at them, Camille reached down, grabbed a carrot, and snapped it in two between her teeth as she surveyed the spread on the table. Surely there was something that needed done, something to put out, something to refill. Something. Anything to give her an excuse to go back into the house—away from the laughter and the happiness that seemed so outside her sphere of awareness.

At that moment Lexie slipped up beside her. "It's going pretty well. Don't you think?"

"Yeah, great," Camille said, sullen although she was really trying to be happy.

"So, you saw her."

"Oh, yeah." Camille arched her eyebrows as she glanced back across the yard. "She's kind of hard to miss."

Lexie reached across her for a green pepper. "So, have you talked to him yet?"

Camille scrunched her nose. "Oh, yeah, of course. I walked right up to him and said, 'Hi, J, remember me.'" She reached for another carrot and then shrugged. "What would be the point? I'm sure he doesn't even remember who I am anymore."

Lexie snorted in disbelief. "Yeah, right."

"Come on, Lex. Look at me." She held her hands out to the sides and then glanced back across the yard. "Now, look at her. Why should he even notice I'm around?"

Slowly Lexie shook her head. "I think you're wrong, and besides that, he'd have to be an idiot to forget about you."

"And I'd have to be an idiot to think he hasn't." Camille looked at the table again. "I'm going to go get some more radishes. If we cut the things up, they might as well eat them."

Without waiting for Lexie's protest, Camille turned and started for the door, but at the second step up, she met Keane coming out.

"Camille!" he said happily the second he saw her. "Hey, I hadn't seen you. Where've you been?"

"Errands," she said with a quiet smile. "I'm supposed to be helping Lexie out, but I think I'm more in the way than anything."

"You? In the way? Never." He leaned on the handrail. "So, what are you up to these days?"

"Working up in Pittsburgh, designing planes."

That news stopped him, and he lowered his gaze at her. "*Air*planes?"

She laughed at the incredulity scrawled on his face. "Yeah, mostly military stuff."

"Wow! How cool is that."

With an off-handed shrug, she looked away. "It's a job. So, how about you? You changing the world?"

"Selling real estate," he said, wrinkling his nose. "Pretty boring, huh?"

"Boring? No. I bet it's great."

He smiled gratefully. "Well, I wouldn't go *that* far."

"Selling people their dreams? I'd call that pretty great."

"Huh." His eyes softened. "I hadn't thought of it like that." He smiled at her. "You going to be around for awhile?"

"All night," she said, knowing that five minutes would be too long.

"Well, when you come back out, come over, there's somebody I want you to meet."

She smiled and nodded. "I'll have to do that." Then carefully she crossed in front of him and went in to the house. After being outside, inside felt much less threatening. It was quiet for one thing—a sensation that her soul needed at the moment. There was enough screaming going on in her body to give her a headache no matter what the noise level in the yard was.

Opening the refrigerator, she pulled out the bag of carefully cut radishes. If she could just keep busy, she could get through this. She looked at the clock as she noticed the fading daylight. Eight-fifteen. One hour to the hayride and then somehow she would find an excuse to leave the party, knowing that no one would really miss her anyway.

That's just the way things were, and she had enough sense to understand that fact.

For a full hour and a half as Seth babbled on about the mechanics business and Julie and Nicole discussed wedding plans, Jaylon sat watching Camille without letting on to anyone that he was. In all his memories she had never looked so good. Graceful. Sure of herself. Gorgeous. She was mesmerizing as she made her way back and forth from the table to the house, talking to anyone lucky enough to meet her in the middle.

He wondered what they were talking about. He wondered if her voice had grown even more beautiful as she obviously had. He wondered how she was doing, what she was doing, where she was living, and so much more that he couldn't even put it into words.

It was like watching a part of his soul that he had forgotten even existed move in front of his eyes. Every motion she made was recorded on his heart. If he had had only a bit less self-control, he would've simply stood from his table and walked right over to her. But he knew instinctively that there were people watching him— with Nicole. He was under the microscope of high school again, and taking risks like going to talk to Camille was dangling his life over the side of a cliff.

Seth slid back into his chair after going back for thirds of the pie now being offered at the main table.

"So, are you two going on the hayride?" Seth asked as he checked his watch. "Nick said the tractor's already out front. They're going to be going in a few minutes."

Jaylon felt Nicole's spirit fall next to him.

"That's so juvenile," she said in annoyance as she crossed her arms.

"That's what I keep trying to tell Seth," Julie said, matching Nicole's tone exactly.

"What?" Seth asked as he forked the pie into his mouth. "I think it sounds like fun."

"Guys," Julie said, rolling her gaze at the growing number of stars above them.

"Tell me about it," Nicole said with a laugh as she leaned back.

The sound of a tractor roaring to life invaded the peaceful celebration surrounding them.

"Well, I for one, want to go," Jaylon said, looking at his fiancée but suddenly finding some courage in the presence of his old friend.

"You girls can just stay here, and we'll tell you all about it when we get back."

The yard around them emptied quickly as partygoers streamed through the gate toward the front.

"I think that's the best idea I've heard all night," Julie said happily.

"Are you serious?" Seth scooped the last of the pie into his mouth. "You really don't want to go?"

"No, no, you go on," Julie said quickly. "We'll just stay here and have fun without you. Won't we, Nicole?"

Seth snorted. "Like that's possible."

"Well, it's more possible than when you're around," Julie said although the tone was teasing.

"Oh! Now that hurt." Seth held his hand over the supposedly gaping hole in his heart, and Jaylon laughed.

"Last call!" Lexie yelled from the back door and then disappeared again.

Jaylon stood along with Seth, but before he took even a step away, he stopped and leaned down over Nicole's chair. "You sure you don't mind?"

"No, I don't mind. You go. Have fun. I'll see you when you get back."

She looked up at him sweetly, and he bent farther down and brushed his lips on hers. Then he pulled back and looked at her again. "You sure?"

"I'm sure." She reached up and rubbed the side of his mouth. "I'll be here when you get back."

"Newlyweds," Seth said, shaking his head. "They're sickening."

Jaylon straightened. "Hey, we're not newlyweds yet."

"Yeah? Well, almost newlyweds are worse," Seth said with a smirk.

"Oh, shut up. We're going to miss our ride."

"I really don't want to," Camille said to Lexie as she stood cleaning Lexie's kitchen. "I'll just stay and clean up a little."

Lexie clamped her arms over her chest as the black hair in her high ponytail waved above her. "I did not invite you here so you could be my maid."

"Invite me?" Camille asked incredulously. "You kidnapped me."

"Fine. I did not kidnap you so you could be my maid. I thought we could have some fun together."

"I am having fun."

"You are not having fun. You're cleaning my kitchen."

Camille looked at her and shrugged as she wiped across the counter with the dishrag. "So I'm cleaning your kitchen. What more do you want?"

"What I want..." Lexie walked over to her and linked her arm through Camille's. "...is for you to come on a hayride with me."

"Ten more minutes," Camille said, trying to get away.

"NOW!" Lexie yanked her friend to the front door.

"Okay," Camille said with a reluctant laugh as she threw the rag back to the counter. "Now is good."

Not once did Lexie release her friend, and by the time they got out to the tractor pulling the flatbed trailer loaded with hay and happy people, Camille knew that getting out of going along was out of the question. So, giving up on that idea, she dutifully climbed aboard and took her seat at the back of the trailer letting her feet dangle off the edge as Lexie left to make sure all was going well with Nick and the tractor.

"Everybody ready?" Nick called just as two shadowed figures appeared from the side gate. "Okay! Hang on! Here we go!"

"No! Hey! Wait! Hey!" the two figures yelled, racing to the trailer just as Nick put the tractor in gear and the whole trailer jerked forward. At the last possible second, the two figures jumped aboard and caught hold of the trailer edge right next to Camille.

Fearing that she would be knocked off either by them or by the jerking of the trailer, she grabbed onto the bale of hay behind her. It was in the next breath that she realized who was sitting right next to her, but the tractor was already going too fast to jump off and run.

"Oh, sorry," Jaylon said, regaining his balance. He ran two sets of fingers through his dark brown hair to push it out of his eyes. "You okay?"

No words would come as she nodded even though her body still clung to the bale. He was so close, the smell of his cologne made her head spin dangerously.

"Who's that?" Seth asked, bending down so he could get a look at Camille.

"Camille," Jaylon whispered when he stopped long enough to see her. The name was obviously supposed to be an introduction, but it hardly made it from his mouth to her ears. He looked stunned speechless.

"Camille Wright," she said as she forced her hand across Jaylon to Seth, but the second her arm brushed Jaylon's chest, she regretted the gesture, and at the first possible opportunity she pulled it back and grabbed back onto the bale as they rolled over a rut in the road.

"Camille Wright?" Seth asked, obviously searching for the connection. "Hey, aren't you...?"

"Umm, Camille," Jaylon said as he cleared his throat. "You remember Seth Taylor."

"Oh, yeah," she said although her voice was drowned out in the roar of the motor. "How are you doing?"

Seth laughed. "Well, I'd have been better without that 30 yard dash."

"And those last two pieces of pie," Jaylon said teasingly.

"That too," Seth admitted.

Camille laughed, fighting not to notice how close Jaylon's arm was to hers or how intense his blue eyes were as they gazed at her.

"So how've you been?" he asked, leaning casually closer to her.

In self-defense she slid closer to the bale although if he advanced any further, she might have to become hay herself to get any closer to it. "Fine. You?"

"Great," he said, and then he clasped his hands in front of him as he leaned onto his thighs. How he didn't fall off, she had no idea.

"Jaylon's teaching now," Seth supplied over the top of Jaylon's bent back.

"Teaching?" She released the bale slightly as she leaned down to look at him. "What are you teaching?"

"Drama." When he looked back at her, his eyes burned two irreparable holes in her soul. "And English."

A smile spread through her heart and to her face as her spirit lost all track of the ground. "Drama, huh? I bet you're great at that."

He shrugged and looked back down. "I try."

"Mr. Allen himself," she said, falling easily into his presence although it made absolutely no sense.

Once again he smiled at her. "What can I say? Drama's my life."

"So, do you like it?" she asked genuinely interested in hearing the answer.

"I love it." His smile lit her heart.

"Drama, huh? Well, I guess that means you just had your Spring Production then?"

"Third week in March. We pulled it out by the bare skin of our teeth."

She laughed. "What was it about?"

"Some dumb farce," he said as if it didn't matter at all. "Two crooks who were totally incompetent. Good thing was we had the right cast for it."

Her eyebrows knit in the center of her forehead. "That was nice."

"That was the truth," he said with a shake of his head. "Our lead, Michael, he was backstage memorizing lines five minutes before we went on."

"Five minutes?" she asked with concern. "No way."

"I swear." He held up both hands just as the trailer hit another rut, and with absolutely no warning he tumbled right into her. Only her strangle hold on the bale saved them both from toppling right off the edge.

"Look out!" she yelled, grabbing onto him with one arm and clutching the bale with the other. People behind them started laughing, and it took more than a moment for him to sit up straight again. "You okay?"

"They've really got to watch those bumps," he said, inching farther away from her. "Hey, McGee! Watch where you're going!"

"Sorry!" Nick yelled from the tractor.

"If I didn't know better, I'd think he was trying to off me," Jaylon said to Camille, but he was smart enough to hold onto the bale next to hers this time. "Now what were we talking about?"

"Incompetent students," Camille said, wishing this didn't feel so perfectly natural.

"Oh, yeah. There's a good topic." Jaylon laughed as he glanced over at her. For one instant their gazes locked and even the bumping of the trailer didn't shake them out of it. Finally he shook his head and trained his gaze into the darkness beyond their feet. "I'm going to try to get on with a college for next year."

"Ah, moving up in the world," she said as the tractor rounded a corner and started back for home.

Jaylon shrugged as a strange look fell over his face. "I'm getting married in May."

That bombshell exploded at her feet before she had a chance to take cover, and in a breath it sent her spirit crashing back to the ground. "Yeah, I heard something about that."

Squeals of delight from their classmates fell between them, but neither could think of a single thing to say for several moments.

"You're going to have to meet her," Jaylon finally said, glancing over at Camille, but her heart wouldn't let her return the look. It hurt too much to watch him tell her that.

"I'm sure she's great," Camille said as she looked away. However, it seemed that on this beautiful night, there was no running from him or from her feelings as her gaze chanced on the stars shining down on them. They looked far too familiar for the sanity of her heart.

"So, I guess you're coming tomorrow night?" he asked softly.

She shrugged, trying to push the whole situation away from her. "I guess."

"You don't sound too thrilled about that."

"About what?" Her smile was small and sad. "About being a wallflower all night? Oh, yeah. That's what I've looked forward to all my life."

"You looked like you were having fun earlier," he said, and instantly her gaze snapped to him in confusion. "I mean...earlier...at the cookout...you didn't look like a wallflower then."

She shook her head and curled her bottom lip in annoyance. "It's like being the only gerbil on the ark."

"Huh?"

Her gaze found the darkness at her feet. "Everybody else has someone. I just..." The darkness slid past her feet. "I don't know."

A light wind whipped across her, sending a stray strand of hair into her face and finding every hole in the knit shirt she had on beneath her flannel one. Instantly she shivered and hugged the bale and her outer shirt closer.

"You cold?" he asked with concern.

"I'm fine," she said with more force than was probably necessary for fear of what he might do to repair the situation. The tractor bumped back into the driveway, and she clutched the bale tighter. "Besides, we're back anyway."

"Yeah," he said, breathing the word rather than speaking it. The trailer bounced through the yard and then rolled to a stop. "Looks like it."

When they were sure it was safe, their classmates started vacating the trailer behind them amid shouts and laughter.

"That was fun," Jaylon said to no one in particular as he slid off the trailer.

Gingerly Camille let go of the bale and slid closer to the edge, trying to figure out how she could dismount gracefully.

"Here, let me help." In the next instant Jaylon inexplicably reached up and took hold of her just under her arms. Gently he lifted her, body and spirit, from the trailer and set her on the ground as every feeling she had managed to deny during the previous minutes gushed to the surface. The next moment lasted only a breath, but it felt like infinity had just engulfed her as her gaze fell into the depths of his.

"You good?" he finally asked.

"I'm great," she said as a sincere smile wafted across her features.

"J.P., dude." Seth clapped him on the shoulder. "We'd better get back, or the women might think we fell off the darn trailer."

"Yeah," Jaylon said with an off-handed nod in Seth's direction, but he looked back at Camille. "I'll be there in a second."

"Okay, but you behave yourself." Seth lifted an eyebrow and an index finger at his friend in warning.

"Oh, shut up. I'll be there in a second," Jaylon said, and Seth laughed out loud and walked away. Jaylon feathered his hair back and smiled down at her. He seemed to back away from her although he didn't move. "So, I'll see you later then?"

"Yeah," she said as her heart panged forward. "I'll be around."

His eyes softened with the news. "Well, take care. Okay?"

"You too."

He stood for one more breath, and then he took a reluctant step away from her, taking her heart and soul with him. Her eyes fell closed as the ripping of her spirit followed him down the driveway and through the side gate. When she opened her eyes again, she looked up at the stars shimmering above her perfectly replicating the shimmering tears on her lashes. "Why, God? Why?"

Jaylon tried to rejoin the party, but the truth of the matter was that everything about him except his body had stayed back at that trailer with her. He looked at Nicole, and he tried to be happy with his life as he laid his arm across her chair. But the more he watched her, the more she just seemed so forced, so artificial—not real and natural and unpretentious like Camille.

They were talking about wedding plans again, and Seth was saying something about planning two years for two minutes. Jaylon laughed, but he wasn't even sure why. His heart and soul were no longer with him. Then without warning, Nicole leaned into his embrace and laid her head on his shoulder. Without any feeling at all he kissed the top of her head and sighed.

She looked up at him as concern coursed through her eyes. "You okay?"

He smiled sadly. "Just a little tired I guess."

Nicole trained her dark brown eyes on him a second longer before looking back to their friends. "Well, I think it's time to get my sweetheart home and tucked in."

"Ahh! Already?" Seth asked.

"We've got a big day tomorrow." Nicole rubbed her hand across Jaylon's thigh before she pushed back from the table and stood.

"Well, take care, you two, and be good," Seth said, wagging his finger at Jaylon.

"Always," Jaylon said with a strange smile.

"Always not!" Seth retorted, and Julie laughed.

With that, their little group broke up.

"We'll see you tomorrow night," Nicole said as she stepped away from the table, still unsteady on her heels.

Seth raised his glass to them. "We'll be there."

Nicole waited a single second so that she could link her arm through Jaylon's, and together they made their way over to the gate where Nick and Lexie stood, engaged in an intense conversation.

"Like I could control that," Lexie hissed just as they walked up. She turned, and her face immediately spread into a forced smile. "You're not leaving already, are you?"

Jaylon shrugged. "I'm not used to staying out past nine anymore. It's one of the hazards of getting old."

"Well, we're glad you could come," Nick said as he shook Jaylon's hand. Then he stopped when he looked at Nicole. "Umm, I don't believe we've been formally introduced. I'm Nick McGee."

"Nicole Byrne." She took her arm from around Jaylon's waist and shook Nick's hand.

"Nice to meet you, Nicole. This is my wife, Lexie," Nick said, placing his own hand around Lexie's waist.

"It's nice to meet you," Lexie said, and although Jaylon was sure Nicole didn't hear the reluctance in Lexie's voice, he heard it loud and clear.

"Well, we'd better get going," Jaylon said as the awkwardness of the situation dropped over them. "Take care, and thanks again. We had fun."

"Thanks for coming," Nick said amiably.

Jaylon put his hand on Nicole's back and steadied her through the gate. On the other side, minus the outdoor lights, the stars spread out above them.

"Well, that was fun," Nicole said, and her voice even sounded sincere. "Did you have fun?"

Although his heart said it was a bad idea, his gaze traveled across the driveway to the back of the trailer. "Yeah, I did."

Long after she'd heard the last of the guests leave and the house quieted, Camille lay on Austin's bed, never so much as bothering to take her clothes off or even to crawl under the covers. She didn't have the strength to do anything but lie there and let the tears wind down her cheeks. Ten years of denial washed over her in wave after wave of grief and pain.

Why did she have to remember? Why couldn't she just forget him and go on with her life? Why couldn't she just be happy for him? She should be. A real friend would be. But then a picture of him and Nicole slashed through her mind, and their laughter ripped her heart right out. He *was* happy—that much was obvious.

And why shouldn't he be? He had the perfect girl on his arm, and he would be walking down an aisle in some church to tie his life with hers soon. It didn't matter when. All that mattered was that there wasn't one single thing Camille could do to stop it.

Their moment in time was over, and she had to find a way to accept that. But as tears that seemed to come from the very depths of her soul coursed from her eyes, she knew that accepting it meant only that she would never stop crying, never stop needing him by her side, never stop reliving their perfect moment together. Never.

And from that perspective, the thought of accepting it and just going on with her life ripped her heart right out of her chest and stomped on it with a six hundred pound Army boot.

Chapter 7

The funk Camille had dove headlong into when he'd walked away from her the night before dogged her every step the following morning. Neither Nick nor Lexie looked particularly happy, but Camille didn't have the heart to even find out what was wrong. Instead she walked around under the guise of cleaning, when what she was really doing was trying to make herself believe that nothing all that important had happened the night before.

Jaylon was just being nice. He was a nice guy, so what was so surprising about that? She smiled when she thought about him teaching, and a memory from many years before wafted through her mind—a young man, standing on a stage in suspenders and a white striped shirt, surrounded by a gaggle of little kids.

Then her mind tripped across Daria's face, and her smile spread farther. She was quite sure that Daria's choice of computers for her livelihood was no coincidence. Allowing that memory full rein, Camille laughed at the memory of a much younger Daria tucked neatly beneath a floppy computer "box-head" as she tramped around the neighborhood saying, "Trick or treat."

Jaylon was talented from minute one. As she wiped off the outside tables in the sunshine, her heart turned over at the memory of standing next to him under the stars by the old trailer. The electricity of his blue eyes shot through her again, and unbidden tears welled up into her eyes. The prospect of never standing next to him again, never being able to look into those eyes again, tore through her like a missile.

Pushing the thoughts of him away, she finished the tables as Nick bounded out the back door. "Need help?"

"I got them cleaned, but I don't think they're going to walk to the shed by themselves." She tested her voice, the statement, the tone. Yes, it sounded normal although she had no idea how she'd pulled that one off. "The party was great."

Nick looked at her skeptically. "You thought so?"

"Yeah, why wouldn't I?" No way could she look at him as they lifted the first table together.

"Well, you kind of disappeared after the hayride. I thought maybe you were upset."

"Tired," she said as the sobs from the night before clutched her throat. "I worked yesterday. Remember?"

"I remember," he said, still looking at her with that skeptical look that unnerved her. "So, you weren't upset then?"

They picked up the next table and started for the shed.

"No, why would I be upset?" It was a stupid question. What she wanted to do was change the subject, but her brain simply wasn't cooperating enough to find a topic to change it to.

"I just thought, you know with Nicole and all."

Camille shrugged as they set the table next to the shed wall. "She's pretty, huh?"

"Yeah," he admitted reluctantly.

"Looks just like Jaylon's type." His name strangled the breath from her lungs.

Nick's face scrunched in concentration. "Now I think that really depends."

"On what?" she asked as they lifted the next table.

"On if you mean to the outside world or to those who really know him," Nick said pointedly.

There was an all-out war going on in Camille's brain. Letting Nick know that she still had feelings for Jaylon was a ticket to a disaster she had no desire to attend, but making him believe she was completely okay with the whole thing was getting harder with each word.

"I think they make a cute couple," she said, choking on the words as they picked up the last table.

"Well, I think that's a pretty sorry reason to marry somebody." He looked at her although she never so much as glanced back at him. "Making a cute couple isn't something you can build your life on."

With a swing, they set the table next to the wall. When she was sure it was going to stay there, Camille straightened, pushed her hair over her shoulder and dusted her hands off. "I think I'm going to go help Lex in the kitchen." She took a step away and then stopped. "Unless you need something else."

"No," he said as the concern tore through the syllable. "I think I can get it from here."

Slowly she nodded and walked out into the sunlight, which had no right to feel so good when she felt so bad. All she wanted to do was lie down and give in to the tears, but for the sake of her friends and the hospitality they had shown her, she wasn't going to do that.

In the kitchen she found Lexie slamming dishes around, making enough noise to shatter an eardrum.

"You know if you break those, you won't be able to have another party," Camille said as she leaned on the counter and tried to laugh.

"Good," Lexie said angrily.

Camille's eyebrows shot up. "Problems?"

The slamming continued. "I should be asking you that."

Camille grabbed a dishtowel to dry the pans already drying in the sink. "Why?"

As Lexie shook her head, she trained an annoyed gaze on her friend. "You're amazing you know that?"

"Please, clue me in. Why am I so amazing?"

Lexie ran the edge of her gloved forearm across her nose. "I heard you last night, you know."

"Heard me?" Camille asked as her drying slowed.

"I was finishing up, locking the doors and stuff, and when I walked by your room, I heard you."

"What? Was I talking in my sleep?"

"No, Camille. You were crying."

The statement hit Camille at point-blank range, but she did her best to shrug it off. "The radio must've been on."

"There isn't a radio in Austin's room."

"It was a car passing by or something."

That statement spun Lexie right around. "You know, you might think you're fooling everybody else, and maybe you are, but I can see right through it."

"Through what?" Camille asked, shuttering at the prospect that someone had heard her after Jaylon had left.

"Dang it, Cami! This is me. Lexie. I'm your friend, remember? Why can't you just talk to me?"

Camille closed her eyes and gathered every shred of peace left from the far reaches of her soul. When they were lumped together in her gut, she opened her eyes and looked right at Lexie. "I'm fine."

"Yeah, that's why you looked like somebody punched you after the hayride last night, and why you didn't come back to the party, and why your eyes are all red this morning."

Instinctively Camille's hands went to her eyes as she shook her head. "You wouldn't understand."

"Understand what? That you're in love with him? I'm married, Camille, not stupid."

"Look," Camille said with as much level-headedness as she could muster, "talking about it isn't going to help anything anyway, so I don't really see the point."

"You're avoiding the inevitable."

"Which is?"

"What happens when you see him tonight?"

Camille shrugged. "It's a big reunion. We might not even see each other."

"Yeah, and you were the one who thought he wouldn't even remember you last night. Great track record."

"Okay, so I was slightly wrong about that, but trust me, he knows what he's got, and what he's got is better than what we ever had together."

"How do you know that?"

"You saw them together. They're happy, and I'm not going to get in the way of that."

"Even though you want to."

Camille's heart turned over as she pushed the words out of her soul. "Even though I want to."

"I think I'm going to go get ready," Jaylon said as he and Nicole sat in her hotel room after lunch.

"Get ready?" she asked taken aback. "We've got like four hours."

"I know, but I've got to iron my shirt, and I'm sure my pants will need some help, too. And my jacket is..."

Nicole laughed. "You act like you're going to your prom."

If only, he thought sullenly. The memory of Camille standing on her doorstep as he placed the corsage on her wrist jumped to his mind. His breath had been swept away at the sight of her. In frustration, he batted that image away. If he didn't find a way to get her out of his head, he was seriously going to go insane.

"I'll be here to get you at six-thirty."

"Is that an order?" Nicole asked, and his frustration level increased on the tone of her voice.

"No, it's not an order. It's a request. I'd like to pick you up at six-thirty, will you be ready?"

She looked at him with concern laced with annoyance. "Yeah, I'll be ready."

Even as his soul pulled him backward, he walked over to her and kissed her on the forehead. "Thanks for coming with me. It means a lot to me."

Her eyes softened. "I'm glad we came."

He didn't say anything. He couldn't. Instead he pushed away from the chair, went to the door, and crossed over to his own room, grateful they had decided to get separate rooms. He needed time alone. Time to think. Time to figure out why seeing Camille again had thrown him so badly.

Once in his own room, he threw his keys onto the little table and flopped onto the bed. His hands ran themselves over his face once, and then they wrapped around the back of his head as he lay back on the pillows. Sure Camille was beautiful, but was beautiful worth throwing away what he had with Nicole?

Nicole. The woman he had thought he was so in love with, the woman he had planned to spend the rest of his life with. She too was beautiful but in a more conventional way. His eyes closed as confusion crashed over him. The wedding was planned right down to the last napkin ring, the guests were invited; the ice sculpture was ordered. Backing out now for something he wasn't even sure was still a possibility was just this side of certifiable insanity.

But were napkin rings, guests, and ice sculptures worth turning his back on the one and only real love his heart had ever felt? Again he replayed their conversation on the trailer in his head, and for all the searching of his soul, he couldn't remember a single thing he'd asked about her. No, it was all about him. How did he always find a way to make everything about himself?

With a kick, he pulled himself off the bed and stalked over to the little closet. He wasn't kidding about his shirt needing ironed. He only wished he could iron out the rest of his life as easily as he could take the wrinkles out of his shirt, but that was a blessing he knew he wasn't lucky enough to have bestowed on him.

"God, where are You going with this thing?" he breathed to the empty hotel room as the hot iron glided over the off-white shirt. "I'm telling You, some real, solid guidance here would be greatly appreciated."

The shower Camille climbed under did little to lift the crushing weight bearing down on her spirit. What she really wanted to do was just get on the first plane back to Pittsburgh and forget Ridgecrest and all of its residents had ever existed. She knew now that she was the cause of the tensions she had felt in the house all morning, and that hurt as much as the prospect of losing Jaylon.

Her thoughts crowded through her head barely having time to voice their intended purpose before being pushed out by even more melancholy thoughts. There was no escaping them. They were everywhere. After doing her best to take a shower, she turned both handles to cut off the water and then stood resting her head against the shower wall. All the energy in her body flowed right down the drain with the rapidly disappearing water until her tears were the only moisture left.

Willing herself to somehow find a way to keep going, she pushed away from the wall and grabbed for a towel. The soft terrycloth was no match for the moisture dotting her cheeks. Jaylon on the trailer. Jaylon under the tree. Jaylon, standing so close she could smell his cologne even now.

It was pointless to keep reliving, and yet it was the only thing her brain, body, or spirit wanted to do. Not really realizing she was moving, she dried herself off and stepped out of the shower onto the bright yellow bath mat. If she could just find a way to lock all of the memories in a box and store them somewhere so far down they would have no hope of ever seeing daylight again, maybe living wouldn't hurt so much.

In the mirror she took a good look into her own eyes, and all she could think was that Lexie was right. Whatever act she had managed to put on was completely see-through. Frustrated with life itself, she stuck her tongue out at herself and then laughed at the gesture. She could change nothing now. Her best bet was to get through tonight with whatever modicum of dignity she could muster.

Tomorrow she could vanish back to Pittsburgh, bury herself in NightViper plans, and just forget everything about this weekend as well as all the rest of her pathetic life. Grateful that she'd at least gotten some practice at dressing up since high school, she dried her hair and then snapped it into a ponytail, which she rolled around itself before clipping it up with a gold pin.

Quietly she padded into Austin's room and pulled the pale blue dress off the hanger. She'd only worn it once—to a cocktail party she and Ben had attended just before he left to pursue greater challenges. As she slipped her legs into the soft satin, she smiled at the thought of Ben.

Nice, safe Ben. He was a lot like Nick—not in looks so much but in the way she related to both of them. With them she could just be a friend, with them she didn't act like a silly, love-struck teenager. She pulled the dress up, wrenched her shoulder to get the zipper up, and spun her arm to get the crick out. Then she stopped. All the blue dresses in the world would never be able to help tonight. No, tonight no matter what she told herself she could do, she knew she would end up in tears.

In fact, even now they were right behind her eyes—stinging just enough to tell her they hadn't gone away. Back in the bathroom, she pulled her small make-up bag out and applied just enough to disguise the dark circles under her eyes. It wasn't great, but it would have to do. A little blush, a little eye shadow, two brushes of mascara, and her face was as ready as it was going to get.

As she threw the mascara back into the bag, she laughed. "I guess tonight we'll see just how water-proof you are."

With that she left the bathroom and sat on the bed to pull on her hose. A sidelong glance at the little clock told her that Lexie would be coming to get her in only a few minutes. Somehow it was easier here—where she didn't have to face anyone and see their concern for her written on their faces. In truth, it wasn't easier; it just wasn't so embarrassing.

A snap, then two and her shoes were on. She walked into the bathroom to examine the entire effect, which actually was better than she could've hoped for. Gently she smiled at herself. "Just smile and you'll be fine." But even then, behind that smile she could see the pain, and she sucked in a hard breath. "Just don't think about him. He's in the past. Leave him there."

The knock sounded on her door, and her smile crossed her face again. "Ready or not."

She pulled her small black purse off the bed and slung it over her shoulder. At the door she took one more breath before she turned the knob, fully expecting it to be Lexie, but on the other side she found a rather timid looking Nick.

"Wow, you look great," he said, surveying her outfit.

Her gaze traveled down his dark gray jacket, light gray shirt and black pants. "You don't look so bad yourself. Where's Lex?"

"Final make-up phase. She said she'd be out in a minute. So, you ready?"

"As I'll ever be."

He smiled in that way that said he hoped everything was going to work out for her. "I'm glad you decided to come."

When she looked at him, she could say nothing else. "So am I."

Chapter 8

The Grand Plaza Hotel. It was a place Camille had only visited once. The night she had gone to the prom with Jaylon. The magic of that night wrapped around her again as she walked through the huge front doors, followed by Nick and Lexie. The hotel had actually been built more than a hundred years before so its grandeur had nothing to do with gold-plated imitations. No, The Grand Plaza was the real deal. A slightly winding staircase led from the ground floor where they now stood up to an unseen floor above which held the Grand Ballroom.

As Camille laid her hand on the handrail and climbed the red-carpeted steps, she could feel him right next to her as though the prom was happening at this moment. In fact, she wouldn't have been at all surprised to see the red and white carnations lining her wrist when she looked down.

It had been an eternity, and yet it was all right there on the surface of her heart. When they reached the landing, Camille looked back at her friends. They seemed happier now although she could still see their discomfort if she looked for it, which she forced herself not to do.

Her spirit didn't need the added pressure. She pulled the calm to her although it barely stayed over her nerves as she stepped through the double doors and into the enormous room where round tables circled a wooden dance floor.

"Umm, Camille Wright," she said at the little reception table.

The young lady manning the table nodded and checked her name off the list. "Hors d'oeuvres are to the left, and dinner will be served shortly."

"Thanks." Camille gingerly stepped away from the table and into the small crowd already gathered. She didn't want to. She thought she could simply walk in without looking for him, but the instant she was in the ballroom, the first thing she did was scan the crowd for his chocolate brown hair, waved back—disheveled and yet perfect at the same time.

"Nice crowd," Lexie said, appearing at Camille's elbow.

"You said two hundred?"

"Somewhere in that range," Lexie said as she linked arms with Camille. "Come on, let's get something to eat. I'm starving."

Camille hadn't eaten much of anything all day, which she was quite sure Lexie had noticed. The more they were around each other, the more Camille realized how little Lexie missed.

"Nick! Lexie!" Keane said, stopping them before they got to the refreshment table. "I wanted to tell you we had such a good time last night. That hay ride was something else."

Nick smiled as he shook Keane's hand. "Glad you liked it."

"It was nice to get a jump on seeing everybody again," Keane said as he pulled Yvonne to his side. "It gave Yvonne a chance to at least meet a few people before we got bombarded tonight."

"I can imagine," Lexie said to Yvonne. "This must be a little overwhelming."

"To say the least," Yvonne said in a small voice. "I just hope there won't be a test later."

"Don't worry, we'll help you cheat if there is," Nick said with a smile.

The group laughed.

"So, Camille, you going back tomorrow?" Keane asked, and Camille's attention trained back on the group.

"Yeah, but not 'til the afternoon."

"There's a good plan," Keane said with a nod.

Camille smiled although the fact that she was one wheel too many wasn't lost on her. "Gone too long and the company might send out a search party."

"Huh," Keane said, "if I was gone too long, they'd probably throw a party."

Nick looked at him teasingly. "In fact, I think we did."

"Ha. Ha," Keane said not really hurt.

"Well, I hate to break this up," Lexie said, "but I've got to get something to eat."

"No problem," Keane said. "See you all later."

"See you," Nick said, and they turned back for the punch. "He's really nice. I never would've guessed that in high school."

Lexie shrugged. "People grow up. I think that's the point of having a reunion."

At the table Camille dutifully placed two crackers and some cheese on her napkin. Somehow she was going to have to eat this or suffer through another nightmare interrogation from Lexie. Carefully she put one small piece of cheese on one small cracker and put the whole thing in her mouth just as her gaze snagged on the door. Her throat never saw it coming, and in a half-second the cracker and cheese lodged itself in her windpipe.

The entire top of her chest and shoulders wound around the offending object as the air in her lungs reversed course. Her whole body coughed, and it seemed that the only direction air was going was out as she choked again and again, doubling over as she reached for the wall to steady herself.

"Hey, are you okay?" Lexie asked with immediate concern.

Camille tried to nod, but all she could do was cough again.

"Is she all right?" Nick asked.

"Get her some punch," Lexie commanded as she laid a hand on Camille's back. "You all right?"

The nod worked better this time, but the coughs still hadn't relinquished their hold on her. Two more and a long breath and once again she felt like she might live to see another day. She blinked back the alarm in her system and swallowed twice, still huddled over herself.

"Here." Nick forced a small cup of bright green punch into her hand.

She drank a little as slowly she returned to equilibrium. Finally she looked at her friends with blurry eyes. "Wow. Watch that cheese. It'll get you."

Both friends looked at her as though they thought she might pass out right there.

"You sure you're okay?" Lexie asked.

"I'm fine," Camille said, but even she questioned that when across the room she caught sight of him again. Black jacket, black slacks, and an off-white shirt casually unbuttoned at the collar. He took her breath away more than any little piece of cheese ever could.

With one hand firmly planted on Nicole's back, Jaylon made the rounds through the crowd. He talked to people who had come the night before and a few who hadn't made it then. Nicole, in her crushed black velvet skirt and mahogany jacket shirt, looked every bit the part of a big city clothing purchaser. He was proud of her, like showing off a trophy he had been lucky enough to acquire since the last time he'd had a reason to rub elbows with these people.

Everyone was so happy about their up-coming wedding. The women wanted to know all the details. The men all elbowed Jaylon at what an impressive catch he had made. As he watched her, he had to agree with them. She was impressive—on the outside anyway. But beneath the surface she wasn't nearly so shiny.

Two of his friends at college had warned him about that happening, so maybe everyone went through that. She certainly looked the part of the happy almost-newlywed. He smiled at her when someone asked where they were going on their honeymoon. However, the second she looked away, his smile faded and he glanced across the crowd in a vain attempt to get some space between them.

It was then that he saw her—the flowing blue dress, hair up so that her graceful neck and the delicate expanse of her shoulders were clearly visible. The wire-framed glasses and soft features. In that instant everything else paled in comparison to her.

"Cazenovia?" Charis, a girl Jaylon barely remembered from high school, asked. "What's that? A community college?"

Nicole wound her arm through Jaylon's. "He's going to try to get on with Syracuse University next year, but it was a little late to apply there now. Besides, it'll be nice to have a year of just being together before we both make the next jump in our careers. Isn't that right, honey?"

"Yeah," he said, straining to make himself keep his feet planted at her side.

"So, what is it you do, Nicole?" Charis asked.

"Oh, I'm a buyer for Macy's."

"No kidding," Charis said as her eyes widened.

"Well, assistant to the buyer," Nicole hedged. "But it's just a matter of time."

"How totally cool is that?" Charis gushed. "So, do you get to go to New York and Europe for the fashion shows and stuff?"

"We're going to New York in May. A couple weeks after the wedding."

"Oh, I bet you are so excited."

"Well, it's going to be hectic, you know. But the good thing is it'll get me out of having to stay at Brickhaven the whole time before we move."

"Wow. Married and career taking off in the same month. My head would be spinning," Charis said.

"Mine does sometimes, you know, but how can I ever be unhappy to be marrying Jaylon?" Nicole nuzzled her nose into his neck as Jaylon fought to keep a smile on his face.

"You are so lucky," Charis said in awestruck admiration. "But I always knew Jaylon would marry somebody amazing. He was always so hot when we were in school. Absolutely. All the girls were after him."

Jaylon ducked his head in genuine embarrassment. The last thing he wanted to do was to relive that part of his high school experience.

"Do you blame them?" Nicole asked with a tinny sort of laugh. "He's still hot."

Charis shook her head. "I'm not arguing with you there."

"I think I'm going to go get us something to drink. You want something?" he asked Nicole.

"Punch." She wound her arm down his and laced her fingers into his. "Don't be gone too long."

"I'll try not to," he said, having every intention of being gone as long as possible.

His feet carried him away from them as he stopped to talk with every person he remotely remembered all the way to the refreshment table. Every moment he spent on the errand meant one more he didn't have to spend hearing Nicole doing her level best to sound superior to his former classmates.

At the punch bowl he poured two glassfuls and reluctantly started back, but he hadn't made it two steps when he met up with Lexie.

"Well, well, look what the cat dragged in," Lexie said not exactly harshly but not exactly friendly either.

"Hey, Lexie," he said, fighting not to hear her tone. His heart wanted to hug her, and his brain didn't veto the action, so he reached over and wrapped an arm around her. "That was a great party last night."

"Yeah," she said barely cordial. "It was some party." She looked past him. "So, where's Nicole?"

"Oh, she's back there talking to Charis Smyth. You remember her, the volleyball player. Short, kind of light hair."

"Oh, yeah." Lexie crossed her arms in front of her. "I remember her."

Jaylon nodded as a veil of tension descended over them. Hesitantly he took a sip of the punch. "I noticed the pictures at your house, so you've got three kids?"

"Two girls and a boy."

"That must keep you hopping."

"Gives me something to do," she said, never melting the ice around her voice. "How about you? I hear wedding bells are in the future."

He nodded suddenly wishing he hadn't stopped. "May 3rd."

She looked like she was about to tell him that had to be the stupidest idea in the history of ideas, but at the last moment, she smiled. "Well, I hope you two will be very happy together."

"Thanks," he said as his heart melted on her words. "You know, I'd better get back over there. She's going to think I went AWOL."

"Yeah, we wouldn't want that, now would we?"

Jaylon stood for one more second and then raised one glass. "I'll see you later."

"Later," she said softly.

It was like pushing an elephant as he coerced his feet into turning for the back. He wondered briefly where Camille had disappeared to, but he quickly decided for the sake of his heart not to dwell on that question for any length of time.

"Jaylon?" a voice in the crowd said, and he turned.

"Mrs. Allen," he said in disbelief. "I didn't know you were here."

"Oh," she said with a shrug, "I always come for a few minutes. Nothing like seeing my old students again."

He gave her a quick hug. "Well, how are you? Classes going good?"

"They're fine." She waved a coffee-colored hand at him, and he noticed the years on her face and in her hands. "But I guess you probably heard already this is my last year at Ridgecrest."

"Last year?" he asked with concern.

"My husband and I bought a little place down in Florida when they offered me early retirement." Mrs. Allen smiled slightly. "Can't pass something like that up."

Jaylon couldn't help but let the concern float through him. "But what's Ridgecrest going to do for a drama teacher?"

She smiled at him. "Oh, there are plenty of other drama teachers out there. I'm sure I won't be too hard to replace."

"Don't be too sure of something like that," he said quickly.

"So, what are you up to these days?"

He ducked and scratched his eyebrow with one punch cup laden thumb. "Well, I'm teaching up state."

The incredulous look on her face told him she hadn't expected that.

"In fact, I was meaning to come talk to you this weekend about some more classroom exercises."

Her eyes shone with pride. "Well, I'll be home all day tomorrow if you want to come visit. We can go up to the school and get some things. Fact, I can give you most of my stuff. I sure won't be needing it anymore."

A pang hit his heart. He couldn't imagine Ridgecrest without Mrs. Allen. "I'll have to do that."

For a moment they stood, and then she looked around. "I'd better get going, my husband's waiting in the car."

"Okay," he said, carefully hugging her so that he didn't spill punch down her back. "I'll be sure to come by tomorrow."

"I'm looking forward to it."

With that, they turned and went their separate directions. By the time he broke through the crowd again, Nicole was in the center of what looked like an entire flock of women.

"Here you go, sweetheart. Sorry it too me so long." He handed her the cup, but his ears immediately picked up on the whispered giggle that swept the group. He looked over at them and smiled. "What'd I miss?"

"Nothing," Nicole said innocently. "They were just filling me in on your high school exploits."

Again with the giggles. He lifted his chin in understanding. "I think I'm just going to go find Seth." Then he looked at the group. "Ladies."

Smiles all around greeted his glance, and quickly he spun and walked away. Some things were simply better off not knowing—like what exploits they were talking about. Yes, that was a big one he was better off just walking away from.

He met Seth and Julie coming in the door and latched onto his friend like a life preserver. "Man, am I glad you're here."

"Nice to see you, too," Seth said with a raise of his eyebrows.

"Where's Nicole?" Julie asked, looking around Jaylon for a sign of her.

"Oh, she's over there, telling everybody our life's story," Jaylon said, at which Julie went off to join Nicole's group.

"So, how goes it, my friend?" Seth asked, clapping Jaylon on the shoulder.

Jaylon considered going with the standard, fine, but when he looked at Seth, he knew he had to talk to somebody. "You got a minute?"

"I got all the minutes you need," Seth said jovially, and then he realized how serious Jaylon had become. "What's wrong?"

In fear that someone might overhear them, Jaylon glanced around. "Could we do this somewhere else?"

"I'm right behind you."

The dread of somehow bumping into Jaylon while she was alone kept Camille right at Nick's side—so close that anyone who didn't know better would've thought it was they who were married. He was her shelter. Her haven, and she wasn't about to let him out of her sight.

"Parts, huh?" Caleb Weber asked Nick as Camille stood at his side, sipping the green punch as slowly as possible. "Like car parts or what?"

"Mostly," Nick said, "but we've got all kinds of things—boat parts, truck parts, a little of everything. How about you?"

"Me? Oh, you know me. I've been in and out of a hundred jobs already. Did a stint on a fishing boat a year or so back off the coast of Alaska. I may go back to that. It's about the only thing I've ever really liked."

Nick smiled politely. "Sometimes life is like that."

"Yeah."

At that moment the speakers squealed to life, and Camille put her free hand to her ear as Lexie, who stood at the microphone on the little stage, looked over to her makeshift soundman in annoyance.

"Sorry," she said into the microphone. "How's everybody doing?"

A small cheer went up across the ballroom.

"Good. Glad to hear it. Umm, I just wanted to tell you we're going to go ahead and start the buffet line right up here in front. So you can come on up whenever you're ready."

Nick looked at Camille with a help-let's-get-out-of-this-while-we-can look. "Well, we'd better go snag Lexie and get in line. You take care, Caleb."

"You, too." Caleb raised his glass to them. Then he turned and disappeared into the crowd.

"Could he be anymore frightening?" Nick asked in Camille's ear as he guided her through the crowd.

She laughed. "I wouldn't know how." There was simply no way to be grateful enough about Nick's presence. At the moment, he and only he was keeping her sane.

The Grand Ballroom was graced not only with beauty inside, but through the double doors opposite the entrance there was a small garden, with a winding trail that led through overhanging trees and potted flowers to a bridge which spread across a small stream lit in hazy blue light. The sky's fading light completed the picture.

"Okay, what's going on with you?" Seth asked when they stopped next to the little bench some distance from the stream.

"I don't know." Jaylon collapsed onto the bench in frustration. "Nicole's great. Right?"

"Yeah." The answer was slow and hesitant.

"Then, why am I thinking about Camille all the time?" He closed his eyes to shut out the implications of that question.

Seth stood without saying a word for a long time. Then he bent to look at Jaylon. "Do you love Nicole?"

"Yeah. I mean I think so."

"You think so?" Seth asked with a raise of his eyebrows.

Jaylon shook his head as he stood and walked over to the doors. "I asked her to marry me. Didn't I?"

Not one second did Seth look anywhere else. "That wasn't the question."

Air escaped from Jaylon's lungs in a whoosh. "She's great. I mean, she's really great."

"But?"

Slowly Jaylon shook his head. "But every time I see Camille, I can't help but think what if..."

"What if you had stayed with her."

"Yeah." Jaylon looked at his friend. "That's terrible, I know."

"No, it's not terrible. Actually I think it's pretty normal. In fact, they have a word for it—it's called cold feet."

Jaylon laid a tired hand against the hard steel of the doors. "But what if I'm making a mistake?"

"Do you think you're making a mistake?"

"I don't know." His patience cracked right down the center as he spun and sat down on the bench again with a sigh. In frustration he ran his fingers through his hair. "How can you know something like that?"

Seth paused, looked at his friend, and sat down. "You know, when Julie and I first got married, I went through the same thing. Every girl I passed, I'd look at her and think, 'Did I give up looking too soon?' I mean I loved Julie, but there was still that question in my head. Then one day, I realized I wasn't being fair to Julie by not trusting our promises as much as I was supposed to."

"So, what then? You just shut everything else off? Like a switch or something."

"Kind of," Seth said softly. "When you make a commitment to someone, really make it—you have to shut the door that anyone else can ever reach you on that level. That's what marriage is about. Or what it's supposed to be about anyway. Giving yourself to one person. The challenge is to figure out which person that is *before* you say those words."

Jaylon sighed. "Sounds easy when you put it like that."

"When it's the right person, it is easy."

For a long moment, Jaylon sat there. Then he looked over at his friend and held up his hand, which Seth met in mid-air. "Thanks, buddy."

"Anytime."

Camille told herself that looking for him was akin to suicide, but she couldn't help it. With little effort, she located Nicole, sitting at a back table with several other women around her. They seemed to be having an absolutely fabulous time. With a shake of her head, Camille focused on the plate in her hands and on the motion of her feet.

Funny how difficult just walking became when your heart was no longer a part of your body.

"Here okay?" Nick asked, motioning to a table.

"Yeah." She set her plate down just as her gaze jumped to the back double doors, and in a breath nothing was okay. Why did he have to look like that? Why couldn't he just look bedraggled and awful? That would make this so much more livable.

Not wanting it to, but having no control over it just the same, her gaze followed him as he crossed the room, buried in deep conversation with the guy she recognized from the trailer. Seth. Whatever they were discussing, it looked like it was of the utmost importance.

She sat down, barely seeing the chair as her heart followed him right to Nicole's table where he reached down the side of her arms and leaned down to kiss her. The entire table of women swooned with the gesture, and Camille shook her head in annoyance.

He was just a big playboy. That's all. It was all for show. And for all she knew, so was his relationship with Nicole. She snatched that thought away from her brain in anger. That was as hostile as thoughts came, hoping someone's relationship would break up just to make your own heart feel better? It wasn't something anyone could think and still call herself a friend.

"The D.J.'s supposed to be here in an hour," Lexie said, sitting down next to Nick. "He'd better not be late."

"Relax." Nick covered Lexie's hand gently. "He'll be here."

Lexie sighed. "I just don't want anything else to go wrong."

"Why? What's gone wrong?" Camille asked with concern.

Both gazes met hers as though they had completely forgotten she was sitting with them.

"Nothing," Lexie said, brushing the question off. "I just hope he shows up." She picked up her fork. "By the way, did you see Matt

Caruthers? He showed up about an hour ago. They said he's a helicopter pilot now." Just before she put a forkful of meat in her mouth, she added, "I think you should go talk to him, Camille."

"Me?" Camille asked, completely surprised at the suggestion. "I don't even know the guy. Why would I want to go talk to him?"

"Well, he flies helicopters for one thing," Lexie said with a shrug. "So, that gives you something in common." One pause. "And he's single."

"Oh, how nice for him," Camille said as she realized a second unsuspecting gerbil had entered the ark. With Lexie on the case, meeting up was simply a matter of time.

She forked through her potatoes and forced two bites down, amid a wash of water.

"Did you ever say if Ariana's coming?" Nick asked off-handedly, and Camille was grateful to him for trying to spin the conversation in a different—albeit equally depressing direction.

Lexie shook her head in annoyance. "I don't think so. Last I checked anyway."

"What ever happened to her anyway?" Camille asked, recklessly swerving to the other side of the road.

"I think she ended up in Buffalo or something," Lexie said, and it was clear she wasn't happy with the new direction the conversation had taken. "Last I heard she was on her third marriage...some casting director I think."

Camille arched her eyebrows, "Seriously?"

"That's what I heard," Lexie said with a shrug. "Oh, look, there's Matt now." Then before Nick or Camille had the chance to stop her, Lexie leaned out of her chair and waved to the tall, black-haired guy standing in line. "Matt! Hey, how you doing?"

He looked over at them, and a question ran through his eyes for a moment. In the next heartbeat it was clear that he didn't want to appear rude, so he crossed the small expanse to their table. "Hi, guys."

In a light gray jacket and dark shirt, he looked every bit the accomplished pilot.

"I'm sorry to drag you out of line," Lexie said gushingly, "but I've got a bet with Nick here that I can talk to more classmates tonight than he can."

Nick raised his eyebrows at Camille as if to say, 'What bet?'

Camille ducked her head to the table to prevent the laugh.

"So, what are you up to these days?" Lexie asked.

"I'm working as a chopper pilot down south," Matt said, lifting one foot to the brace on the chair next to Camille's.

"No kidding," Lexie said. "Did you know that Camille designs helicopters?" Lexie looked at her friend just before she reached over to her. "Isn't that right, Camille?"

Trying not to choke for the second time that evening, Camille put her napkin to her mouth to finish chewing. "Umm, actually it's airplanes. I design airplanes."

It was Matt's turn to be impressed. "No kidding? What kind of planes?"

"Military stuff mostly."

Matt spun the chair next to Camille and sat down. "Military stuff? Like what?"

She coughed slightly and barely managed to look at him. "Well, we're working on a new one for the Air Force right now—kind of a second generation F-19."

"And you're designing it?"

"Yeah, me and a team," Camille said.

"She's the team leader," Lexie pointed out. "Isn't that right, Camille?"

Camille shot her a would-you-shut-up look. "Umm, well, yeah. The original leader left to do consulting work so I kind of inherited the project."

"That's awesome," Matt said clearly glad he had taken the time to come over. He glanced back at the dwindling line. "Umm, I'd better go get something to eat before it's all gone, but could I...I mean would you mind if I join you?"

Camille expected Lexie to jump in with a big, dramatic welcome, but the question was so obviously directed at Camille, even Lexie wouldn't try that one.

"Umm, no. I mean yes. I mean that sounds great," Camille said, choking on the words and her smile.

He grinned and stood. "I'll be right back."

"K." She watched him walk far enough away from the table so that he couldn't hear her before she leaned across the table. "What do you think you are doing?"

"Trying to fix you up," Lexie said as she smirked at her friend. "And it looks like it's working."

In frustration Camille shook her head and shoveled food in her mouth. How had she ever allowed herself to be talked into any of this? She must've been insane to ever get on that plane bound for Rochester.

From the moment Matt walked away from her table, Jaylon followed his every move. He shouldn't worry. This night was supposed to be about talking to old friends, reconnecting. It was just the level of that connection he was concerned about, and the sight of Matt walking back to her table only a few minutes later didn't do one single thing to calm Jaylon's anxiety.

He tried to keep his attention focused on his own table and the conversation going on around it, but that was difficult. The only thing that helped anchor it there was Seth, who was obviously keeping a watchful eye on his old friend. It had been a long time, but not that long, and Jaylon knew that Seth could still read him like a third-grade textbook.

So, throughout the rest of dinner, Jaylon did his best to stay up with the conversation and not glance back across the room to her table. He tried, and for whole entire minutes, he actually succeeded, but then in a careless moment his gaze would slip across the room and land on her.

The soft curve of her face when she smiled and the eyes that could say volumes with one single glance called to him like the yell across a chasm. Although they were as good as standing across an abyss from each other, those moments felt more real than any single second he had at his own table.

He wondered what they were talking about. They were obviously having a very good time although when his mind traced back to high school, he couldn't remember ever having seen Camille so much as talk to Matt. He smiled absently at something Julie said as he willed his attention to stay at his table.

With the next glance, however, his attention stuck on Camille's table when he realized that Matt's other half seemed not to be attached to his side. A picture of a tiny rodent stepping onto the ark slipped through Jaylon's mind, and his heart fell. What if Matt didn't have an "other half"? What if he was still looking...just like she was?

That thought yanked his attention to her table again. They were laughing about something. Why had they sat so far away? He wished he could hear what they were saying—hear how desperate his own situation was becoming.

"No, we'd love for you to come," Nicole was saying at his side. "Isn't that right, honey?"

"Oh, of course," Jaylon said with something only vaguely resembling a smile. "Yeah, we'd love for you to come." Where, he had absolutely no idea.

With Matt sitting next to her, the dinner seemed to fly by. Camille asked every question she could think of about flying as she had never actually flown anything in her life. The irony was, safely on the ground, she designed vehicles meant only for other people to soar in.

"I'm working on getting a copter they flew in Vietnam," Matt said as the wait staff cleared their table.

"What for?" Nick said incredulously. "That's not something you can just set out in your front yard."

Matt pulled himself forward with his elbow on the table. "Actually I've got this lease on a building in Raleigh that I've considered making into a museum."

"A museum?" Lexie asked in fascination. "For helicopters?"

Matt nodded. "I've got tons of stuff—documents, pictures, old replicas. It just seems a shame to keep them all for myself. I think sharing them would be something I'd really like to do. But I can't very well have everybody trekking through my house to see them, so that's my great dream. Set up a museum and have an old 'copter to actually sit right in the middle of it."

"Sounds awesome," Nick said sincerely. "You'll have to let us know when you get it up and running."

"I'll do that," Matt said.

A rather harried young man appeared at the edge of their table at that moment. "Ms. McGee?"

Lexie along with everyone else looked up. "Yes."

"Umm, I'm with Discman's. Charlie got sick, and I'm his replacement. Do you want me to go ahead and start? Or would you rather wait?"

Lexie looked to Nick for guidance.

"Why don't we go ahead and start?" Nick said, looking out across the tables. "It looks like everybody's about finished."

That made no difference in the young man's nervousness. "Umm, would you mind coming up there for a few songs, just so I can make sure I know what you want?"

"Sure," Lexie said, and Nick instantly stood to pull her chair out. "We'll be right back."

Then before Nick could sit back down, Lexie grabbed his hand and pulled him with her.

Camille looked at Matt as Lexie and Nick walked away. She could feel the set up fall around her. Slowly she shook her head. "That Lexie. She's not always the most subtle person in the world."

Matt smiled. "Yeah, I kind of noticed that."

"How could you not?" Camille laughed, genuinely glad to not be sitting here by herself.

The music started, and she smiled. Songs could always bring back such clear pictures for her. This particular one conjured up a memory of sitting in her room with Lexie when they were sophomores or something—long before either of them had a life.

"I haven't heard this song in forever," Matt said. "They used to play this over the loud speakers in the gym all the time." He shook his head. "That old gym. I wonder if it's even still there. Have you been over to the high school?"

"No, I've tried to stay as far away as possible."

"I hear you there. That's one part of my life I'm definitely glad is over."

Her gaze fled across the room as her heart ripped in two. She wasn't glad it was over. Given the chance, she would go back and relive every single second of it for the rest of her life.

That song ended, and a slower one took its place.

"Hey, what do you say we check out the dance floor?" Matt asked.

"I might step on your toes."

He pulled one piece of his pant leg up. "Boots." Then he looked down at her sandaled feet. "I'd be more worried about *your* toes."

She laughed. "Then I say, 'What're we waiting for?'"

Jaylon knew Seth was watching him, but he didn't really care. Camille with Matt Caruthers? Until that moment Jaylon had never had anything against Matt, but in that instant, he could very easily have dropped the guy off the edge of a cliff.

"We're going to have a live band at our reception," Nicole said with an air of superiority. "None of this D.J. stuff for us. I mean how much talent does it take to put a CD in and push play?"

Jaylon was trying not to listen.

"The committee said they couldn't find a band," Julie said, "but I don't think they looked very hard."

"Well, they certainly did a bang-up job on the rest of this little celebration," Seth said, leaning back in his chair.

"They ordered food," Julie said in annoyance. "It's not hard to make you happy."

Not taking the bait she was dangling in front of him, he leaned over to her. "You ought to know."

She made an irritated noise at him and turned to watch the dancers. "They look like they haven't danced in ten years."

"Oh, my gosh," Nicole said as if a rock star personified had just stepped up, "Jaylon and I went out to the Lost Horizon last month. Ugh! That place is unbelievable. Talk about some people who can dance now. It was amazing."

Jaylon remembered that night during which he was treated to three hours of Nicole's friends—all of whom lived together, none of whom were married. In fact, it was more like spending an evening playing rotating dates. First two of them seemed to be together, then those two would each be with someone else. The thought of it sickened him to the core.

"Want to dance?" he asked Nicole if for no other reason than to have something to do besides think.

"I guess so." She laid her hand in his. "Maybe we can show these people some real moves."

Please, Nicole, please, he begged silently as she led him to the floor. *Do not embarrass me here.* His timing could not possibly have been worse because the second his foot hit the dance floor, the beat changed to a pulsating drumbeat that he couldn't remember having ever heard.

On a good night, Nicole's idea of dancing looked more like an exotic dancer with a pole, but tonight she obviously had something to prove. As embarrassment seeped through him, she slid around him so close a molecule couldn't have gotten between them.

In the clubs was one thing. This was something else entirely. He tried to smile at some of the others on the dance floor, and they smiled back although they didn't have to broadcast what they were thinking. Thoroughly regretting the rash decision of asking Nicole to dance, he laid his mind outside himself and simply prayed that the song would be over before he was completely humiliated.

It took longer than he had hoped, but finally God got around to granting his request, and the beat slowed.

"Dance with me, darling," Nicole said, hanging her hands on his neck and pressing her body next to his.

With his hands on her waist, he tried to relax and enjoy the music, but every gaze in the place was on them, and he knew it. Being on stage was one thing—that was at least predictable. This was about as unpredictable as it got.

"I can't wait 'til we're doing this at our reception," Nicole said in his ear softly, and his whole body cringed at the thought. "But I don't think I'm going to want to dance too much that night."

Again embarrassment seeped over him as he pulled away from her as far as he could get without physically removing himself from her presence. Three weeks, and this would be for real. Three weeks, and they would be tied together forever.

Forever. It sounded like such a long time.

Camille kept her focus on Matt although she couldn't help but notice Jaylon and Nicole on the dance floor. It was too bad she had never been flashy like that. There was no way she could ever pull off that dance. One-on-one with her husband alone in a bedroom, she would never be able to pull off that dance.

"Boy, it's getting hot in here," Matt said after their third dance. "You want some punch?"

"Sounds good," she said as he led her back to their table.

He helped her with the chair. "I'll be right back."

She nodded as she laid her chin on the edge of her wrist to watch the dancers. Her mind drifted as it always did to being in Jaylon's arms—gliding as though gravity had no hold on them. At that moment she would've traded every other second of her life to feel that again.

"Here we go," Matt said, setting the punch in front of her and jolting her out of her reverie.

"Thanks."

"So, tell me," Matt said when he'd sat down at her side. "A great catch like you...how come you don't have Mr. Perfect sitting here next to you?"

Dreamily she shrugged, trying to move the haze in her mind away as easily. "I guess luck hasn't been on my side."

He laughed a little at that. "I hear you there." He nodded slowly as he took a drink. "I hear you there."

Chapter 9

When midnight came, Matt begged off the celebration. He had a sixty-thirty flight the next morning that required him to be awake as he would be the pilot. Camille said good night to him, grateful for having had a friend to enjoy the evening with yet knowing it would go no further than that.

She sat at the table, watching Nick and Lexie dance, and the envy invaded her heart again as her gaze fell to her empty glass. It seemed that seeing her friends happy should've made her happy, too, but as far as she could tell, it just didn't work that way.

With a sigh she realized there was precious little she could do about anything in her life at the moment, so she stood, knowing that no one would so much as notice her absence. Her feet carried her to the garden's double doors, and she turned to look at the dancers only once more. Just before her heart had a chance to take hold of that image, she pushed her way outside.

The air was cool, and her arms, minus sleeves, immediately protested. But being in there, with them and yet totally alone was just too hard. Even freezing to death seemed a better choice at the moment. A dreamy step at a time she walked past the little bench, through the trees to the bridge. Its plain wooden planks clicked against her heels as she stepped up it, laid her hands on the railing, and simply let the dreams in her heart take her away.

How many rounds of let's-see-if-we-can-humiliate-Jaylon he had endured he had no idea, but the idea of simply getting away was nearly intoxicating. They had left—Camille and Matt. One minute they were dancing, and the next he couldn't find them anywhere. He tried to convince himself it didn't matter, but convincing himself of anything anymore was becoming this side of impossible.

"I'm going to get some air," he said to Seth when the ladies had vacated the table bound for the restroom.

"You want some company?" Seth asked clearly troubled by his friend's strange mood.

With a sad smile, Jaylon shook his head. "I just need to be alone for a little while."

Seth looked at him, and then he nodded. "We'll be here."

"I know," Jaylon said.

Casually, although he didn't notice it, he put one hand in his pocket and made his way through the guests to the double doors. If he could just get outside, get some good, clean air into his lungs again, he was sure the cobwebs that were clinging to his brain would clear.

He pushed through the doors and slipped outside. The instant the doors closed behind him, he was glad he had come. His spirit took in his first real breath as he started down the little path. It was quiet out here. So quiet that even the traffic out front seemed only to blend with the wind in the trees.

It was really too bad someone couldn't bottle this place and sell it. In the next breath he rounded the corner, and every other thought ceased—for there, standing in the wavy blue light, stood every dream he'd ever had.

For one moment and then another he didn't move, he couldn't. All he could do was stand there in the middle of this vision and watch her. Everything about her was exactly like he remembered and yet so, so much better. The small shoulders, the regal chin, the wisp of a waist. In fact, even as he stood there, he could feel every curve of her under his fingertips.

Once again, it all came back to him—holding her under the tree, watching her blossom on stage, feeling her soul meld with his. In one reckless second he took his life in his hands and stepped toward the bridge. One, two, three steps, until he was standing right at the base of it, gazing up at her as though she really was just a piece of some unbelievable dream. His foot slid up the first plank to begin his ascent up to her, but the second his footfall sounded, she jumped and spun toward him with a gasp.

"Sorry," he said as a smile spread from his heart to his face and beyond. The earth stopped on its axis as he was suddenly caught up in the depths of her eyes.

Her smile brought more memories with it. "You've really got to stop doing that. You know?"

His heart pulled him up to her side where he had just enough presence of mind to turn and lean back casually against the railing as he crossed his arms. Side-by-side they stood for the space of time it took for their souls to connect again.

"So, what're you doing out here?" he asked as he tried to simultaneously imprint this moment on his memory and yet not look like he was.

She looked back out at the shimmering water. "It was getting kind of stuffy in there."

He gazed at her, amazed at his luck. Never had he ever thought he would get the chance to be this close to her again. And this time, he wouldn't waste the chance by talking about himself. "I didn't get to ask you last night, what're you up to these days?"

The blue light reflected off her glasses. "Designing."

"Designing what?"

"Airplanes," she said so softly it brought back a memory of her sitting under a tree, ecstatic that she was going to be able to follow her dreams.

He was happy to see that she had made those dreams come true. "Here?"

"In Pittsburgh." She looked at him for a split second, and then she returned her gaze to the water.

"Pittsburgh? I bet that's great."

She shrugged. "It's okay. Kind of lonely sometimes, but I can't complain."

He waited a full minute, trying to decide whether or not to ask the question that was on a perpetual loop in his brain. "So, I guess that means you haven't gotten married then?"

"Married?" Her gaze turned toward him incredulously. Slowly it fell from his as she shook her head. "No. I haven't gotten married." She laughed like the wind. "I have a cat though."

There was no way to comprehend how his heart didn't burst right out of his chest. "A cat?"

"Max. He keeps me company." She stopped and then laughed again. "Pretty pathetic, huh?"

He shrugged and looked over his shoulder to the water below. "Well, I've got 110 kids running around me every second of the day, and that gets kind of lonely sometimes too."

She looked at him with a questioning gaze before returning her attention to the water. "Yeah, but you have someone...special." Her words drifted out barely audible over the stream.

His heart went out to the sadness permeating her voice. Every word was couched in a melancholy so deep it felt all-but bottomless, and he leaned back over the railing to get a good look into her eyes. "Hey, you okay?"

She looked at him, and in that second he saw the palpable sadness in her eyes. "I'm trying to be."

No rational explanation would ever account for his next move as he gently swung his body around and wrapped an arm around her shoulders. "Hey. It's all right."

In the next breath she was in his arms, pressing into him as though he was her only shelter from an angry storm. No part of him could deny how perfectly they still fit together. That moment flowed into the next as he simply held her letting the quiet tears stream out of her heart. "It's going to be okay."

She sniffed into his jacket, and he felt her head move from side-to-side as the moment lingered. Finally, she pulled away from him and wiped her eyes. "I'm sorry."

Concern overwhelmed his entire being as her presence moved away from him. He ducked his head to the side, wanting only to assuage the anguish that seemed to pour from her. "No need to be sorry. These things can do that to you."

With only a single glance up at him, she turned and dropped her gaze to the water. The fight to hold her composure was evident. "It's just so much pressure, being here again. I feel like I'm under a microscope."

He could relate. "I know what you mean there."

Disgustedly she shook her head. "I should be used to it by now—the pressure, but I always feel like I'm just one cubic inch away from cracking."

His gaze softened as he watched her, but he never moved. "Pressure creates diamonds you know?"

A sad but surprised smile crossed her face and then fell away. "Yeah, but it also crushes things not strong enough to withstand it."

Warmth spread through his body. "Well, I wouldn't worry too much about that, you're the strongest person I know." *And the finest gem*, his mind whispered although he didn't put that thought into words.

Noise from the dance invaded the quiet air around them as someone pushed through the doors, and her gaze jerked past him to the path beyond although the door wasn't visible from the bridge. "We'd better get back. I'm sure Nicole's wondering where you are."

The name cracked over him like a thunderbolt. It was crazy, he knew, but he didn't want to go back. He wanted to stay out here in this dream and never move again. "Yeah. I guess so." Reluctantly he took a step back down the bridge before realizing she wasn't following him. "You coming?"

She looked at him with a sad smile. "I'll be there in a minute."

His soul wanted nothing more than to stay there with her, but he knew that option was out of his grasp. "Save me a dance?"

She smiled, considered, and finally nodded. That was all he needed. Voices coming down the path brought him back to reality, and half-heartedly he put one hand in his pocket and went back in to find Nicole.

The water, along with her spirit, seemed to continually come back to the same place. She loved him. He loved somebody else. And there was nothing she could do about that. When two other classmates joined her on the bridge, Camille knew her time there was finished, so with a sigh, she stepped off and walked back through the trees, hoping even as she did so he would be there to stop her.

She ran her hands up and down her arms, feeling the chill of his absence more than the chill of the night. It was a chill she knew would be with her forever. Back in the Ballroom, she walked to her table and sat. There was no use running from it. This was her life, and there was no escaping it.

The dancers moved in front of her like reflections on a mirror. Real, and yet somehow—not. Her eyes watched them even as her heart traveled to other places—the trailer, the tree, and now the bridge. One more memory to store with all the others. One more moment to hold onto when the lights were out and she was alone.

She was alone now. Sitting here, in the midst of two hundred people, she was completely alone, and yet her heart couldn't even cry about that fact. There were no tears left.

"One for old time's sake?" Jaylon asked, suddenly appearing at the edge of her table, extending his hand in invitation to her.

If this was a dream, she thought as she looked up at him, she really didn't care. Her hand reached up and laid itself in his, and all she could feel was the electricity she had somehow convinced herself would no longer be there. As he led her to the dance floor, the party, the crowd, everything dropped away from her consciousness.

Once there, he stopped, turned to her, and gently took her in his arms. It was like living again. Her brain managed to somehow keep them a respectable distance apart although her body was doing absolutely everything it could to get closer to him.

Cautiously she glanced at him, knowing what that would do to her heart, and yet not looking was killing her just the same. For one heartbeat their gazes met and locked.

"I've missed you, you know that?" he asked so softly she couldn't be sure her brain hadn't just whispered them for him.

But her heart smiled for her, and she breathed in being with him again. "I've missed you, too."

Nobody had to tell her, she knew she was standing right in the middle of the best moment of her life.

They hadn't made it even halfway around the dance floor when that song ended and the D.J. announced the last song of the night. Reluctantly Camille smiled at Jaylon. "You'd better go find Nicole."

His hand was still entwined with hers. "Yeah, I guess so." However, he never so much as moved. Then without warning, he wrapped her in his arms and squeezed so hard she thought her lungs would burst. With one more squeeze, he released her and backed away. "You take care of yourself. Okay?"

"Yeah," she said, struggling to gather any amount of rational thought left. "You, too."

With one more swing, he released her hand and walked back through the dwindling crowd. Her brain hurt, her body hurt. Everything about her hurt. She watched him as he stepped up behind Nicole, ran his hands down her arms, and kissed the top of her head.

In self-defense Camille ran her hands over her own arms and wished it wasn't nearly so cold.

"Hey," Lexie said as she and Nick walked up. "You ready to go?"

Camille looked at her friend with eyes blurred by tears. "Yeah, I'm ready."

In trying to act normal enough so that Nicole wouldn't notice his bleeding heart, Jaylon lost track of Camille, and by the time the last song ended, she was long gone. He tried to tell himself that was for the best and that now he could move on with Nicole in peace. He tried, but the absence of his soul told him differently.

On the way up to their rooms, Nicole was aglow. "I am so glad that's over. Did you talk to Keane? When's he going to list the place?"

If it was possible to crash further, Jaylon's spirit did. "I don't know. I didn't get a chance to ask him."

Nicole dimmed for one second. "Well, that's all right you can call him first thing Monday morning."

The elevator dinged on their floor as Nicole squeezed his arm. "This is just so great. Just think in three weeks, we'll be stepping off the elevator in Syracuse as Mr. and Mrs. Jaylon Quinn. Isn't that exciting?"

"Yeah, exciting," Jaylon said as he fished for the key in his pocket.

At her door they stopped, and Nicole's lashes dropped seductively. "You know, we're here now, and we're alone..."

"I'm tired," he said, backing away from her.

"Tired?" she asked in irritation.

He backed farther away. "We've got a long drive tomorrow, and I need to get up early to go see Mrs. Allen."

If Nicole could've looked any angrier, Jaylon certainly didn't know how. Quickly his brain locked back into gear. "Besides, in three weeks we've got the rest of our lives to be together." He advanced on her, deciding a good offense was the best defense. His lips connected with hers as he pressed them both against her door. The heat of her body froze every inch of him. This wasn't who he wanted to be here with, but he had proposed and going back now seemed foolhardy at best and utterly stupid at worst. When he finally broke from her, his gaze softened. "I'll see you in the morning."

She looked into his eyes. "I can't wait."

And he knew she meant more than just waking up to the sun. "'Night."

He felt her gaze follow him to his door, and he knew if he gave her even a glance, there would be no talking her out of her brilliant idea. So as quickly as he could with the shaking of his hands, he opened the hotel room door and slipped inside.

Once inside he collapsed against the door and closed his eyes. Why did life have to be so unbelievably complicated? If he just hadn't come. If she just hadn't come. If ten years before could've just been erased from his mind...

But logically, his brain asked, "What? What if it could?" Would Nicole be any more his soulmate if he had never met Camille? Would he then be able to give his life to her knowing it was the best decision of his life?

No answers. Only questions. He needed to think, and one place had always been the perfect place to think. Carefully, he peered out through the peephole, but there was no sign of Nicole. Steeling his nerves, he reached for the doorknob and gently turned it. In the hall, nothing.

Easily, quietly, he slipped out and left the hotel behind.

Not even Lexie and Nick could jolt Camille out of her dream world. Tomorrow she would go back to reality. Tonight she just wanted to hold onto the dream of his arms around her as long as possible. The ceiling in Austin's room was no match for the stars outside, and that's where her heart wanted to be. To hold on one more moment before she let go forever.

As quietly as possible she pulled on her jeans and the flannel shirt from the night before. They felt good. Her feet made no noise as she walked down the hall to the front door. Hoping they wouldn't be mad even though she knew they would never understand, Camille lifted the keys from the hook by the door and stepped outside.

A tree, under the stars, one more moment and then her life could go on without him.

Chapter 10

Straining to see through the darkness, Camille drove the little SUV as far down the path as she felt was safe. Her hand slid the gearshift to park, and she climbed out, mesmerized by the stars and the sight cloaked in darkness. It had always had a way of lifting her heart and allowing it to soar.

Peace wrapped around her as she laid a delicate hand on the tree trunk. Somewhere far below she could hear the water, and her spirit was again standing on a tiny bridge looking down into a shimmering blue pool. She put her hands on her arms as she slid down the length of the tree to the roots.

It always felt safe here—like nothing bad could possibly get to her. That was a feeling she had so rarely felt in her life, it was amazing to her every time it invaded her consciousness. She closed her eyes and allowed her dreams full rein. What she would've said if he had come without Nicole. What she would've felt if she could've let herself. Here, she could feel those things.

Desire. Love. Acceptance. Joy. If only...

A noise. Her eyes flew open as a set of headlights swept across the grassy plain beyond. Immediately the peace was replaced with an overwhelming sense of fear. She looked around for something to use as a weapon. It was she who was trespassing, of that she was completely sure. Maybe the owners had just gotten back. Once again on her feet, she crept to the edge of the tree as the headlights cut off plunging the area into darkness.

Terror reached up and twisted around her chest as she surveyed her options. Her vehicle was now blocked in, and she was a good 20 miles from town, walking out here in the darkness was a prescription for disaster, but something told her it couldn't compare to what was coming.

"Hello?" a voice from somewhere near the vehicles called. "Who's out there?"

That voice, and confusion crashed over the fear. "J?"

He stepped around the front fender of her vehicle, and the fear in her body stood down. "Camille?"

"Yeah," she said reluctant only because of her embarrassment at having been caught. When she could see him more clearly, she realized he hadn't so much as changed from the night's soiree. The black pants, the black jacket. Perfection even at three o'clock in the morning.

"What are you doing out here?" he asked when he neared her position under the tree.

"I could ask you the same question," she said, folding her arms across her chest.

"Well, for one thing I'm not trespassing." He laughed softly as his face was lit with a smile. "Which is more than I can say for you."

Her bravado crumpled a touch. "Oh, yeah?" She shrugged, leaving her shoulders up to huddle into. "Well, it's three o'clock in the morning—I didn't think anyone would mind."

His face was set in an amused smile as he approached her, and then two feet away he stopped. "I could have you arrested right here, you know."

She scowled. "You act like you own the place."

Slowly he laughed again. "Well, actually, I do."

"You do?" she asked, as her eyebrows knotted. "Oh, I'm sorry. I didn't know." Her heart slammed into her ribcage and thudded in her ears.

His gaze fell, and his smile was replaced with a sullen acceptance. "Grandma gave it to me when she passed on."

"Oh," Camille said, stricken with the news. She searched his face for the sorrow she knew was there. "I'm sorry. I didn't know she was...when did she die?"

"Seven, eight years ago." He shrugged. "She's better off now."

"Yeah," Camille said although she wasn't at all sure that was the right response. Frantically her brain searched for some other safe topic. "So, how's your dad?"

A strange look crossed Jaylon's face as he sighed. "He passed away about five years ago."

"Oh, no." The grief on his face made her want to put her arms around him. Instead she shoved both her hands into her pockets and stood her ground. "I'm sorry. I didn't know."

Jaylon shrugged as his hand relocated to his pocket. "It was real sudden. One heart attack and he was gone."

As she looked at him, she saw him—the real Jaylon, standing completely alone in the world, and it tore her heart out. "So, this is your place then?"

"Yeah." He looked away from her as he stepped past the tree to the slope edge. "For now anyway."

"For now?" she asked, telling herself she shouldn't step to his side but doing so just the same.

He swung his gaze to her and smiled sadly. "I'm probably going to put it up for sale on Monday."

"For sale? Why?" she asked with overwhelming concern both for him and for the fact that if he sold it, she couldn't come out here anymore. Of course that was ridiculous. Pushing all that away, she forced her concentration to him.

He looked out across the dark chasm for a long moment. "We're trying to buy a house in Syracuse. It doesn't make much sense to hold onto this when the money could be used somewhere else."

Dismay clutched her chest. "But, J, this was your grandmother's. How can you just sell it?"

The exhale was hard. "I don't need it anymore. It's time to let it go."

She took that news into her soul—wanting to argue, yet knowing that wasn't her place. "So, you're really going to sell it then?"

"Yeah." The word barely found the air. "I talked to Keane the other day. He's going to be handling everything, so I don't have to."

Her head nodded even as her heart protested. He was selling the land, but it felt like it was her soul he was putting on the auction block. Slowly she turned back to the tree, walked over, and sat down on one of the roots, pulling her knees up to her chest. He felt so far away from her as he stood on the cusp of that slope, one hand in his pocket, looking out into the infinite darkness beyond.

"It's going to be hard," he said, never so much as looking at her, "not coming back here anymore. I can't imagine not being able to stand here and think about things. It's going to be like selling a part of myself."

She laid her temple on one knee as she watched him. "Then why sell it if it's that important to you?"

He glanced back at her as though he hadn't realized he'd spoken those words out loud. A step at a time, he approached the tree and sat down on the root next to hers. He rested his wrists on his knees. "Mind if I tell you something?"

"What's that?"

Life paused as the wind rustled the trees above them. "I never thought my life would go this way."

Her gaze traveled the length of his silhouette. "What way?"

He shrugged. "The way it has. Teaching. Brickhaven...Nicole."

The name made her cringe, but she shoved that down. This was about being his friend, not about her. "Life doesn't always lead us where we thought it would."

Of every, single person in the entire world, she knew that better than anyone.

He rolled his head to the side to look at her. "What happened to us?"

Her arms squeezed her knees closer to her chest. "We went in two different directions. It's nobody's fault. That just happens sometimes."

The night whispered past them as his gaze slid down her face. "I miss us."

She smiled, knowing even as she looked at him that she had to let him go, let him be happy. In her heart she prayed for the right words, not even knowing what those words might be. "We had our moment, J. It didn't last forever, but that doesn't mean I regret it." Her gaze slid past his face to the stars beyond. "You want to hear something weird?"

"What's that?"

Never would she have said the next words in the light of day nor even admitted them to anyone but him. However, somehow, she knew she had to say them, knew he needed to hear them so he could go on, knowing he had changed her life for the better.

"Want to know what I always think just before I stand up to give a presentation?" she asked softly. "I mean it may be for 500 people in a huge conference center, or it may be for the top military brass in the country, but just when I get to feeling like there's no way I can stand up there and act like I know what I'm talking about, I always think, 'It's just you and me. Okay? You and me in your kitchen. No big deal. Just like in your kitchen.'"

His words from so long ago filled the air between them.

"Weird, huh?" she asked with a small laugh. "But I'll tell you what. I'm grateful every day for the time we had. It's because of you that I'm the person I am today. I would never trade that for all the forevers in the world."

A sad smile coursed through his eyes as he looked over at her. "Do you mean that?"

She thought for only a second before she nodded. "Yeah, I do."

The wind brushing through the trees provided the only noise. She had come to make peace with their time together. She had come to let him go, and in a strange way she now felt like that might be a possibility.

"You know, I'm glad I came this weekend," he said quietly.

"Yeah," she said, allowing the dream to wrap around her again. "So am I."

The midnight black was ceding to the first rays of the dawn when Camille climbed the porch steps and slipped back into the house, making sure to hang the keys back right where she'd found them. She was sure that no one had so much as noticed she was gone until she tiptoed past the kitchen and found two gazes trained solidly on her.

"Morning," she said, straightening as she saw no way to keep going, pretending she hadn't seen them.

"Morning," Nick said over his coffee cup.

"Where've you been?" Lexie asked, and the concern in her voice was obvious.

Camille shrugged. "I went for a drive. Sorry. I'll be sure to pay you back for the gas." The pretending stopped, and she looked at them both. Lexie looked ready to spit nails.

Shifting from one foot to the other, Camille spun her brain trying to come up with a logical excuse, but the way they were looking at her no excuse would make up for the disaster she'd caused. Finally, defiantly she shook her head. "What?"

"Did it ever occur to you that we might be worried?" Lexie asked barely concealing her anger.

The carefully built scaffolding holding Camille upright swayed beneath her. "I'm not sixteen, you know."

"Camille." Nick stood and held his hands up in an effort to calm the rising tensions in the room. "Lexie was just worried."

"Well, I'm old enough to take care of myself. I don't need you or anyone else to run my life for me."

Lexie's face fell as she stood and turned for the counter. "I'm sorry for caring."

"Yeah? Well, I'm sorry for being here." Too much hurt. Too much trying to hold everything together, and knowing it was coming apart. In one crash it all broke over her. She ran for her room, feeling exactly like the 16-year-old they had so much as accused her of being.

She didn't need this, not after the night. Not after watching Jaylon drive away for the last time. What she needed was to be alone. What she needed was to go back to Pittsburgh to her real life—back to being an adult, back to living life on her own terms, back to reality.

Because one thing was completely obvious, she had somehow stepped into a parallel universe, and this one hurt more than reality ever had.

Feeling like he hadn't slept in days, Jaylon made it back to his hotel room just before the sun came up. Without wasting time to even undress, he collapsed onto the bed and fell asleep. It didn't matter. Awake or asleep, she was always right there, just behind his eyelids and just beyond rational. And he was beginning to think she always would be.

For all intents and purposes, sleeping was pointless. Camille came to that conclusion an hour before she was scheduled to leave for the airport for her return flight to Pittsburgh. The sounds outside her bedroom door told her that the kids were back although presumably they were trying to be quiet for her sake.

Wanting to see the kids and seeing no way to spend time with them in her current cell, she brushed all her feelings under a secured carpet and walked out to the living room. "Morning."

Nick looked up and smiled as genuinely as he could. "Morning. How'd you sleep?"

Camille shrugged as she crawled onto the floor where Samantha and Austin were playing ball. She snagged the ball midway between the two. "My ball." Instantly both kids laughed and jumped on top of her. "No, no! Help!"

In two heartbeats Lexie appeared from the back. "Hey, shhh! Camille's still... oh."

"Morning," Camille said, not knowing what else to say.

"Morning," Lexie said, sounding less than enthusiastic about that greeting. "What time's your flight?"

"Two-thirty," Camille said. She looked at her friend, and although her own spirit hurt, she could see that in her anger, she had hurt her friend, too.

"Okay," Lexie said with a small sniff. "Then I'd better get some dinner on, so you can eat before you leave."

Camille scrambled to her feet and followed Lexie to the kitchen. "You don't have to. I can grab something at the airport."

"Airport?" Lexie asked, without arguing further, she pulled two pans out of the cabinet.

"And you don't even have to worry about taking me. I can call a cab."

"We already talked about it," Lexie said evenly. "Nick's going to take you in. We'll just eat first."

Camille wanted to argue, but hurt and anger were already as plain as the words Lexie spoke. The last thing she wanted was bad feelings over this weekend hanging between them. The likelihood that this would be their last day together invaded her consciousness along with a palpable sadness.

"You need some help?" Camille asked.

When Lexie looked at her, Camille saw the "no" snap to her eyes.

"Okay, microwave is more my style these days," Camille said, baiting her friend with a small smile. "But maybe this other way of cooking is like riding a bike."

"Or like falling off of one," Lexie said, accepting the offering of peace. "You can start the macaroni."

Gratefully Camille accepted the bag of noodles Lexie placed in her hand. At least their last moments together would be peaceful.

The knocking on Jaylon's door brought him right out of the bed like a shot. His head felt like someone was pounding on it with a jackhammer. Quickly he crossed the still-darkened room to the door, which he opened without even checking the peephole.

"Jeez. You look good this morning," Nicole said with a sarcastic scowl. Then her gaze slid down his still-dressed frame. "Did you already go into town?"

Jaylon ran a hand through his hair, trying to shake out of his dreams. "No, I guess I overslept. What time is it?"

"Almost noon. I thought you were going into town this morning."

"Yeah, I thought so, too, but I guess I was more tired than I thought."

Annoyance streamed over Nicole's face. "So, are we going now or what?" She looked at her watch. "Check out time's like now."

Rational thought escaped from him as he tried to work through a gang of problems attacking his brain simultaneously. "Yeah, just let me throw my stuff together. I'll be out in five minutes."

"And then what?" Nicole asked.

"And then we'll talk about it."

"Thanks for everything, Lex," Camille said, hugging her friend as they stood at the front door. "I had a good time."

The look in Lexie's eyes said she knew the depth of that lie, but instead of voicing that thought, Lexie smiled. "I'm glad. Don't be a stranger. Okay?"

Camille nodded although deep down she knew they would probably never see each other again. At least until the next reunion, for which she promised herself right then and there that she would be conveniently busy.

"Take care of yourself," Lexie said softly as she pulled her friend close once more.

"You, too."

"That's it." Nick stepped back in. "Everything's loaded."

Camille smiled down at the children surrounding Lexie's legs. "You guys take care. Okay?"

Two sets of eyes stared at her in wary puzzlement. Finally her gaze dropped to the carpet and then swung to Nick's. "I guess I'm ready."

He nodded mutely, and she looked back only once before stepping in front of him and out the door.

"Be careful," Lexie said to her husband as he bent to kiss her good-bye.

"I'll be back in a while."

Forcing her feet to keep walking so she wouldn't have to hear any more of the conversation that was tearing her apart, Camille walked under the carport and climbed into the passenger's side of the vehicle. Without her realizing it, her hands came up to rub her arms. A few more hours and she could cry in peace. A few more hours and she could be lonely without anyone trying to cheer her up. She couldn't wait.

When Nick climbed in the other side, he waved once at his wife who stood on the front porch. Then, doing her best to smile, Camille waved to the figures standing on the porch. As they drove out onto the road, Camille allowed the act of cheerfulness to evaporate away from her. Tiredly her head dropped back against the headrest, and she closed her eyes.

"Tired?" Nick asked.

"Exhausted."

"You were out pretty late last night."

"Trying to figure my life out."

"Did it help?"

She shook her head slowly. "I don't think anything will help at this point."

He drove a little. "Did you ever get to talk to J?"

Two pictures invaded her consciousness simultaneously. "A little."

"That didn't help?"

"I don't know." With one dive, her spirit shattered onto the ground. "I don't know anything anymore. I think if I could just do this. If I could just talk to him. If I could just see him again, then I can go on with my life and forget about him."

"But that's not working?"

"Yeah, that's one way of putting it."

He looked over at her with concern. "What's the other?"

"That I'm going to be miserable forever."

"Is this going to take long? I wanted to go by Mom and Dad's before you drop me off," Nicole said in that petulant tone that made Jaylon's nerves stand on end.

"I just want to get some books from her," he said as he drove up Mrs. Allen's driveway.

"I really don't see the point. You're not going to be teaching there that much longer anyway."

Jaylon parked the car and started out when he realized Nicole hadn't moved. "You coming?"

"I don't even know her. I think I'll just stay here."

In complete frustration, he climbed out and slammed the door a little harder than necessary. "Fine. Stay there. What do I care?" He walked to the front door and rang the bell.

Minutes passed before Mrs. Allen appeared at the door and swung it open for him. "Jaylon."

"Hi. Umm, is this a bad time?" He looked past her into the house.

"No, no, come on in." Mrs. Allen glanced past him to the car. "Your wife doesn't want to come?"

"Oh, she's not my wife. I mean we're not married...yet. She's my fiancée."

"Fiancée? Well, congratulations."

"Thanks," he said but didn't sound like he meant it. "She's a little tired. Too much excitement I guess. Besides, I can't stay long. We're headed back."

"Well, that's okay. I went up to school earlier, and I pulled these out for you just in case," Mrs. Allen said, going over to the piano bench. She lifted several books and handed them to Jaylon. "And you don't have to worry about getting them back. I won't be needing them anymore."

He smiled sadly. "So, you're really leaving then?"

With a sigh, she nodded. "I'm sure I'll miss it, but when an opportunity like this comes your way, you've got to grab on and go for it."

His spirit reached out to hers even as sadness wrapped around him. "Thanks...for everything."

"I'm glad you went into teaching. Those kids will never know how lucky they are."

"Well, I think I'm only just beginning to realize how lucky I was." Despite the books in his hands, Jaylon leaned over to her and gave her a quick hug. "Good luck with everything."

She looked down at the books in his hands. "You, too."

Together they walked to the door, and she opened it for him. "Oh, and I hope all is wonderful with your wedding, too. I'm sure your fiancée is terrific."

"Terrific, yeah," he said, not realizing how halfhearted his voice sounded. "Well, thanks for these."

"You're welcome."

He stepped out of the house. "I'll see you later."

"Yeah, later," Mrs. Allen said with a small wave.

Jaylon stepped off her front porch as his nose caught the hint of rain in the air. He looked out past Mrs. Allen's budding garden to the coming storm. Quickly he climbed into the car, stowed the books in the backseat, and started the motor.

"It's about time," Nicole said, and that tone was back.

He didn't bother to reply as he put the car in drive and left Ridgecrest and all its inhabitants in the rearview mirror.

"I wish there was something I could do," Nick said as he sat with Camille in the terminal. "I hate for you to go home hurting like this."

"Tell me why this is happening. Why can't I just forget about him?" Camille looked down at her fingers as they played with the edge of her boarding pass.

"Well, I can't give you an exact answer," he said as his gaze traveled out to the planes beyond the windows blurred by the gray sheets of rain falling from the ominous sky, "but my grandma used to tell me, 'Nick, do you know what 'why' backward means? It just means Your Holy Will.'"

He paused as his gaze dropped to the carpet. "It used to get to me when she'd say that because she always acted like that was supposed to just take care of everything. But you know what, the longer I'm here, the more sense it makes."

His gaze swung back to Camille. "I don't know what His plan is, and sometimes when I'm in the middle of it, I'm thinking, 'God, this really wasn't what I had in mind.' But then when I look back, I almost always end up seeing something I learned from that experience that I really needed to learn. Most of the time it wasn't pleasant, and sometimes it was downright painful, but I can tell you, remembering that saying's gotten me through more than one scrape in my lifetime."

The speaker over their heads beeped to life. "Flight 542 to Pittsburgh, Pennsylvania, now boarding at Gate 39."

Simultaneously they stood as the crowd around them began standing as well. Camille reached down and grabbed her purse from the chair. "I guess that's me."

"Sounds like it." Nick shifted awkwardly in front of her as a reluctant smile crossed his face. "Well..."

She looked at him and smiled. "Well..."

Gently he reached out for her and enveloped her in his embrace. "You take care of yourself. Okay?"

"You, too." She breathed in the strength of his arms, knowing that in the next second she would once again be on her own. Letting him go was like letting the branch go as you're tumbling down the side of a cliff. Her face wanted to smile, but all her heart could do was cry. "Tell Lexie thanks for everything."

"I will."

Then she let go and backed away from him feeling their spirits tear from each other.

"We will be seating passengers 1 through 100," the flight attendant said.

"I guess I'll see you sometime," Camille said barely able to meet his gaze.

"Yeah, sometime."

Camille waved once more before turning to join her fellow passengers. With a heavy, tear-laden heart, she boarded the plane and left Rochester, Ridgecrest, and that moment in her life behind.

It was the missed sleep, Jaylon tried to convince himself when he snapped at Nicole for the third time, igniting a conflagration he wasn't sure he had any hope of putting out. "Look, I don't want to go see your parents tonight. All right? They're hard enough to deal with when I'm awake. I'm exhausted, and I just want to go home."

Nicole's side of the car fell into silence as the strain of keeping himself together crashed over him. When his senses came back, he looked over at her.

"I'm sorry. I didn't mean it like that," he said in frustration as they neared Syracuse.

"Yeah? Well, how did you mean it then?"

"I just meant an hour or two there, means I won't get home before nine. I'm exhausted, and I've still got papers to grade."

Nicole clicked her tongue. "You've always got papers to grade, and I haven't seen Daddy and Mom for four whole days. I just want to stop in and say, 'Hi.' Why is that such a crime?"

He sighed out of true exhaustion. "It's not." His hands continued to guide the car further into Syracuse although no part of him wanted to direct it where she wanted to go. "But could we just say, 'Hi' and then get going? I mean I really do need to get some sleep."

"I thought you had papers to grade."

"I do! And I have lesson plans to get ready and a shower to take, and I'd like to get to bed sometime before the sun comes up."

She folded her arms in front of her. "I went with you, I don't see why you can't come with me."

His resolve to get out of the visit to her parents' house was crumbling. "I didn't say we couldn't go. I just don't want to stay forever."

"We hardly ever get to see them. You always have something else to do."

"Well, we're going now. Aren't we?" His exasperation with her, her parents, the entire situation was about two degrees from boiling right over.

"Yeah, but not because you want to."

It took every sane part of his mind to keep from screaming at her. He didn't want to go. He didn't want to go because he was tired, but he also didn't want to go because they treated him like the hired help—not like the man who was to marry their daughter and certainly not like a son. But with his last shred of good judgment, he kept those words to himself.

The streets of Syracuse slipped by the windows as his spirit and body said the only place they really wanted to be was in bed. He looked at the clock 4:30. If he was really lucky, they could be back on the road by 5:30, but even as he thought it, he knew the possibility of that actually happening was slim to none.

In her parents' driveway, he put the car in park, wishing he'd at least had it washed. Next to their shiny, smoke-colored Lexus, his car looked about a hundred years old. He got out and waited for Nicole at the front of the car. She didn't look particularly happy when she met him there, but they turned and walked to the front door just the same.

However, just before he reached for the doorbell, she turned to him and started her normal attempts to make him presentable. She straightened his shirt collar and jacket before running a hand through his hair.

"Perfect?" he asked, trying to find how special he felt when she had done it the first time.

She shrugged in exasperation. "It'll have to do." With that she reached over and rang the doorbell.

As his spirit shrank next to hers, he fought to smile when the door opened. They were led through an enormous foyer to the sitting room. Like a bird alighting on its perch Nicole sat down on the white chair. Everything, including the book sitting open on the piano, was choreographed to elicit the feeling of being in absolute perfection.

Nervously, Jaylon reached up and straightened his own collar. He always felt so inadequate when he was around her parents—like they were just waiting for him to mess up so they would have an excuse to throw him out.

"Darling," Nicole's mother said, sweeping into the room. "We were expecting you two hours ago."

"Sorry. Jaylon had some errands to do before we left." Nicole hugged her mother and then looked around. "Where's Daddy?"

"Oh, they had some problem down at the plant. That manager he hired in October has been nothing but trouble." Mrs. Byrne turned her attention to Jaylon. "How was your reunion?"

"Very nice," he said, nodding to her slightly. He didn't offer more because he knew two words was as much as he ever needed to say on any given subject.

"Well, I got a call from Acacia yesterday. She's expecting us to be at her studio for pictures tomorrow morning at nine sharp. Is your dress all ready?"

"It's hanging in my extra bedroom. I guess we can meet there, or do you want me to come get you?"

"I think you'd better come get me. You know how I hate morning traffic."

"You hate all kinds of traffic," Nicole said, visibly lightening in the presence of her mother.

The one and only problem was that Jaylon felt nearly non-existent in her presence, and it was not a good feeling.

"Your father is supposed to be home for supper later," Mrs. Byrne said. "So, I'm sure you'll want to stay to see him."

Nicole never so much as looked at Jaylon. "Of course we'll stay. We have all the time in the world."

Camille retrieved Max from the Hathingtons' and padded over to her own door—a suitcase, a purse, a hanging bag, and a cat in tow. With a sigh she unlocked her door and stepped back into her life, the heavy mantle of which dropped on her like a boulder.

She hit the light, and the first thing she saw was the set of plans spread across her table. "Back to reality."

It felt like the very last place she wanted to be.

All the time in the world turned into nearly ten o'clock, and by that time, Jaylon honestly felt like his eyes might permanently close at any moment.

"You take care getting her home," Mr. Byrne said to Jaylon as they stood at the front door saying good night.

"I will," he said, feeling like he might go to sleep with each nod.

"I'll see you in the morning, Mom," Nicole said as she quickly hugged each parent.

"I'm looking forward to it," Mrs. Byrne said.

They said their good nights and stepped out into the cool New York air. When they were in the car, Nicole's smile had returned. "I'm so glad we're only going to be a few miles from them at Hatherly. We'll be able to do this every weekend."

Oh, joy, Jaylon thought but said nothing.

The rest of the evening could very easily have been nothing but a dream as he took Nicole home, kissed her good night on her doorstep—of course he couldn't come in, the infamous dress was in that apartment. Also, she needed her beauty sleep, which to be honest, he was perfectly happy about because it meant he could get home that much faster.

He didn't remember the 45-minute drive home. He didn't remember making at least two of the turns he must've made, but somehow he was suddenly in his driveway wondering how in the world he had managed to get there.

There wasn't even enough brainpower to contemplate that question, so instead of pondering it, he grabbed his carry-on and climbed out of the car. Not even the stars shone as brightly here, but he pushed that thought from his mind and clicked the lock to let him in the back.

"Just don't think. The less you think, the less it hurts," he told himself as he walked through the house without bothering to turn on a light. In the bedroom he dropped the suitcase to the floor and crawled gratefully into bed.

Then, for the second straight night, he fell asleep, exhausted in mind, body, and spirit, wearing the same clothes he'd been in for more than 36 hours.

Chapter 11

"Rai," Camille said into the phone Monday afternoon as she sat at her desk five-plans deep, "have you sent the cockpit finals to me yet?" She listened to his answer even as her hands dug for her request through the stack. "I don't know. I can't seem to find them anywhere. Do you mind sending them up again?" Her frustration was mounting with each second. "I know. I promise I won't lose these. Okay. Thanks."

The phone crashed back to the cradle with a bang. "Liz!"

"Yeah?" Liz asked, appearing at the door.

"What happened to the engine designs outlining the new thrust augmentation system?"

"They were on your desk," Liz said.

Camille dug and dug, but her hand came to the desktop before she found what she was looking for. "Well, they're not here now."

Liz shook her head. "I'll go look out here."

Aerospace terms crowded Camille's mind like jammed airspace over JFK when the radar's down. Drag, thermal fatigue, ballistic conditions, cryogenic propellant; delta wings, net thrust, drift rate... They all circled around her head with dizzying velocity. Why had she ever thought she could handle this? How had she ever convinced herself that she could do this?

"Did you find it?" Camille called to the outer office.

"Are you sure you didn't take it with you over the weekend?"

The weekend. Camille didn't even want to go there. "It was here when I left. Someone must've taken it." She grabbed for the phone again feeling the control slipping from her grasp. "Kali, hey you didn't take the engine designs for the thrust augmentation system, did you? I can't find them anywhere."

"Enough!" Jaylon yelled over the students who seemed bent on arguing no matter what the question.

"But if Karen..." one of the girls said.

"I said, 'Enough.' For the rest of the class, I just want you to read quietly. You've got through chapter seven for tomorrow."

"But we've got soccer tonight..."

"Through seven," he said, fighting but barely maintaining control. Without another look at the students, he sat down at his desk wishing he could just put his head down and sleep. Sleep. It was a necessity he simply couldn't find anything other than brief snatches of, and when added together, those snatches hardly constituted anything even remotely resembling enough.

The night before ghosts had floated through his brain the entire night appearing and then vanishing so that by morning when he woke up, his head was pounding like a base drum. He bent his head over the papers in front of him, intending on at least getting some grading done, but even that was a challenge. His mind simply wouldn't stay on anything for more than a few seconds, and the one thing it would stay on, he was determined to push so far away from him that it would never come back.

Ever since Jaylon had mentioned selling his grandmother's land, Camille had been batting away an idea that had popped into her head immediately. It was silly. What would she possibly want with land in New York? However, the longer she tried to work, the more it became clear that if she didn't do something about that land, it wasn't going to let her get anything else done.

"Liz, could you come here a minute?" Camille asked into the intercom.

In moments Liz was standing in the doorway. "Lose something else?"

"No. Could you get me a list of real estate offices in Ridgecrest?"

"Real estate?" Liz asked with concern. "You planning on abandoning us too?"

Camille shook her head. "Just bring me the list as soon as you get it."

Liz raised an eyebrow but nodded. "Will do."

The second Liz was gone, Camille sighed. "Okay, Wright. Somebody's working on it. Now can we please get something else done?" Over the plans her hand shook slightly, and she shook her head. "Stop it. Okay? Just stop it. You've got to focus."

"Boy, you look positively partied out," Kandice Thorton, a high-strung sprite who happened to be one of Jaylon's fellow teachers, said when he sat down at the lunchroom table after a full morning of wrestling with unmanageable students.

The missed sleep gnawed at his eyelids. "That's one way of putting it."

"I hate to see him after the wedding if he looks like this after one little reunion," Lucas Duncan, a man nearly twice Jaylon's age, said. "We may not have an English teacher those last four weeks."

"Maybe they just decided to start the honeymoon early," Kandice said teasingly.

"Too many parties," Jaylon said, defensive at even the implication of Kandice's words.

"Private or public?" Kandice asked, and Jaylon made a face at her.

"I can't really figure it out," he said, fighting to steer the conversation in a different direction. "I used to party all the time in college. A different party every night, but I never felt like this."

"You were younger then," Lucas said. "Trust me. It gets worse."

That wasn't what Jaylon wanted to hear.

"Here's your list," Liz said, laying it on Camille's desk next to the sandwich with three bites missing. "That wasn't terribly hard. Ridgecrest must not be very big."

"Yeah," Camille said as she picked up the list and scanned it.

Liz walked to the door and then stopped. "Oh, Ben called. He'll be here next Tuesday to go over everything with you."

"Okay," Camille said, but she hardly heard the statement. She was too busy trying to figure out which firm Keane might work for. One second and then two, and Liz stepped back out of the office, closing the door softly behind her.

Immediately Camille picked up the phone and dialed the first number.

"So, how are wedding plans?" Kandice asked, causing Jaylon to wish he had taken his lunch outside.

"Pretty good. Nicole's having her pictures done this morning I think."

"You think?"

He shrugged. "I do what I'm told, when I'm told."

"Practicing for being a husband already," Lucas said, laughing. "Smart man."

"I try," Jaylon said although he wished he could laugh about it as easily as Lucas did.

"Keane Dinsmore, please," Camille said when she had made the connection to the fifth and last office on the list. If he didn't work here, her brilliant plan could just join the others on the failed idea heap.

"One moment, please," the receptionist said.

In a heartbeat the phone was ringing, presumably in Keane's office, and Camille's determination shrank inside her. What was she doing? Keane was going to think she was crazy. Her hand faltered as her brain screamed at her to hang up the phone. There were bad ideas, there were terrible ideas, and then there was this one.

"Superior Real Estate, this is Keane," he said in one continuous string of words.

She hesitated for a full second before yanking her courage back to her—courage that had no trace of rational behavior anywhere in it. "Hi, umm, this is Camille Wright... from this weekend."

"Camille! Hey. I didn't expect to hear from you again so soon."

"Yeah, well, this is a little unexpected for me, too." Her fingers filed through her hair, fanning it out and then smoothing it down. "Umm, listen, when I was in Ridgecrest this weekend, I found some land that I'm wanting to look into purchasing."

"Oh, thinking about moving back?"

"Kind of," she said, knowing it was pointless to go into the real reason she wanted that land.

"What land are you talking about? I'd be happy to look into it for you."

"It's out on 1575."

"1575? Huh, that's interesting. I've just been working on a tract out there. Do you know what the coordinates of it are?"

"Well, not exactly. I know it has an old house on it, and there's a creek that goes right along side of it."

"How far off the main highway?"

"A mile, maybe two."

Keane's side went silent. "I swear you have to be talking about the same land I just came from. Which side of the road?"

"Left if you're coming from Ridgecrest," Camille said, pinpointing the land with her heart.

"That's got to be it." Keane left for a split-second. "I can't believe this. I'm working with the owner of that land to put it up for sale."

"Oh, really?" she asked as her heart fell. She tried to get cheerfulness into her voice, but it hurt. "That's great. Umm, do you know how much is being asked for it?"

"I'd say in the 850 to 950 range although we haven't really settled on anything yet."

"How many acres?"

"23."

The business was easy. It was the current just below the illusion of normalcy that Camille was having difficulty. She punched the numbers into her calculator and did a quick mental check of her asset sheet. $20,000. It was well within her financial affordability. The only outstanding question was if she could afford it emotionally.

"Now, I have to tell you, it hasn't formally been put on the market yet," Keane said carefully.

"But it will be?"

"I'm expecting it to be."

She nodded although he couldn't see her. Slowly her pencil turned end-to-end as she considered the deal. "Well, I'm definitely interested. Can you call me as soon as you know for sure?"

"As soon as I know something definite, you'll be my first call."

"I'd appreciate that."

Jaylon came up with every excuse in his arsenal not to make the call to Keane during his day on Monday, so by the time he got home, he wasn't at all surprised to see his answering machine blinking twice at him. Reluctantly he hit the button and waited for the tape to rewind and stop.

"Mr. Quinn," a voice he didn't recognize said. "We've scheduled your interview with Mr. Stanton at Cazenovia for April 25th at 2:30. If there's a conflict, please call us to reschedule as soon as possible."

The voice gave the number, and the machine beeped to the next message. "Jaylon, hey, this is Keane. Great news, man. I've got someone interested in that land we talked about. How does 850 hit you? Give me a call."

850? Jaylon threw his briefcase onto the table and yanked out the calculator that for three solid years had only been used to figure grades. Quickly he punched in the numbers and stood gaping at the result.

It was far more than he could ever have hoped for. Enough for a down payment in its own right. The chair caught him on the way down as his knees buckled beneath him. This was real. If he accepted this offer, that land would no longer be his.

In one snap, his mind was back there with Camille, and every single dollar staring up at him from the calculator seemed minuscule next to the thought of selling that property. His mind said he was silly for having cold feet now. This was, after all, the answer to all the financial worries he had about Nicole. Sell one property, buy the other. How much difference could there possibly be in what he owned and what he didn't?

Nonetheless, his heart said there was a very big difference. He hadn't grown up in the house on Hatherly—more to the point, he had, and he didn't want to go back. The thought of once again living in his father's house that looked so perfect on the outside but felt so utterly scathing to his spirit on the inside made him recoil. Thankfully he had managed to make peace with his father, but he had never made peace with that whole experience, and he was sure he never would.

A decision seemed totally out of his grasp, so instead of dwelling on it, he did what he was getting really good at: he pushed it away from his mind, hoping it would simply go away and never come back.

Any sane mind would've had the plans memorized by that point, every bolt, every fold, every tiny curve, and yet it was becoming increasingly obvious that Camille's mind was anything but sane. At her kitchen table she reworked one cut-away of the design, trying to perfect it and yet somehow always making another problem that she hadn't foreseen.

It was like a giant jigsaw puzzle with no real "right" answer. Throwing the pencil to the table in frustration she walked into the kitchen for a drink and a break. But in reality she hadn't had a break since her feet had landed in Rochester. Her spirit churned inside her until her stomach began to feel like she'd been on the world's most dizzying roller coaster.

When she made it back to the table, she stood, drinking her water and staring at the plans. They, much like her life, were impossible. She thought about the call to Keane. She didn't regret the move exactly, it was more a despondent, nagging thought that Jaylon could even consider putting the land up for sale that tugged at her.

He loved that land. She could see it when he stood there. Her body slid into the chair even as her spirit traveled back to the slope. She stood next to him, put her arms around him, and wished again that she could make the sadness in his eyes dissipate. Even in high school, at his lowest moment, he had never looked that sad.

Her brain went through all the things that could cause him to look so miserable. It pushed Nicole to the back of the file and pulled the sale of the land to the forefront. That had to be it. It had to be. Nothing else made any sense. But if selling it was killing him as much as it seemed to be, why would he even consider it?

Why. There was that word again. Overtaking even Jaylon's position in her mind, Nick was suddenly there. "Why backward means—Your Holy Will."

She turned the words on end as easily as she always did with her pencil. Your Holy Will. In truth, she had never been a religious person, hadn't set foot in a church six times in her entire life. But still in the dark of night, when no one else was listening, sometimes, she talked to God. Mostly in terms of making futile requests for something to work out in her life.

There never really seemed to be an answer, and most of the time she had just given up even asking. But here, thinking about Nick's words, she couldn't deny that with one exception everything she had ever really asked for had been realized—eventually.

Her mind turned her present situation over as her fingers drummed absently on the table. Asking for help with this one seemed ridiculous to the nth degree. God didn't really care if she was with Jaylon or Fred Flintstone. No, asking made no sense, so with a push, that thought landed somewhere below taking out the trash and dusting the furniture. She stood from the table and dumped what was left of her water on the pathetic looking ivy on her counter.

The best thing to do was to just go to bed, go to sleep, and maybe by some miracle tomorrow would be better. It wasn't likely, but at the moment all she was hanging onto was hope, and that was just enough to keep her standing.

Chapter 12

"Knock, knock," a voice said at her door as Camille sat at her desk the next Tuesday going over the final set of plans for Friday's meeting. The blueprints were due to be printed in an hour, and she was determined to get this last glitch fixed.

However, the plans were forgotten in the greeting as she looked up and smiled. "Ben." The sight of her one and only life preserver was enough to stand her up, walk her to him and give him a hug.

"I thought maybe you'd want a run-through," he said, hugging her to him. He was a good bit taller than her, dark and thin, but the hug felt as good as any one ever had.

Her arms released their hold on him, and she stepped back. "You read my mind."

"I love it when that happens," he said with a broad smile. He stepped in and closed the door behind him. "So, what are you working on?"

"The wheel casing. Everything else seems to be fitting in just perfectly, and then there's this tiny little problem of the edge of this wheel not quite having enough clearance to make it in and out of the hold."

Ben bent over her shoulder as she mapped out the problem. It was nice to have someone who understood right there. Ben. Her safety net. Somehow she hadn't realized how much she'd missed him until that very moment. She looked up into his gray-green eyes, thinking he really was quite handsome.

"Boy, you've changed a bunch of this. Where'd the wing extensions go?"

"Axed about three weeks ago. They were causing too much drag on our models. In a 360-degree turn they kept creating this uncontrollable instability with anything but the slightest winds, so we nixed that and housed some wing buffers in the back of the design. That'll give the wings enough expansion to maintain flight but not drag the plane down in precision moves."

"Impressive," Ben said with a nod. "And this thruster?"

"Kali's been working on that non-stop for two months. The idea is to use the heat from the first thruster to provide additional thrust for increased velocity using the same amount of fuel."

Ben shook his head clearly impressed. "Is it working?"

"So far." She laid her hands on the desk and looked up at him. "What do you think?"

He smiled down at her with a look that said he was more impressed than he had figured he would be. "I think they gave this position to the right person."

Camille took the compliment as she took all compliments— letting it brush by her without touching any part of her. "So, tell me what you'd do about this wheel casing. The thrusters aren't going to do us much good if these wheels won't get under that carriage."

"Well, let's see what we can do about that."

Keane had left numerous messages during the previous week, but Jaylon always found a way to get out of returning his calls. The biggest distraction was the wedding and his impending trip to Cazenovia. Nicole provided another distraction but not in the way most brides-to-be do.

"I want them all to get their final fittings by Friday," Nicole scolded Jaylon over the phone when he thought he was safely at home away from all the insanity in his life. "Have you talked to them?"

"Well, yeah."

"When?"

"When I asked them in October."

"*October?*" she practically screamed. "No wonder Mr. Tuxedo doesn't have their measurements."

"I was going to get around to calling them," Jaylon said.

"When? Two weeks after the wedding?"

He laid his temple on his two fingers. "Well, this whole thing just seems to be sneaking up on me. But I promise I'll call all three of them tonight."

"Where have I heard that before?"

Frustration exploded in him. "What does that mean?"

"It means it took me three months to get you to call Cazenovia, and I'm sure you still haven't called Keane back on that land."

"I'm working on it."

"How? Mental telepathy?"

Jaylon leaned forward on the chair in his kitchen. "I'm trying to keep up with all of this, Nicole. It just all seems like it all has to be done right now."

"That's because *it does!*"

"I know. I know. And I'll get it done. I promise." He fought the sigh with a hard clamp of his emotions.

"Get what done?" she asked suspiciously.

Air. It left the room. "What we talked about."

"What did we talk about?"

She was backing him into a corner, and he knew it. "The tuxedos. I'll call the guys right now."

"And Keane?"

"Keane." His voice drifted out as the exhaustion he hadn't been able to shake invaded his body again.

"You know, while you're pussyfooting around, the Hatherly house is going to sell, and then we'll have to start all over."

"Okay. Okay. I'll call Keane."

"Tonight?"

He sighed. There was no way around it. "Tonight."

The restaurant lights were so dim that seeing what happened to be on her plate was nearly impossible. In fact, Camille had to strain to see Ben across the tiny table. "I guess business is going well?"

"Oh, yeah. We've got conference orders coming in faster than we can process them."

"That's good. How was the one in...?"

"Boston?"

"Yeah. Bridges, right?"

"No, that one was Cincinnati two weeks before that."

It was like taking a tour she had no idea she'd signed up for. "Oh, what was the Boston one about?"

"Nuclear fusion for BU."

Camille shook her head. "How do you possibly keep it all straight?"

Ben laughed. "I've got a really good secretary. She hands me my tickets and my papers and points me in the direction I'm supposed to be going that weekend."

Taking a bite, she worked on the interested tone in her voice. "So, you're up to every weekend then?"

With a small sigh, Ben's gaze fell to his steak and then picked hers up again. "Every other at least. You wouldn't believe how many people I see in a week."

She laughed softly. "Kind of a change from Baker and Marsden, huh?"

He smiled at her over their dwindling entrées. "Yeah, there I only saw you."

Camille knew she was flirting with fire as she smiled, but she was so tired of hurting, she almost didn't care. "You make that sound like a bad thing."

"Bad?" His laugh was hearty. "Oh, no. Believe me, that was a good thing."

Her gaze reached for the security of his as all the doubts about herself fell in around her. At almost 40 he was what she would've termed newly distinguished. His hair was only beginning to show gray, and he was settled in a way that should've been an attraction. She couldn't help but wish she could feel more for him than she did. "Was it?"

The smile fell. "Of course it was. Why would you even ask that?"

She forked through her steamed vegetables as she shrugged. "I don't know. I've just been kind of down the last couple of weeks. It's been kind of rough."

Nothing but sympathy and concern wafted across the table. "Why?"

The glance up knifed through her with the look on his face. She shouldn't have said anything. "A lot of reasons." She'd wanted it to sound nonchalant, but it didn't.

He laughed softly as his soft, compassionate eyes begged her to trust him. "Well, that's specific."

Looking away from their table, she shook her head and pursed her lips. "It just feels like I'm doing this high-wire act, and nobody even notices I'm here."

"Ah," he said, nodding, "nobody to say, 'That's brilliant, Camille. I don't know why I didn't think of it before.'"

She smiled having heard those exact words come from his mouth infinite times in the past. "Something like that." The incessant fight she'd been waging with herself since she got on that plane tugged at her eyelids. Her entire spirit felt like it was slogging through a mud pit.

His side of the conversation stopped for a long moment, and his gaze fell to his plate. "I didn't know you even missed me."

It was her turn to look up in surprise, and regret rammed through her heart. "Are you kidding? Of course I've missed you. You could see right through every problem I ever had with one glance. I always thought you must be God or something."

He laughed. "God?"

Her eyes smiled. "Well, close." She shrugged. "You know what I mean. You were always there anytime I had a problem. When I got so frustrated I wanted to throw the plans out the window, I could walk into your office and in seconds you had solved it for me." Her words slowed as the heavy mantle of responsibility bowed her shoulders. "Now, I'm the one they come to with problems, and I just feel so...inadequate."

Ben looked at her in the dim light before he smiled and took a drink. "You want to know a secret?"

She was too tired to care. "What's that?"

A moment elapsed as he mulled over his next words. "It was a snow-job."

In shock her gaze snapped to his. "A snow-job?"

"Yeah, I had you snowed. I had everyone snowed. Well, almost everyone." He shook his head slowly, and the light caught on the whisper of gray right over his ear. For a long moment he simply stared at his drink. Then his gaze chanced up to hers. "I didn't know the answers; I just started talking and prayed that what was coming out of my mouth would have some shred of something you could use. Funny thing was, you always managed to see the answer somewhere in the middle of all my ramblings."

She stared at him in confusion. "But you had such a grasp on this stuff, on the plans, on the project."

"No," he said softly. "You had the grasp on it, I just made sure to give you enough latitude so you could figure it out for yourself."

Camille's mind bent around the words. Not once had she ever seen it that way.

"That was the reason I got out." Ben's gaze never left his glass. A moment and he glanced up. "Well, one of the reasons."

Still, searching for evidence of what he was telling her, Camille stared at him. "I don't understand."

"For four years all I ever did was play catch-up with the rest of you. You and Rai could design circles around me, and if I could've ever admitted it, I knew that. When this whole NightViper thing came up, I decided it was time to cut my losses."

Not happily, she crooked her mouth. "Yeah, and dump it in my lap."

His gaze soft and knowing held her. "I knew you could handle it. I didn't want to get in your way."

"You weren't in my way."

"Yeah, I was." He leaned forward, and his brown suit jacket suddenly looked too small for his shoulders. "It was just a matter of time anyway."

"A matter of time 'til what?"

"'Til Isaac gave my job to you."

Camille shook her head as if that could never have happened. "Isaac wouldn't have done that."

Ben tilted a brown eyebrow at her. "Isaac is a smart man, Camille. He knew how important those designs were, and he wanted his top person on it. He just didn't want to come out and tell me that. So, he named you my assistant, and then he quietly nudged me into this new job."

"He fired you?"

"No, he expanded my life options." Ben laughed softly. "And I'm grateful for that. I'm so much better at this than I ever was at design."

"But every time you helped me..."

"You helped yourself. I was just there as a sounding board."

She tried to take in what he was telling her, but it was all so different from what her own experience had told her that it was difficult. "You know, in high school it was so easy. I'd do my work, collect my grade, and move on. It wasn't about anybody else's job— anybody else's business. Now, I've got all these people counting on me, and I'm afraid I'm going to let them all down on Thursday." It was the most honest she'd been with anyone including herself.

"How could you possibly do that?"

Her heart snagged on the concern. "Well, for one thing I could have missed something on the plans, something simple that a real designer would've caught."

Ben laughed. "You are a real designer."

Camille shook her head. "I don't feel like one. I feel like at any minute Isaac's going to come into my office and say, 'Who are you trying to kid, girl? These are the worst designs I've ever seen.'"

"Yeah, right. Isaac thinks you hung the moon. He wanted this NightViper thing so bad, he could taste it, but to be honest with you, I don't think he would've taken it without you."

She laughed. "Oh, now I know you're lying."

But he never lost the seriousness in his face. "Why? Why is that so hard to believe?"

Her heart slid through the answer, and it took a long minute for her to get the words around the knowledge in her spirit. "Because no matter how much I've ever done, nobody's ever bothered to notice."

Ben looked positively shell shocked. "But you graduated Suma Cum Laude from Princeton. How could nobody have noticed that?"

"Oh, yeah. They said, 'Congrats, Camille.' Next." She flipped her hair over her shoulder for emphasis.

He narrowed his eyebrows as concern slid across his face. "Next?"

"Yeah, like 'How are you going to top that one?'"

Confusion dropped over him. "Why would you have to top it?"

She reached for her tea. "That's the only way people ever notice me—when I do something really spectacular. Only thing is as soon as I've done that, I have to do something even more spectacular for them to notice me the next time." She took a drink as if saying it made no difference.

"But people are noticing. Isaac noticed. I noticed."

Setting the glass down, she let her finger run down it slowly. "That's why I liked having you around, you always seemed like you were impressed with my work, and I never had to beg very hard for a compliment from you." She bent her head over her glass at that admission. "Man, that sounds selfish."

Ben shook his head. "Human. It sounds human to me. So, the plans?"

Camille felt her teeth come together in a tight knot. "I don't want them to just be right, I want them to be perfect."

"And if they're not?"

Her frame shuttered at the prospect. "Confirmation I guess."

"Confirmation of what?"

She looked up at him, hitting nonchalance with no trouble at all. "Confirmation of what everyone else has known all along—that I'm not enough, and I never will be." It was the first thing she had said with any real conviction.

"And what if they are perfect?" Ben asked carefully. "What if everyone says how wonderful they are?"

For a long moment she stared at the liquid in her glass. It was like watching the unstable elements of her life slide over one another "Then I'll be right back where I started. I mean how do you top a billion dollar airplane?"

As Ben sat in silence, Camille replayed the conversation wondering why she felt the need to tell him that. He was going to think she was absolutely out of her mind. People didn't want to hear about your insecurities—especially people who had hundreds of thousands of dollars riding on a speech you were scheduled to give in less than a day.

It was the epitome of dumb moves. She didn't even have to look at him to see that. Chalk another one up for all-time stupid moves of her lifetime.

"It makes a lot of sense," Ben finally said as he folded his hands on the table.

She arched an eyebrow at him. "What does?"

"Thinking that people will only like you if you're perfect. I mean why would anyone want to put up with someone who isn't perfect?"

Camille nodded although by the tone in his voice she knew he wasn't finished.

"After all perfection is structured, it's safe. So if you're perfect, you're safe," he continued slowly. "But people aren't structured. Are they? Personalities aren't structured. Not even yours. No, people are complicated, and that means they aren't safe.

"So the only way to make them safe is if you give them absolutely no reason to be upset with you, but even then they're not safe." His reflection about life stopped, and he looked right at her. "Are they, Camille?"

She was listening, but she couldn't so much as even nod. Somehow he had put a voice to what only her spirit ever whispered.

Slowly he shook his head. "What you're missing is that the people who really love you, don't love you for how much you do or for what you accomplish. They love you for you."

Her gaze attempted to bury itself in the burgundy tablecloth. Anything to get away from how close he was getting to her heart.

"I bet there's somebody you love—somebody you would do absolutely anything for."

Silence descended on their table as her heart landed on the answer to his unspoken question.

"One," she said softly, thinking of Daria, six hundred miles away and yet wrapped around her heart just the same. She glanced up at him with a smile. "My little sister."

"Your little sister," he said, smiling gently. "And I bet the only reason you love her is because of all the wonderful things she's accomplished."

Camille stared down at the rose napkin right next to her finger. "She's in college working on her computer programming degree."

"So, she'll graduate, at some point then? I guess you're waiting until then to really love her."

She shook her head solidly. "I already love her."

"Okay, then, when she finishes her first program, then you'll love her more."

"No. I mean I'll be proud of her, but I won't actually *love* her any more."

"So, when she finishes her fifth program, then you'll really love her."

"No," Camille said, now clearly seeing where this was headed.

Ben stopped and considered his next words carefully. "What you're not seeing is that people don't care about you more just because of how successful you are. They don't love you based on your accomplishments."

"But they recognize you more."

He shook his head. "Not the people who really love you—they love you no matter how many wonderful things you do. They love you not because of your accomplishments but because of you." He sat back, scrutinizing her. "And I'll do you one better. I'll bet your sister isn't the only one who loves you like that."

Camille could hardly breathe. She knew what he was saying, but it had never felt that way. "It just seems like everyone wants something from me—like they'll be mad if I don't live up to what they want me to be."

"There are always people who want things from you. I deal with about seven hundred of them every day, but those aren't the ones I'm talking about. I'm talking about the ones closest to you—the ones who really love you."

She tried to grasp his words, but they felt slippery beneath her fingertips. "But how do you know? I mean how can you tell who is your real friend and who just wants something from you?"

"Well, first you stop looking at them, and you start looking inside yourself. Who do you feel like that about? Who do you feel that you would love even if they never accomplished a single thing?"

A list materialized instantly on her heart. Lexie, Nick, Daria, Ben...

"Those are the ones who love you no matter what you accomplish, and they're the ones that will be there no matter if you make it big or just make it really small."

Her soul wrapped around his words even as her head protested. "And the speech?"

He shrugged. "Hey, speeches will come and go. It's who you are to the person you go home to after the speech that counts."

If only it were that easy, she thought sullenly. If only...

"Yeah, Keane, sorry I haven't gotten you called," Jaylon said to the answering machine that had accepted his call. "Umm, I need to talk to you about that land. When you get in, call me. Thanks."

Quietly Jaylon hit the phone's reset button and dangled the receiver between his knees. Sitting on the floor wasn't his normal "doing business" position, but this wasn't any ordinary transaction. This one meant that life as he had known it was ending. Permanently.

He thought about the new owners. What would they do to the land that felt like such a central part of who Jaylon had always thought he was? Would they tear down the house? In his mind he surveyed the house. Probably. It was falling apart anyway. Would the tree get to stay? Or would it too be sacrificed to progress?

Progress. It was such a strange word. He felt like he was going forward, but nothing he did felt like progress anymore. It just felt like more of the same—forever and ever. With a sigh, he let go of the reset button and dialed the first groomsman's number.

They weren't friends really, barely acquaintances from college. Guys he had shared a few beers and laughs with. In his position friends were hard to come by. Thinking about that made his chest ache, so he forced his brain not to think as he dialed the phone. Just get through this. Just make it to the 3rd. Just...

"Shane, hey, this is Jaylon...Quinn."

Camille thought about Ben's words long after they had said good night at her doorstep. Her list of people was short, but she couldn't deny that every, single person on that list cared about her—the real her. The person she was when the designs were finished, and everyone in the office had gone home.

Her gaze traced across the wallpaper opposite her bed. Ben was right. In her heart she could love Daria no more even if she won the Nobel Prize, and when she turned that equation around, she knew that Daria felt the same way.

Lexie and Nick had done practically everything in their power to get her to have fun during the reunion, and what had she done? Sulked the entire time. Even when she left, still they stood there—solid as though they would be there for her forever.

The sight of Jaylon walking away from the trailer dealt her heart a glancing blow. The biggest lesson of her life was that no one stays forever. It was clear she had a choice to make. The road in front of her diverged, and it was now up to her to make the decision which one to travel down.

The safer looking one offered the choice of holing up in her office from that point on and letting her friendships fall by the wayside. Yes, Lexie could be persistent, but at some point even she would get tired of always being the one to call, always being the one to suggest that they get together, always putting her hand out in offering—and more than once getting it slapped for the effort.

The other road, far less clear, far more dangerous-looking, wound almost immediately around a blind corner. She had never been one to reach out to her friends. In fact, in almost every case it was her friends who had made the initial move. Even when they got to know one another, Camille had the habit of hanging back, waiting for them to steer the friendship in whatever direction they saw fit.

She went along, half-hoping they wouldn't notice how hard it was to be her friend. In every relationship she'd ever had, it was she who did the bending when someone had to be flexible. Until now, she had always thought if she didn't, they would no longer want to be friends, but in light of Ben's words, she wondered how accurate that assessment had been.

Was it possible that those people who loved her really loved her no matter what she did? Her mind traced over Lexie, and Camille had to admit that she had made more than one mistake where her friend was concerned. Yet when asked who her best friend was, there was only one name that came to mind.

Nick, Daria, Ben—they had all stood by her, accomplishments or none. Then there was Jaylon, who her brain said she hadn't thought of in two weeks; although, her heart knew differently.

Her mind flew back to a time she had tucked neatly out of sight. Drama class, her senior year. She laughed at the very thought. Even now, she could see him sitting there on the stage playing Wink Murder with the intensity of a professional cat burglar. He was such a natural on-stage, always in the moment, always carrying his lines off effortlessly.

It had been a long time since she'd allowed herself to think about that year, but now lying on her bed, she let her mind float over it. Her heart took the reins, and in a breath she was back—memorizing lines with him in her kitchen, learning to project her voice, dreaming under the stars in his arms.

When she thought of him, she didn't feel the judgment she had felt most of her life. No, with him there was just acceptance. "You're the strongest person I know." His words, uttered so softly on a hazy, blue bridge floated back to her.

If only she could find a way to hold onto that tomorrow when she was standing in front of Military Intelligence Officers who could crush her with one look.

"Pressure creates diamonds."

In the darkness she smiled. "Well, J, I guess we're going to find out if I'm a diamond or just a lump of coal."

Her mind traced back over the designs. They were ready. She was sure of that or as sure as she could possibly get. Even the wheels now fit like they'd been made to all along. The only question left was: Was she ready?

"Jaylon," Keane said two seconds after Jaylon picked up the phone. "I didn't wake you, did I?"

"No." Jaylon slid the papers off his legs. "Just grading some papers."

"Listen, sorry I've been missing you. I think when you're there, I'm not and vice versa. It's kind of a vicious cycle."

"Well, I haven't exactly been beating your door down either. Don't worry about it." Jaylon paused to gather his courage. "So, you have a buyer then?"

"Yes, Sir, I do. She's offering 850 per acre."

"850, huh?" Jaylon said as in his mind, he looked out over the glittering city with the devil by his side.

"I think we could get a little more though if you want me to try."

"No, no, 850 is plenty."

The devil in his head whispered, "All this can be yours..."

"Jaylon?"

"Yeah," he said, pushing the devil away, but he was going nowhere.

"So, what do you say? You ready to make the deal?"

Jaylon's spirit clutched his chest with a screamed, *No!* as he gripped the phone. If he didn't sell it soon, Nicole would be furious. Nonetheless, he couldn't deny that he, himself, wanted nothing more than to just hang up the phone. Her tug was powerful, but she was little match for his soul on the other end. "Tell you what, don't do anything yet. I'll call you after the wedding, and we'll get to work on it then."

"I can't be sure the buyer will still be interested then," Keane said slowly. "She could retract her offer."

"Well," Jaylon said, breathing again for the first time in two weeks. "I guess that's a chance I'm just going to have to take."

Chapter 13

Nerves, the sort even Camille wasn't accustomed to, accosted her the moment she woke up Friday morning. They were with her as she showered, as she dressed, and as she sat at the little vanity, trying in vain to get her hair to look somewhat sophisticated. Her hair was too thin to do anything very dramatic with. She had known her hair was hopeless ever since her mother had burned her ear with the curling iron when she was eight.

"Hold still or I'm going to burn something really important," her mother had said. That was her mother, constantly finding ways to make even your worst moments...well, worse. "Of course you fell down. The way you walk, I'm surprised you don't just stay down... A bicycle? You don't need a bicycle. I don't even have health insurance, how would we ever pay to patch you up again?"

Camille wasn't sure why her mother's voice seemed to pick these particular moments to invade her thoughts. It was as though even now her mother had the power to diminish her daughter's spirit with a judgmental glance or a callous word. How many times had Camille tried to escape from those words? She had lost count. But it didn't matter, they were with her at every step.

Deciding she could do no more with her hair, she stood and pulled on her shoes. Today would mean the difference between securing her job and joining the homeless in the unemployment line. It wasn't a comforting thought.

"Don't mess this up," Nicole said as she sat across an early lunch from Jaylon. "This is important."

He had made the mistake of stopping in to see her on his way to the Cazenovia interview. It was what grooms-to-be did, he told himself. However, the second she had him in her crosshairs, he completely regretted the decision.

"I'm not an imbecile, Nicole," he said nearly losing his grip on control. "I know it's important."

"You know you wouldn't have to do this if you'd just accept Daddy's offer."

"I don't want to accept 'Daddy's offer.'"

"Well, I don't want to live on food stamps either."

"We're not that bad off. I've got a steady paycheck."

"Yeah, well in a week, you're going to have a wife, too."

Don't remind me, his brain said. "We'll be fine."

"Like I said, 'Don't mess this up.'"

"Just like in your kitchen," Camille whispered to herself as Ben made his introductory comments. "No big deal. Okay? Just you and me in your kitchen." She looked out at the stern faces, watching Ben's every move, and she knew that in moments they would be trained on her.

Perfection is structured, Ben said in her head as she watched him. *It's safe. But people aren't structured. They aren't perfect. Not even you.*

She, of every person on the planet, knew she wasn't perfect, but it had been her number one goal to make everyone else believe that she was for most of her 28 years. Slowly her gaze slid over the rock hard faces. *People aren't perfect.* The words streamed through her brain. It was the other half of the lie her life had been predicated on. When she looked at other people, she believed that they were far superior to her, and so she was left scrambling, trying to make up the deficiencies in her own being.

"They aren't perfect. It's an illusion," she said to herself softly. "They're human—just like you."

"And with that, I'll turn the microphone over to Ms. Camille Wright, lead designer on the project."

Every gaze in the room turned to her as she stood and walked to the podium. Steadily her hands opened the folder, and then she took one moment to look out over the faces again. Only this time there was something different that she hadn't seen before looking back at her. A vulnerability she had felt in her own soul but admitted to no one. "Good afternoon."

A couple heads nodded slightly.

"I'm going to approach this a little differently than at our last meeting. You all probably know as much as I do about this plane by now, so instead of me going back over it, I'll simply tell you the modifications we've made since we talked last. Then I'll open the floor for suggestions on further improvements."

She looked around the room, and when no one objected, she smiled. "We'll start with the wing extensions."

For one second her gaze caught on Ben's, and she knew every word he had told her was true.

No matter how hard he tried, Jaylon couldn't stop his knee from bouncing. Up and down, up and down, until he thought it might fly right off his leg. His sweaty palm wrapped around the folder which held his resume and two letters of recommendation. For whole moments at a time he pondered the question of why he could get up on stage in front of thousands of people and not feel a hint of nerves, but the prospect of going one-on-one sent him into orbit.

"Mr. Quinn?" the secretary said. "Mr. Stanton will see you now."

The words sounded like a death knell.

"We think we can get extra propulsion from these heat boosters positioned in the thrusters. Instead of allowing the heat to simply dissipate, this device will allow the pilot to open the heat shields and the radiation produced from the thrusters will be transferred to a set of panels designed to transfer that heat into added energy. This, in turn, will allow for increased flight time without increasing the fuel necessary to maintain that flight." Camille looked out over the group. "Questions?"

"How does this heat system work in relation to the current technology?" the Chairman of the Joint Chiefs of Staff asked.

She had never liked fielding questions before. They had always seemed to be aimed at finding the very weakest points in her designs. Of course, that was the point, but until today she had dreaded questions like this with the intensity of the noonday sun. Today, however, they didn't seem nearly so personal.

Confidently her gaze locked with the chairman's. "As far as we're concerned it is the equivalent of going from a candle to the light bulb. Let me show you why..."

"We'll be making our selection in the next few weeks," Mr. Stanton said as he led Jaylon out of his office. "We'll give you a call."

One handshake and he was gone. We'll give you a call. Jaylon closed his eyes, knowing it was the worst interview of his life. There wasn't one actual thing he could point to as being really bad. It was more that it was all really bad. His focus was off. His brain was off. Everything felt off.

He pushed that as far down as he could until he got outside again. He felt like a fraud—like an actor walking around in character, and not doing a very good job of carrying off the part. Nicole would be furious when she found out, but as much as he knew that, he couldn't find a piece of himself that was disappointed. Fearful of her reaction was closer to the truth, but even that couldn't get all the way to his core.

No, at his core he was too numb to feel much of anything. He climbed into the Z28 and gunned the engine. The numbness was his shield, his way of blocking out the things he really wanted to feel but knew he shouldn't. Things like he didn't want to teach at Cazenovia and he didn't want to sell the property and he didn't want to get married.

In one snap he chopped that line of thinking in half. He was getting married, he was going to sell that property, and like it or not he was going to have to find a job at Cazenovia—or somewhere very similar—or risk being humiliated by his wife for the rest of his natural life.

How his life was no longer his own, he didn't know, but it was hers now. In every way that mattered, it was hers, and he no longer had the presence of mind to even care.

"That was by far the best presentation I've ever seen you give," Ben said in a voice registering absolute disbelief.

"Why, thank you," Camille said demurely as she laid the plans and her briefcase back on her desk.

"You looked invincible."

"No, I looked human." She looked at him from the vantage point of his former desk. "That was the point, wasn't it?"

Going to Nicole's after the Cazenovia interview seemed akin to hitting a self-destruct button, but Jaylon knew he couldn't hide forever. He parked the little blue car under the covered parking, and he climbed the steps to her apartment, wishing that running in the other direction was an option. Any direction other than the one he was traveling would've been welcome.

At her door he knocked softly, hoping in his heart-of-hearts that she wouldn't be there. No such luck, he heard noises on the other side and shifted even as he took a wishful glance at the stairs.

"Jaylon!" Nicole said happily as the door swung open. "I wasn't expecting you 'til later."

He stuck one hand in his pocket and forced a smile onto his face. "Sorry."

"No, I'm glad you're here. Mom came today, and she dropped off the catering list. We need to go over it and make sure they haven't left anything off." After a quick kiss, Nicole sashayed off down the hall. "It's right there on the table. Why don't you take a look at it while I change?"

"Okay," he said so softly she had no way of hearing it. With reluctant steps, he walked over to her table and sat down. He picked up the top three pieces of paper and scanned them.

The off-beige linen paper was the one she was talking about, but it wasn't the one that caught his attention. Slowly his eyes narrowed as he looked at the paper in his other hand. "Balance due: $21,585" stared up at him. He shook his head to get his brain working again. But still it was there. $21,585.

At that moment Nicole stepped into the kitchen. "Man, work was a bear today. We got a whole shipment of lingerie in that Ms. Soren wanted on the floor like yesterday." She looked down at her fingers. "My fingers still hurt from putting all those tags on."

"What's this?" Jaylon asked, strangled by the question as he held the paper up for her to see.

Nicole stopped her replay. "Oh, that's mine." She took it from him and stuck it with some other papers on the back cabinet.

"Twenty-one thousand dollars?" he asked, fighting to wrap his brain around that figure.

"Oh, you know how hard those things are to pay off. I'm working on it."

"Working on it?" he asked incredulous at the number but more disbelieving of her cavalier attitude toward it.

She shrugged helplessly. "You play, you pay."

"Yeah, but $21,000?"

"You act like I did something wrong," she said as the enthusiasm dropped from her voice.

The screaming questions in his brain left him near speechless. "When were you planning to tell me about this?"

"I was going to pay it off." Like nothing had happened she reached into the cabinet for a glass. "You want something?"

He wanted something all right, but it wasn't a drink. "How do you think we'll ever get the loan for the Hatherly house?"

"Oh, yeah. I was going to tell you, Daddy said he'd co-sign the loan with us if we're having trouble."

Jaylon snorted softly. "I bet he did."

"What?" Anger snapped into her voice. "It's no big deal. Everybody does it."

"Everybody is not us!" His point brought him right off the chair.

"I'm telling you, it's no big deal."

"It is a big deal." He stood looking at her, and all he could think was he had never liked her much in the first place. "To me, it's a very big deal." With a shake of his head, he turned on his heel and stomped out. $21,585.

Ben took Camille out for a celebration dinner, and for the first time when she looked at him, she didn't feel fear. She could be honest with him and with herself. It felt like floating on the clouds.

"Thanks for the talk the other night," she said, and this time she didn't need the meal in front of her for a shield. "You'll never know what that meant to me."

His smile was soft. "I didn't do anything."

But she wasn't going to let this go without getting all the way through it. "Yes, you did. You gave me back my life, and I definitely consider that something."

He laughed. "That's a little dramatic."

"That's the truth," she said, unwilling to let him laugh it off. "Until we talked, I was so busy seeing how everybody else was so superior to me, I didn't stop to see them for who they really were. It was a contest."

"Who won?"

She considered that and then shook her head. "No one. We all lost." Her gaze faded from the table as she withdrew into the rehearsal she'd been having in her head all day. "I need to tell you something."

He didn't sound at all concerned. "What's that?"

In fistfuls she pulled her courage to herself before she looked up at him. "Listen, Ben, you're a great friend..."

"Oh, no," he said instantly, "not the you're-a-great-friend speech."

Her smile didn't make it all the way to her face. "I don't think it's fair to make you think there's something here when there isn't."

He looked at her sadly, and it took more than a moment for him to get a voice to the words pleading from his eyes. "There isn't?"

She sighed as she looked at him and shook her head. "No."

"Not even a little tiny bit?"

The confidence in her decision solidified in her heart. "Not even a little, teeny-tiny bit. But I need to tell you, I'm grateful for all you taught me. I wouldn't be the person I am now without you, but hanging on, making you think I feel something that I don't just isn't fair to you—or to the future Mrs. Ben Conrad."

Sadness permeated his smile. "You think she's out there?"

"Are you kidding? I know she is, and she is beyond lucky."

His smile dimmed ten more watts. "And you're sure you're not her?"

She nodded. "Yeah, I'm sure."

Camille wasn't sure who the girl walking up to her apartment was, but she was quite sure it wasn't the Camille Wright she had known her whole life. Quietly she unlocked the door and stepped inside. Ben, her one and only lifeline, was gone, and she wasn't falling apart. No, she was happy for him. He was free, and now so was she.

With no plans to occupy her thoughts, she snapped on her computer and pulled up her email. There was a short note from Daria saying she'd aced another test. Pride swelled in Camille's chest, but in her heart just under the pride was a love she had never really realized was there. It poured into her soul and wrapped around her like a blanket.

The second email was a message from Lexie. A slight case of fear threatened in the corner of her mind, but Camille pushed that away. Lexie was her friend—one of her they-love-you-no-matter-what friends. The email slipped up onto her screen. "Just thought you might like to know, you're a lifetime."

In confusion Camille clicked on the tiny paperclip in the corner and laid her chin on her wrist to read the message. The email talked about how people come into your life for a reason, a season, or a lifetime. As she read, there were friends she could clearly put in each category. Some had come along to teach her one lesson, and some had come with a myriad of them in tow.

At the end of the email, Lexie had added, "Like I said, 'You're a lifetime.' Thanks for being my friend."

Without a second thought, Camille reached for the phone. Some things were best said out loud.

Jaylon's mind was in turmoil. He thought as hard as his brain would let him before it emitted an ear-splitting signal that said it was about to explode, but still he couldn't come up with one single person he could go to for help. Until he had seen that number on that paper, he had somehow convinced himself that they could make it work, that Nicole would start being reasonable once they were married.

How he thought that would ever materialize, he wasn't at all sure because from the second minute he had known her, she had never been reasonable. Standing in the Macy's manager's office as the alarm mania swirled around her, she had been anything but rational.

"You can't hold me here. I'll call my lawyer! I'll call my daddy's lawyer!"

"Miss, if you'll just give me your receipt so we can match up the items, I'm sure we can clear this up," the manager said.

"Here." Jaylon handed his own receipt and bag over. "Do mine first."

The manager, clearly not enjoying the little incident, smiled gratefully. With Jaylon using every opportunity to look at her, the manager began digging through the bag, matching the receipt items to the contents and checking for hidden scan alarms.

"Ah, here it is." The manager peeled the little sticker from the tie's fold. "These little suckers are hard to see."

"May we go now?" Nicole asked, in what at the time had sounded like haste but now sounded like arrogance.

"Of course." The manager replaced the tie. "So sorry for the inconvenience."

"Not a problem," Jaylon said and then followed Nicole out of the office.

She hadn't exactly stopped, but determination was never one of his weaknesses. "Hey! I didn't catch your name."

"Nicole Byrne." Not once had she ever stopped.

"It's nice to meet you," he said, offering her a hand and then checking his watch. "I'm really sorry about all of this. What do you say, let me take you to lunch to make up for it."

Bags still swinging, she slowed. "That wasn't your fault."

"More mine than yours, come on. Just a bite."

However, that bite had turned into much, much more, and now he was staring down the barrel of $21,000 of her debt. Not to mention the debt they would incur if she somehow talked him into accepting her father's charity.

He chafed at the thought of being indebted to that man forever. Not once had he ever felt on-level with him, and buying this house with his money wouldn't help that situation at all.

In the bathroom Jaylon pulled his shirt off intending to take a shower, but the mirror caught his gaze. His eyes. He stopped and looked at them. They looked so tired, so sad. They looked exactly as bad as he was feeling.

Nothing in him wanted to go down this road, but he wasn't sure he had what it took to start over either. It was a question he was sure would only be answered when he stood in a church and tied his life to hers. He had never dreaded a moment so much in his entire lifetime.

"I can catch the red-eye tonight," Camille said as the excitement invaded her chest. "Unless you don't want me to come."

"Of course we want you to come!" Lexie said as though hesitating even a second might let Camille change her mind. "I can send Nick if you want."

"No, I've got some errands to do tomorrow, so I'll just get a car."

"Are you sure?"

"Just leave me a key out so I can get in the house when I get there."

Chapter 14

There was no need for a key because when Camille pulled up to the little house at two o'clock in the morning, the lights were still on. With a smile, she parked and pulled her carry-on with her as she climbed the steps. Softly she knocked, not wanting to wake anyone who might be sleeping.

In seconds the door swung open, and Lexie in full surprised exuberance enveloped her.

"What're you guys doing, landing planes?" Camille asked, pointing to the lights.

Lexie's smile spread all the way to her voice. "We didn't want you to miss us."

"No chance of that."

Nick stood from his chair and offered an arm for a hug. "Just couldn't stay away, huh?"

"You got it." The second he let her go, her gaze chanced upon the cards lying on the coffee table. "What're you playing?"

"Gin," Lexie said dramatically. "And he's whooping me."

Camille dropped her carry-on to the floor. "Deal me in."

At four a.m. Nick surrendered and left the two of them still giggling in the living room. It had been ages since Camille had felt this light.

"Okay, what gives?" Lexie asked, slumping back onto the couch.

"Gives?" Without looking at her friend Camille gathered the cards.

"Taking the red-eye? That's not like you."

Camille straightened the cards, tapping them together. "I wanted to see a lifetime friend of mine. Is that a crime?"

Lexie smiled at the reference. "You were the first one I thought of."

"Same here." The straightening slowed. "That's why I had to come tell you in person."

"You fly 300 miles because of an email?"

Camille's heart dropped at how awful she'd been. "Well, that and to say how sorry I am for how we left things."

Lexie's gaze fell to the coffee table. "Oh, that."

"Yeah, that." How she would ever put it into words, she didn't know. All she knew was that she had to try. "You know, Lex, I never would've made it last week if it wasn't for you and Nick."

"You mean you wouldn't have come if it wasn't for me and Nick."

The laugh was barely, but it was there. "That too. But I'm glad I came."

"You didn't look very glad."

"Yeah? Well, let's just say I've gotten a better perspective on things this week, and I've decided it's time to make some changes in my life."

That pulled Lexie's curiosity up. "Like what?"

"Like being grateful when my friends knock themselves out trying to make me happy." Camille smiled at her friend. "Thanks for that."

Slowly Lexie shook her head. "I just wish it would've worked out better."

Peace flowed through Camille's soul. "No, it worked out exactly the way it was supposed to."

Jaylon awoke Saturday morning having no idea where Friday night had gone. It was like he was on some time machine that someone had pushed the fast forward button for. Inside he was screaming, "Help! Let me off! Let me off!" even as his body hurdled down the corridor of doom.

He was supposed to meet Nicole for a pre-bridal shower brunch in Syracuse, but he knew already he wouldn't have the appetite for it. His rational side considered calling her, but his perpetually vanishing courage wouldn't let him.

By this point his only prayer was for the earth to literally open up and swallow him whole. Minus that miracle, the only end to this ride that he could see lay at the top step right in front of an altar. In frustration he pushed that thought away. He wouldn't think about it, maybe then it would just leave him alone.

The clock blinking on the little countertop microwave said if he didn't hurry, Nicole would be eating brunch solo. With all the sanity he could muster, he pulled himself out to the car.

"Just think, J," he told himself sarcastically, "next week your windows will say, 'Just married.' Oh, joy."

"Thanks for meeting me," Camille said when Keane stepped into the front of the office. "I'm sorry I couldn't come on a better day."

"No problem," Keane said. "Always happy to help a friend."

"I appreciate that."

"So, you want to take my car?"

Camille nodded. "Mine's rented, and I can't seem to find the mirror adjusters so maybe we'd be better off in yours."

"My car it is then," he said with no hesitation.

"You're late," Nicole hissed when Jaylon folded himself onto the stark white chair at the Woodland Country Club.

"Last minute stuff," he said quickly.

"I talked to Mr. Tuxedo. All the guys made it in this week." For as happy as that news should have made her, it didn't show.

Jaylon ducked his head, trying to hide his own unhappiness. "That's good."

"We're supposed to meet with the minister on Thursday at 4:30. You're going to remember that. Right?"

"Thursday at 4:30."

Nicole nodded. "And Friday we've got rehearsal at 6, but we really need to be there about 5 to get things set up."

"Six," he said dutifully as he perused his menu.

"Five," she said as anger flooded her face.

"Five," he repeated like a trained seal.

"Saturday, we'll start pictures at one. I figure you guys can go first so I can have more time to get ready..." Her voice trailed off. "Jaylon, are you listening to me?"

Without even looking up, he nodded. "The crab legs look good."

"Hey." She snatched his menu away from him. "This isn't about food."

He looked at her, fighting to keep the anger rising in his stomach down. "I thought we were here to eat."

"We're here to coordinate our schedules!"

His face scrunched in annoyance. "We're getting married not planning a bank heist."

"This is the most important week of my life, and I'm not going to let anyone ruin it for me—and that includes you."

"Well, excuse me." Jaylon yanked his menu back. "I'll just sit over here and eat and try not to get in your way."

"Yeah," she said irritably. "You do that."

"This is really a beautiful piece of property," Keane said as he drove down the two tire tracks that had already begun to fade. "The creek is just gorgeous."

Camille didn't need the speech. She knew how beautiful the place was right down to the twists of the tree roots.

"I don't think the house is livable though," Keane said when they had gotten out of the car and started down the path. "It's too bad. It looks like it was a nice place at one time."

On the slope edge Camille laid her hand on the rough bark and gazed out across the gash in the earth. Home wrapped around her, and rather than fight it or deny it, she pulled it to her. "So, it's not on the market officially yet."

Keane shook his head as his hand settled in his pocket. "Not yet, but I expect it to be next week sometime."

Her spirit saw Jaylon standing with Nicole in the front of a beautiful church, and for all the screaming of her brain, she couldn't push that image away. In fact, with only one small modification, she didn't want to push it away, she wanted it right there with her forever. "I don't even want you to list it. When they're ready to sell, I'm ready to buy."

"He's considering upping his asking price to $950," Keane said tentatively.

"Doesn't matter," she said, letting the dreams take her. "Whatever they ask, I'll pay it."

For a moment they stood, she letting the feeling of the place seep into her wounded heart; he watching her.

"You don't back down when you see a good thing, do you?" Keane finally asked.

"I did that once," she said as a shredded tear wound its way through her words. "I'm not about to do it again."

"Just put it on my Mastercard," Nicole said, slipping the tiny piece of plastic into the black bill book.

"Yes, Ma'am," the waiter said with a nod.

"Mastercard?" Jaylon asked, barely waiting until the waiter was out of earshot. "Wasn't the bill I saw last night a Visa?"

Nicole shrugged. "You put it where it fits."

Where it fits? his soul shrieked, and only by some small miracle did he keep his wits about him. "How many cards do you have?"

"Five or six," she said off-handedly. "I lose count."

Not one microbe in him could fathom what he was sure she was telling him. It was an all-out fight to keep his voice down. "Well, what kind of balances do you have on those?"

"Oh, nothing like the Visa," she said confidently. "Only four or five thousand on each. Seven or eight at the most."

"Seven or..." He couldn't keep his eyes from going wide with the shock.

"Thank you for dining with us," the waiter said, laying the book back on the table.

"Thank you." Nicole smiled sweetly. When the waiter left, Jaylon watched as she opened the book and added a king's tip to the already over-priced bill.

She looked over at him. "Ready?"

"Do you have any idea how much you've got charged?" The weight of the situation dropped on him like an anvil as he stood to follow her out.

"I don't know," she said with a shrug. "I pay the minimum each month. What does it matter?"

He wanted to scream at her, but he was in too much shock to say even a single word. Instead he followed her out to the cars, where she kissed him good-bye and smiled softly.

"I'll see you tomorrow," she said, squeezing her body to his. "One more week."

"One more week," he repeated, wanting nothing more than to run. One more week and then a forever after that. That thought alone was enough to send him careening over the edge.

Long after Nicole was gone, Jaylon sat in the Woodland Country Club parking lot with his hands on the steering wheel watching the patrons come and go. He remembered when he was younger, sitting with his father in a club just like this one. He'd hated it then—all the show, the fragile façade he'd had to put on so everyone else would think his life was perfect.

Inside, things were never perfect, but his father had trained him well. Nobody wanted to know that things weren't perfect. They expected you to act in a certain way, and that was just how you acted. Even as he looked out his window now, he could see the veneer draped carefully over the people who stepped through those doors. It was a life he had done everything he could to get away from—until Nicole.

The thought of her brought with it the picture of that Visa bill, and five or six others just like it stared at him from the shadows. Why hadn't she told him about the debt? More to the point, why hadn't he asked? Was it too practical to talk about such things when romance was in the air? Or was the real answer that he didn't want to know? Was the illusion all he really wanted to see—regardless of what was really staring him in the face?

His mind traced over his own meager savings. It wasn't much, but he was at least on the plus side of zero—for six more days anyway. With one more glance out the window, he could take no more. He fired up the Camaro and backed out, seeing as little as possible.

He didn't want to see. He didn't want to think. All he wanted to do was drive so far away that Nicole and her debts and her idea of the perfect life could never reach him again.

"I'll let you know when it comes open," Keane said when they were again seated in his office. "And just for my information, at what point will this be out of your league?"

Camille sat for a long moment, and then she smiled at him. "I'm sure you'll do the right thing by everybody."

Slowly Keane nodded and matched her smile. "I'll try."

The country flashed past the Z28's windows. Going all the way back to Ridgecrest was crazy. It made no sense. He should be in Brickhaven, getting everything ready for the wedding. However, that thought chopped itself in half. The wedding. He didn't want to think about it or Nicole or anything else in his life at the moment.

What had Seth said about cold feet? Well, Jaylon's were beginning to get frostbite. The thought of tying his life to Nicole's sent his soul reeling in fear. If she had conveniently forgotten to mention something like $21,000 in debt, what else had she conveniently forgotten to mention?

Convenient. It was a good word when it came to Nicole. She had never been one to delve into anything remotely considered difficult. He had heard the stories about her college experience—going from one major to the other looking for something that didn't require too much of a challenge. She had settled on retail fashion for the simple fact that after six years it was all she had left to try.

Even then she had only barely scraped by, and he wasn't at all sure that her eventual graduation wasn't more because of her father's donations to the school than about Nicole's pursuit of knowledge. Of course, how she got the diploma didn't matter to most of the world anymore. What mattered was that she had it and to all outside observers seemed to be doing quite well with it.

However, that bill coupled with the others she had so easily tossed off as meaningless hounded him. At what point did she stop being Daddy's Girl and start being Jaylon's wife? At the wedding? After the wedding? In six months? In six years? Never? One thing was for sure, she certainly hadn't stopped yet.

As he turned the car and headed the last 30 miles to Ridgecrest, he wondered if her father knew anything about her growing debt. It seemed unlikely in-so-much as if Mr. Byrne did know, Jaylon was sure he would already have baled his daughter out of the hole she had dug for herself.

The muscles in Jaylon's chest constricted over his lungs as the feeling of being in the same room with Mr. Byrne came over him. It was silly to have a feeling so deeply entrenched in the psyche that the mere thought of the person would bring it up, but that was precisely what happened any time the older man's existence crossed Jaylon's mind. It was like a giant foot had taken up residence on his chest and would gladly squeeze the life right out of him if he so much as breathed wrong.

Nature had turned to city and then back to nature outside his window, and for all the rationalizations of his brain, his heart knew he was headed for the only place on earth he wanted to be—the only place that still made any sense. In ten minutes flat the car was making the last turn onto the two tracks and winding its way down the path.

He noticed the tracks but immediately crossed off their existence as belonging to Keane when he came out to look over the property. As irrational as it seemed, the fact that anyone else had been here—on his land—felt like they'd trespassed on his very soul. He didn't want anyone else here. He wanted to be here. Just him, and no one else.

The cool, late April air wrapped around him as he crawled out of the car and started down the path. If he could just stay here, just forget about the rest of the world, then his life could feel right again. Out of all the confusion, that was the one thing he was completely sure. Once this was gone, once it belonged to someone else, he would never feel right again. Never.

His body slid down the length of the tree, and he laid his head in his hands. Everything hurt. His head from not letting the tears fall. His heart from forcing it to feel things it didn't and from not letting it feel things it wanted to. The ache seemed to sink right into his soul—into the hole that had become his being.

The emptiness fell in over him, and he no longer had the strength to fight it.

Chapter 15

Nick and Lexie weren't expecting Camille back until five, and although she had other things she could be doing that would be far more productive, she didn't really want to tackle any of them. What she wanted to do was go sit and live for another moment.

She was scheduled to fly out later that night so this would be her one and only chance to come out here by herself. All the rationalizations and excuses in her mind made no real difference. She knew the second she'd gotten back in her car after leaving Keane's office where she was going.

The little rental car had already bounced through the turn and started down the tracks when she first saw the Camaro sitting at the end of the path. It wasn't wholly unexpected. In fact it had been there in all of her dreams, but the sight of it still caused her heart to drift skyward. She fought to tell herself he was probably just here to get the place ready to sell. That made sense to every part of her other than her heart.

Parking her car behind his, she climbed out and secured her hands in the pockets of her jacket as she started down the trail to the tree. It was strange, but this time she didn't feel like she was trespassing—more like she was checking up on her own land. It wasn't hers yet, but in a week it would be, and that apparently changed things for her heart.

"I didn't expect you to be here," she said when she was only a couple feet from the tree.

In a blink Jaylon whirled around and stood. Instantly she saw the crushed look on his face and the trails of the tears that had ceased but had left their shadows behind just the same.

"Camille." He swiped at his face as he turned back to the slope in embarrassment. "What...? Where...? What are you doing here?"

She heard the questions, but all she saw was the pain in his eyes. It knifed through her. "J, what's wrong?"

"Nothing." He stepped away from her even as his hands continued wiping.

"Nothing?" she asked not believing that for a second. She paused and then stepped to his side unwilling to let him run. Her advance stopped when she was right next to him. Carefully she bent her head to look at him even as he did everything he could to avoid her gaze. "Doesn't look like nothing to me."

He shrugged and smiled thinly. "I'm fine."

"Uh-huh, and I'm the Queen of England. Come on, J. What's wrong?"

His teeth ground across the inside of his lip, and even from two feet away she heard the battle raging in his head.

"Just a bad case of cold feet."

Nicole. Camille's heart coiled around the name, and she had to force the air into her lungs. "I hear that happens to everyone."

"Not this bad," he said quietly, but she heard it just the same.

Her heart slipped out of its casing and slid down into her stomach. "Why? What happened?"

For a second his gaze swung to hers, and the steel blue of his eyes tore right through her. Then his gaze dropped, and he turned to look down the edge of the slope in the other direction. "I found something out I'm not sure I can deal with."

Camille kept rational with her in a tight grip. "Something... about Nicole?"

Slowly he nodded, and she had to fight not to simultaneously go to the worst possible thing he could be talking about and to also not rip Nicole's head off her body for causing him so much pain.

Her gaze followed his down the slope side. "That's why you're here."

He nodded.

She waited, but when he said nothing, she had to ask. "What happened?"

The question threatened to tear down every wall she had managed to build between him and her in the last weeks. Seeing anyone in pain had always ripped her soul to shreds, but seeing him in pain hurt her own soul as badly as anything anyone had ever done to her had.

The words strangled themselves out of his core. "She wants me to give everything, but she's not willing to give anything."

Camille's gaze traveled down the length of the slope. "The land."

"Among other things." He stuffed one hand in his pocket. "I just always thought marriage was supposed to make you happy."

"Marriage doesn't make life go away."

"Huh. Bad time to learn that," he said with the tiniest of laughs.

"So what do you want to make go away?"

He glanced at her, and then she watched as he visibly deflated. "Everything."

She smiled at that. "That's pretty general. Got anything specific in mind?"

The remaining strength in his body seemed to melt away as he stepped over to the tree, sat down, and rested one elbow on his knee. "Let's see. Quitting, changing jobs, moving, buying a house, selling the land, trying to be something I'm not..."

"Wait, wait, wait." She put her hands in the air to stop the list as she stepped over to the tree. "One at a time."

"Yeah, that'd be nice." He shook his head. "It's not what I thought it would be."

Careful not to twist anything important as she did so, she lowered herself to the root next to his. "What's not what you thought it would be?"

"Life." His hands dropped to his sides as he leaned back against the tree. "This."

She watched him for a moment, trying to find a good place to start. "Okay. Well, let's start with the job. Why do you have to quit? I mean it sounds like you like teaching, right?"

"Oh, yeah. I like teaching." Then he deflated again. "Well, most of the time."

"Then why do you have to quit?"

"It's too far to commute from Syracuse."

She worked to get the pieces together in her mind. "So, you're moving to Syracuse then?"

"In June as soon as school's over."

Camille nodded, feeling the news but surprised at not being crushed by it. "And you don't want to quit?"

"No. I don't want to take a job just to make somebody else happy."

"Somebody else...?" she started and then crashed into a beautiful blonde model. "Nicole."

He nodded. "I know. I'm getting married. Things are supposed to change. It's just I don't want them to."

"You don't think the change is going to be better than now?"

"It's not that." The wind brushed through the trees above them as it blew strands of hair into his face. However, he never moved. "I just want my life—what I want—to be important to her. That's all."

Camille's eyebrows narrowed. "And it isn't?"

"It doesn't feel like it is."

She wanted to tell him to get out. That getting married when you don't feel important to the relationship is a mistake. However, she couldn't tell how much of that speech had to do with what he was feeling and how much of it had to do with what she was feeling.

"Have you talked to her about this?" Camille asked, hating how calmly every word that was coming out of her mouth sounded.

"What am I supposed to say, 'I hate what you're doing to my life'?"

Camille's gaze traveled to his profile. "Do you hate what she's doing to your life?"

His teeth ground across his bottom lip. "Sometimes."

"Then yeah," she said softly. "I think she needs to know that."

Skepticism rained through his eyes when he looked at her. "That's not something a bride wants to hear right before she walks down the aisle."

"Well, would it be better after she walks down that aisle?"

It took a moment for him to answer. "No."

She didn't want to dig, but she knew he needed it. "And is this going to go away after you walk down that aisle?"

He thought for another long moment. It wasn't clear if he was thinking of an answer or just fighting to get one out. "No."

Calm understanding slipped into her spirit. "Then she deserves to know it now, J."

Pain scratched across his face. "But I don't want to hurt her."

"And you're going to not hurt her by lying to her?" Camille asked pointedly. She watched his head drop under the weight of the question, and although the next words threatened to push her sanity to the bottom of the river and drown it there, there was no stopping them. "Look, if you really love her, you have to trust her to help you make it work for both of you—not just for her."

Camille's gaze traveled down the expanse of the land as her spirit released him. This was his decision, and regardless of how she felt, she wasn't going to push him into making the decision she wanted him to. He had to make it regardless of what she wanted. "Being miserable to make someone else happy doesn't work, J. Eventually it just makes everyone miserable. You deserve to be happy, too."

He leaned his head back against the tree, closed his eyes, and shook his head. "I'm just so confused."

She watched him, not impassively but calmly. "About what?"

"About what I should do." His lip curled inward. "It's just that I've come this far, and turning back now seems..."

"Silly?"

"Yeah something like that." Slowly his head moved side to side. "I just don't understand why this is all happening now. I mean I was so excited about getting married before..."

"Why it's happening," Camille said, breaking into his statement with a soft laugh. "Well, it's happening for the same reason everything else does. It's happening to teach you something. Your job is to figure out what."

"What? Like that I'm destined to be miserable my whole life because every time something seems to finally be working out, I do something stupid to mess it up or the timing's all wrong, or..."

"Everything happens for a reason." She breathed in as she looked out across the slope. "Like us. I was so mad about us not working out, I made everybody else miserable."

"Everybody?"

"Well, Lexie and Nick. I took it out on them, which of course wasn't fair. I just wanted it all to go away. But instead of owning up to that, I got mad, hoping nobody would notice what I was really feeling." She smiled and shook her head. "Thankfully they didn't exactly let me by with that."

"Yeah," he said, seeming to step back from the brink as he looked at her, "this isn't exactly Pittsburgh, is it? What's up with that?"

Her mind considered lying and then realized she would be selling him short too by not being honest. "I don't know. I guess I realized how awful I had been to them, so I came back to say I'm sorry."

He considered that for a moment. "But out here isn't Lexie's."

"No, but it's part of the process of making peace with my life... and figuring out where I go from here."

He waited a long moment before he narrowed his gaze at her. "And where do you go...from here?"

She thought about that question and then closed her eyes. "Forward I guess. I've been stuck in miserable for too long now. I've been pushing people away and doing everything I could think of to get them to leave me alone."

Concern flashed through his voice. "Why would you do that?"

Ben's face drifted through her mind, and she smiled. "Because I thought it was easier."

"Than?"

Her eyes opened, and she looked at him softly. "Than letting them get close to me and then watching them leave." By the crumpled look on his face, she knew that statement had hurt him although she hadn't meant it to. "I wish it could've been different between us too, but it wasn't. I've accepted that."

"How?" he asked, sounding like accepting that was all-but impossible.

"Well, I spent a lot of time asking why. I mean what's the point of getting close to someone if they're just going to leave you anyway? I couldn't figure it out, but Nick told me something that made a lot of sense."

"Oh? What's that?" Jaylon asked, clearly searching for something to grab onto.

"He told me that the answer to 'Why?' is always, 'Your Holy Will.' That there's a reason. There's a lesson. The only question is: Can you stop long enough to listen to what the lesson is? For some reason, that made a lot of sense to me."

They sat, listening to nature talk to itself around them. Finally, reluctantly she looked at her watch. She was due at Lexie and Nick's half an hour ago. "I hate to say this, but I've really got to get going. I've got a flight out tonight."

Jaylon nodded and followed her up from the tree roots as he shifted, obviously not wanting to say good-bye to her. "Take care."

In all her nightmares this moment had ripped her apart, but now that she was living it, it wasn't nearly as bad as she had imagined. "You too." Tenderly she leaned in to his embrace and held him for a long moment. "It's going to be all right, J. You'll see."

As she let go of him, she looked into his eyes, and it was the first time she had seen even a trace of peace there.

"You know what?" he asked as he gazed at her. "I think you just might be right."

She smiled. Her gaze dropped from his as she let go of him, and her feet started back for her car. Once there, she waved once, got in, and backed out, glancing only once more at him standing under the tree, one hand in his pocket, watching her go. It was an image she knew would be on her heart forever.

Jaylon didn't move as her car backed out and then disappeared past the trees. "Your Holy Will." He laughed softly. "Well, God, I sure wish you'd clue me in on Your plan because right now, I'm really confused."

What had she said about stopping long enough to figure out what the lesson was? That was supposed to be the point of this afternoon—stopping long enough to figure things out. The plan was definitely not to run into her.

Strange thing was she was a long way from Pittsburgh, and if she was visiting Lexie, why had she come out to the slopes? He traced back through the conversation but couldn't really come up with an answer to that question.

Exhaustion flowed over him, as he sat down on the tree root and traced back over everything. "There's a lesson there..."

Nicole floated through his mind, followed almost immediately by Ariana. If he had learned the lesson with Ariana—as he thought he had—why had Nicole shown up? Nicole, with her ten thousand demands and the relentless understanding that he would never be good enough for her.

As ache stabbed into his heart, he thought about the night he had asked her to marry him. It was one of those moments in life that you're supposed to remember forever, and there was little chance that he would ever forget it—but not for any of the right reasons.

Against the onslaught of the sinking sun, he closed his eyes as his mind went back to her apartment.

"I've got something to ask you," he had said, and now he could hear the fear mix with the excitement he had felt. This was it. The moment he had worked so hard to arrange. Slowly he slid the box out of his jacket and cracked it open. "Nicole, will you marry me?"

He could still remember her face. Excitement until she looked down. His heart fell at the mere memory.

"Yeah," she said, looking at him. "I'll marry you, but I always kind of thought I'd get to pick out my own ring."

It was a lie. He knew it from that moment as well as he knew it now. Had that ring been "enough," she would've put it on and never looked back. As it turned out, however, that ring—his lifetime gift to her—had led to their biggest fight so far.

"Tiffany's?" he remembered asking. "I don't see why it has to be from Tiffany's."

The incredulousness in her eyes seared him even now. "Of course you don't."

In the present he bit into his bottom lip as his memory traced over the journey to the ring he had ultimately purchased for her—a flawless half-carat, that wasn't nearly as big or flashy as the one she wanted, but one that had put him in debt for the next several years anyway.

Even that wasn't enough. He knew it every time she showed it to someone, always with the qualifier, "We're going to get something bigger as soon as he gets into something other than teaching."

Two slams in one simple statement. She was good at it. She'd had a lot of practice. And one thing was completely clear: if he went through with this wedding, she would have plenty more opportunities to run him into the ground.

He didn't want to think about that. This trip was supposed to be about finding a solution to this mess, but the only solution he could see seemed to be to tell Nicole to get lost. The only problem with that was he wasn't sure he could ever do that. It was just easier to keep going, to not make waves, and to keep hoping things would get better.

With a push, he lifted himself off the ground and dusted his pants off. His stomach said it had been hours since he'd eaten anything, and grudgingly he decided he'd better get something to eat when he went through town. The mere thought of going back to Brickhaven and her screamed through his soul, but he beat the reluctance down. He was going to go back, and one way or the other, he was going to be happy about it.

Going back to the car, he tried not to feel himself walking away from everything he had ever loved, but it was difficult. A hazy fog of reluctant acceptance descended over him. If Camille had just said, "You really shouldn't get married. We still have a chance..." What? Would that have made anything better? Would that have solved anything?

No, she had let him go. She had gone on with her life. He wondered if she ever really thought about back then, but even as he thought it, he knew he would never have the guts to ask her. Besides, he would probably never see her again anyway. That thought made him shift in the seat. Trying to drown out the whispers of his mind, he flicked the radio on and turned it up. Anything to make himself stop thinking.

His fingers drummed on the steering wheel as he forced his mind to concentrate on the words of the song. "I can't help but see...the way you look...tonight..."

In an instant he was back standing on a bridge in hazy blue light with Camille in his arms. Why couldn't life just be simple? Why did he have to let her go ten years ago? How big of a fool could he have been to believe that he could ever find anyone better than her? Than Camille...than his soul mate...

Almost on its own, the car turned into the Basel Restaurant where only a few cars were parked. Eating alone had never really been his idea of a fun way to spend a Saturday night, but this Saturday night, all he wanted was to be alone. Versus the alternatives, alone looked very good. Quickly he parked and climbed out of the car—his legs aching with every movement they made.

His hand found the confines of his pants pocket, and just before he got to the door, he ran his fingers through his hair. He was a mess, but everyone else didn't have to know that. With a determined swing he opened the door and stepped inside where he met up with the hostess.

"One?" she asked, looking past him to his non-existent date.

"Yeah," he said, again running his fingers through the top of his hair.

"This way." She turned, and he followed her short black skirt past the first two tables to a booth in the center of the restaurant. "This okay?"

"Yeah," he said, wishing he were Nicole who could make a scene and get any table in the restaurant she wanted. As he slid into the booth, his mind said the table that he wanted was the one in the darkest corner available. He could just go hide there and disappear. It seemed like a good option at the moment.

Absently he looked over the menu. It seemed strange to order a hamburger in a place like this. Nicole would laugh holes through him if she heard him do anything so inane.

"Hi," the waitress said as she slid up to the edge of his table, "what can I get you?"

"I'll have a burger," he said with a defiant smile, "extra tomatoes, fries and a Dr. Pepper."

She wrote the order down. "Anything else?"

"Not right now. Thanks."

When she left, he leaned back in the booth, proud of taking a stand against the tyranny of Nicole's presence in his life. Too bad he couldn't seem to do that with her around. Slowly his mind traced over their relationship as his soul realized how much of himself he had lost in Nicole. The more he looked, the more he noticed the holes gnawed through what he used to be.

"J?" someone from the next table over asked.

Instantly his gaze swung to the table next to him, where Nick, Lexie, and Camille had suddenly appeared and were taking their seats around the little table. Disbelief cracked through him. "Hey, what are you guys doing here?"

"Us?" Nick laughed. "What are you doing here?"

"A guy has to eat. Doesn't he?" Jaylon slid out of his booth to step over to their table where he watched them get comfortable. "But I certainly didn't expect you all to show up."

"Date night," Nick said.

"Two dates?" Jaylon raised an eyebrow. "Lucky you."

"Two dates—yeah, that would be nice." Nick laid an arm over Lexie's chair casually. "No, this is my date. The other one just showed up on my doorstep."

"Hey!" Camille said mockingly wounded. "That wasn't very nice."

Jaylon laughed as he looked at Camille. He smiled and barely caught himself from winking at her. "Like I said, 'Lucky you.'" His gaze dropped from her face, knowing that looking at her too long might literally slice his heart in two. "Well, I'd better let you all get back to dinner..."

"Why don't you join us?" Nick waved at the empty seat. "We've got an extra place."

Jaylon knew Nick was just being nice, and considering their history, that was more than he could've asked for. "Oh, I wouldn't want to intrude."

"Who's intruding?" Nick never so much as flinched. "Besides we didn't get to talk much at the reunion. Come on. I promise, I won't let Camille bite."

"Hey!" Camille said again as her eyes widened in warning at Nick. Then in the next instant she caught Jaylon in her soft gaze, and he was taken in just as he had been that first day on the steps in drama class. "Come on, J. I'll make Nick behave himself. I promise."

All rationalizations got lost in her eyes. He knew he should say no, make some excuse to go back to his table. He shouldn't be here, talking to her—again. But here, talking to her, made more sense than everything else in his life. "Okay. If you're sure you don't mind."

Nick held his hands out to the sides. "Do we look like we mind?"

Forcing himself to look across the table and away from her, Jaylon sat and trained his gaze on Lexie. "So, Lexie, looks like you got parole tonight."

Lexie looked at him with not too kind but questioning eyes.

"From the kids," he clarified before her gaze burned him to cinders.

"Oh, yeah. That's why God created grandmothers," she said, and he saw a tiny piece of the ice chip away from her.

He smiled—glad she would give him even a tiny chance to show he wasn't a total jerk. "I meant to tell you all thanks for the party the other night. It was really fun—especially the hayride."

The words were out of his mouth like a shot, and although honest, they hit far too close to what he really wanted to say. Feeling that, he ducked his head to the table.

"I'm just glad nobody fell off," Nick said jovially.

Jaylon's gaze trailed up from the table and said thanks to Nick for saving him from himself. "A couple of those bumps I kind of thought you had planned."

"I'd say I did, but I'm afraid I'd get sued."

"It's a possibility," Jaylon said as his waitress came back, looking puzzled by the impromptu rendition of musical chairs. Carefully she set his drink in front of him. "Thanks."

She looked at the rest of the table. "Umm, could I take your orders?"

In no time she had the orders and was headed back for the kitchen.

"I talked to Mrs. Allen at the reunion," Nick said, clearly understanding his role as lead conversation-maker. "Did you know she's retiring?"

"She is?" Camille asked, her disbelief crowding out her obvious reluctance to join the conversation. "Why?"

"She's moving to Florida." Jaylon took the straw out of its wrapper. "It's hard to imagine that place without her."

Nick laughed. "Yeah, her and that dumb old chalkboard."

"Man, I wonder how many miles she made dragging that thing across the stage," Jaylon said, joining the laugh.

"Six trillion while we were there at least," Nick said. "Class. Please, class. Can we get started now?"

Camille giggled at the horrible impression. "I bet that's exactly what J sounds like now."

"I do not," Jaylon said defiantly. "I'm much cooler than that."

"Oh, yeah." She nodded. "And I'm sure you don't play Magic Box anymore either."

In a breath he was back on a stage, surrounded by little kids and her.

"Magic Box?" Nick asked with confusion.

"Yeah," Camille said, but her voice had drifted away on the memory just as surely as Jaylon's mind had. "J used to run a Theatre Arts program over at the youth center. We got to play Magic Box a lot."

"The youth center?" Nick looked at Jaylon. "I didn't know you worked there."

Jaylon shrugged off the admiration in Nick's voice. "It was something to do."

"I've been thinking about taking Samantha to the youth center," Lexie said. "But I don't think they have the Theatre Arts thing anymore. At least that wasn't on the little hand-out they gave me."

"Sam in Theatre Arts?" Camille asked with a raise of her eyebrows. "Now there is a scary thought."

Jaylon laughed at the seriousness of her voice as the waitress set the other three drinks in front of their owners. "Why's that?"

"Take Nick," Camille said gravely, "and multiply him on a bad day by twenty."

"Oh." Jaylon nodded knowingly although he wasn't sure what was so bad about Nick in the first place.

Nick shook his head in disgust. "You give a girl a roof over her head, and..."

Camille pointed a warning finger at him. "Be nice."

"Me?" Nick asked, wounded.

"Yes, you." She wagged the finger at him. "You behave yourself."

Nick lowered his voice and gaze to Jaylon. "You see what I have to put up with?"

Despite every sane piece of his mind, Jaylon smiled at her, and his heart traveled ahead of the words. "Yeah, I do."

Chapter 16

As he drove back to Brickhaven later, Jaylon thought about Camille, sitting there, joking with Nick and Lexie like everything in her life was fine. It was such a dichotomy from the way she had looked on the bridge. That night she had looked like one wrong word could shatter her into a thousand pieces. Now, she looked almost...happy.

He thought back to his own emotions over the last few months, and from that perspective her actions made complete sense. That was how he felt—like what he was feeling this minute had nothing to do with what he would be feeling the next minute or the next second for that matter.

As he drove past the "Syracuse 50" sign, his thoughts tripped back over Nicole. For nearly two hours he hadn't thought of her even once. No one had asked about the wedding, which he knew was more for Camille's sake than for his own, but he was grateful just the same.

The wedding. A brick through the head couldn't have been as clear as the signals he'd been getting on what now seemed like a minute-by-minute basis. Marrying Nicole was a mistake. Regardless of whether Camille was available or even interested, Nicole's life was not where he wanted to live.

Compromise was one thing, but giving up everything that made him who he was—was another. The decision played in his mind, batting back and forth as he tried to catch it. It was the right decision. He knew that. The only question was how to tell Nicole.

Even the prospect of that confrontation made him shiver, but some things couldn't be helped. He looked at the clock on the radio. It was already nearly eight o'clock, but he knew telling Nicole couldn't wait another day—not another minute. He wanted to be free from her.

As his soul broke away from the weight of being with her, he felt lighter than he had since he'd slipped the second ring on Nicole's finger. Ever since that moment she had been an anchor, pulling him to the bottom. Link by link, he unhooked himself from her, and every link that dropped away sent his spirit soaring higher into the heavens.

All the tension from the afternoon dropped away from Camille as the plane lifted into the night sky. She had done what she had come to do—make peace with Lexie and find a way to let Jaylon go. True, she still couldn't think of him pledging his life to Nicole without a twinge tweaking her heart, but at least the simple thought of him didn't bring a flood of tears and regret.

"God, I put J in your hands. Keep him safe for me, and find a way to bring him peace."

That was all she now asked—that and not one thing more.

As the blue Camaro rounded the corner to Nicole's apartment for the fifth time, he closed his eyes and gathered all his courage to him. Now would be better than later, he reasoned—although he really didn't want to live through the next few minutes.

Frustrated at being frustrated, he finally parked and forced his feet through the lobby to the elevator and right to her door. However, the sight of the numbers on that door and the knowledge of what was coming when it opened nearly sapped his remaining determination. He looked back at the elevator once and then before he could think about it too long, he turned and knocked three times.

The decision made and the initial action taken, he took a breath and stepped back. After a few seconds he looked at his watch and knocked again. Suddenly he heard the locks, and in the next breath he found himself staring into the moment he had done absolutely everything to avoid.

"Jaylon! Where have you been?" Nicole asked, and the second thing he noticed right after the anger in her voice was the white sheath snagged with a golden belt draped over her body. "I've been trying to call you for three hours."

"You have?" he asked as she grabbed his elbow and pulled him into the room.

"Of course, didn't you get my message?"

"Message? No, I haven't been home. What message?"

"Ms. Soren called this afternoon. There's a party for the buyers tonight."

"Tonight?" he asked.

Nicole looked at her watch. "Right now."

He looked down at his attire. "But I'm not..."

"I got your tux. It's right back here."

"My tux?"

She pushed him down the hallway to the bathroom. "From the rental company. They knew your measurements, so I just..."

Trying to figure out where this whirlwind had come from, he allowed himself to be pushed into the bathroom. "There's no way we're going to make it on time."

"Well, it's better than not showing up at all. I told her we would be there." Quickly she grabbed her shoes, checked for anything else she needed, and looked at her watch. "You've got ten minutes."

"Ten..."

But she had already closed the door. Then just as quickly as she was gone, she was back. "And don't forget to shave."

Again he was alone. In disbelief he looked at the tux hanging on the shower rod. "Oh, by the way, Nicole," he said to his reflection in the mirror, "I wanted to tell you something..."

Something was going to have to wait—just like it always did when it was about him.

"Hey, Max," Camille said when she pushed into the apartment. A feeling of dreaded loneliness dropped around her as she knelt to pet the cat, but even kneeling required too much strength, so seated on the floor her back resting against the side wall, she pulled her knees to her and took a really good look at her life.

A chair, a threadbare couch, a second-hand rug purchased for $20. One thing was clear, she didn't like a single shred of it. She needed to talk to somebody. In desperation, she dragged the phone off of the desk and dialed Daria's number. All she wanted to do was to check in with her little sister. To hear a friendly voice. To connect to a world she felt hopelessly disconnected from.

"Hi, is Daria Marek there?" she asked the person who answered the phone.

The wait until Daria answered seemed infinite.

"Hello?"

"Dar, hi," Camille said as the gratefulness ran through her. "How you doing?"

"Hey, sis. I'm fine. How are you?"

"Oh, you know me," Camille said softly. "I'm fine."

"Liar."

Camille laughed. Her sister had gotten very perceptive. "Okay, I'm lying."

"What's wrong?"

Her next question seemed utterly ridiculous, and yet she really wanted the answer to it. "Do you think I give up too easily?"

"What kind of a question is that?"

"I don't know. I just...umm, I met up with Jaylon Quinn this weekend, and..."

"Jaylon?" Daria nearly shrieked. "From theatre?"

"Yes from theatre."

"Where is he? What's he doing? Is he still as good-looking as he was back then?"

"He's getting married next weekend."

That one sentence stopped Daria cold. "Oh, Camille, I'm sorry."

"Yeah, so am I."

"Want to talk about it?"

"Not really."

"Okay," Daria said slowly. "Then what do you want to talk about?"

"I don't know. Anything but that. How's school going?"

Pinpoints of light illuminated the darkened room beyond as Nicole stopped Jaylon at the door of the restaurant.

"You know, I kind of like this little preview," she said seductively as her hands worked to straighten his tie and jacket. "I'm going to have to keep my eye on you tonight."

Something told him that shouldn't be a problem. Nicole missed very few of his faux pas, and he was sure they would be in abundance tonight.

"Very nice." She appraised him one more time. "Now, remember this is important. Okay? If I'm going to make assistant, I need this to go well."

He nodded for no other reason than to make her stop talking.

"Great." She smiled at him and then stepped back so he could open the door for her.

For one moment before he reached around her for the door, he could've sworn she had nearly-black hair and a Cleopatra dress on. Quickly he shook that image away from his consciousness and pulled the door open.

A hush crossed the room, followed by a "they're here." In the next second applause erupted across the room as Jaylon stood, looking into the faces of people he had never met before, trying to get a handle on what was happening.

"Congratulations!" a woman, he recognized as Ms. Soren, said as she swept up to them. "We were beginning to think you weren't coming."

"Oh," Nicole said as she accepted a fake kiss on the cheek, "we wouldn't have missed it."

Missed what, Jaylon still didn't know.

"Jaylon," Ms. Soren said, holding her hands out to him. "You have got to be the luckiest man in the world."

"Thank you." He accepted her hands and her air kiss as he fought simultaneously to smile and not to run.

"The happy couple," Ms. Soren said to the rest of the group, and a cheer went up. She turned back to them. "Come, eat, mingle."

Jaylon stole a sideways glance at Nicole, who looked positively glowing. He didn't want to do this; he didn't want to be here. If he could just be someone else... that's when it hit him. They wanted a show. Nicole wanted him to be the happy groom-to-be. He had played characters before, and for the sake of getting through this night, he knew that was his ticket out.

It wasn't rehearsed, but he fell into the part with little trouble. With Nicole planted firmly on his arm, he made the rounds of all her office friends. The act called on every piece of training he'd ever had, but it worked. He laughed like his happiness knew no bounds. Even Nicole seemed to be buying it, so all that acting training hadn't been for naught. That was at least good to know.

The act worked most of the night. Jaylon simply let Nicole's digs roll off of him like so many lines a scribe had written that had no real connection to his life. However, a small voice in the back of his mind kept reminding him that this was in fact reality—not some play on which the curtain would fall and he could go back to his own life.

During the evening he fought that voice, but when the clock wound around past midnight and the tensions of the day began to catch up with him, even acting became agony.

"So, you're a teacher then?" a man Jaylon couldn't remember ever meeting said.

"For now, but he really wants to work at the college level," Nicole broke in before Jaylon had a chance to say even a word. "Syracuse University."

"Syracuse? Wow. That's quite a step up," the man said.

"Well, he's sick of working with the little hoodlums on the high school level, you know? They are just so childish."

Childish. That was a good word for the woman standing right next to him. With one glance at her, Jaylon could take no more. "Excuse me."

Determination surged through him as he stepped away from them. He set his drink down on one of the little tables and strode for the doors. However, Nicole wasn't going to let him get away so easily.

"Where do you think you're going?" she hissed when she caught up with him.

"What do you care?" he asked off-handedly. "You don't need me for this."

Her gaze narrowed at him. "Mind telling me what that means?"

Three feet from the doors, he stopped and turned on her. "It means I don't need you to answer for me. It means I'm sick of trying to stay in this little box you want to put me in."

Nicole glanced over her shoulder. "I was just trying to make conversation."

"No, you were trying to make me better than you think I am, and I'm tired of it."

"Jaylon," she said, her voice melting like butter. "Come on. I'm sorry."

"Of course you are," he said, and his voice was hard as stone. "You're always sorry—except you're never sorry enough to stop putting me down."

Like a begging puppy dog, she smiled at him. "Do we really have to do this here?"

"Do what? Be honest with each other?"

"I am honest."

As he looked at her, he knew the full meaning of that statement. "Yeah, I know. You honestly think I'm someone you have to make excuses for. Well, I don't need you or anyone else to make excuses for my life."

Nicole pushed one side of her blonde hair over her ear. "I wasn't making excuses."

"You weren't? It sure sounded like it to me."

"Umm." She glanced over her shoulder again obviously trying to decide if it was worse to simply walk out or to have a fight in clear view of everyone. "Could we do this somewhere else?"

Recklessness took over his soul. "Why? Reality a little too honest for you?"

"I just...umm, these people are my co-workers," she said as she leaned into him with a whisper. "I'd rather them not know every little detail of my life."

He regarded her for a moment and then shook his head in annoyance. "Where do you want to go?"

Her gaze traveled back over her shoulder. "Somewhere else, but we need to at least tell them thanks first."

Never in his life had Jaylon been in more disbelief. He had taken his stand, and still there were things more important to her than him. "You tell them thanks. I'll be in the car."

"Jaylon..."

But he had already pushed out the doors into the cool night air beyond. Not once had he ever been so rude, and truthfully it wasn't her co-workers he was mad at, but to have to keep up that charade for even one more second had the capacity to rip him in half. It was all so fake, so phony, so...his father.

"The Camaro," he said to the parking attendant as he forced his body not to lash out at the light pole standing there. In this state he felt like he could bend the metal with his bare hands. There was anger with her to be sure, but more than that there was anger with himself. How had he ever convinced himself that he loved her? How had he ever convinced himself that she loved him?

Simultaneously the Camaro rounded the corner and a very irritated Nicole stepped out of the building. Jaylon didn't even wait for her before he went over to his side of the car and got in, waiting just long enough for the attendant to open her door. Once she was in, he never even looked at her as he gunned the engine, put the car in drive, and sped away from the curb.

"I have never been more embarrassed in my life," Nicole spat.

His whole body went rigid. "Welcome to the club."

"They were nice enough to throw us a party...that you almost missed by the way."

"I wish I would've."

"What is up with you?"

Jaylon set his jaw. "I guess I finally came to my senses."

"Well, it looks like you've lost your mind to me."

He looked at her derisively. "It would."

Nicole shook her head in incredulousness. "What's the deal— six days before the wedding and you flip out on me?"

His hands grasped the steering wheel tighter. "There's not going to be a wedding."

"What?" The shriek was enough to wake Manhattan.

Pulling rational to him, Jaylon slowed to a stop at the red light. "You heard me. I don't want to marry you."

"You don't...?" she started in utter disbelief. Then she turned to look out her window. "Well, now's a great time to decide that."

He glanced over at her. "Would you rather I waited until next Saturday? I know how much you like to make a spectacle out of yourself."

She whirled on him, livid. "What's that supposed to mean?"

"It means I've seen how you are." As much as he'd always thought he'd have to scream the words to get her attention, he wasn't screaming at all. Telling the truth came much easier than he expected. "You aren't interested in how things really are, Nicole— all you care about is how things look to everybody else. Well, let me tell you, from where I'm standing, things look like crap."

"You're insane."

"To ever believe I loved you, yeah, I'm insane."

Hurt and anger mixed in her eyes, concocting a dangerous combination when she looked at him. "Are you on something?"

He looked at her and smiled. "That would be convenient, wouldn't it?"

"Well, it would certainly explain why you're acting like a lunatic."

"How about this for an explanation? I just took a really good long look around me, and I've decided this isn't what I want for my life."

She put her hand to her head in frustration. "I don't believe this."

"What?"

"You! It's like you're a different person all of a sudden."

"No," he said softly. "I'm finally myself."

The car pulled up to her apartment, and when he killed the engine, the darkness swathed them in its folds.

"I think we should sleep on this," Nicole said after several minutes, and he heard the fear in her voice. "I mean we're both tired and..."

"If you think sleep's going to change my mind, you haven't been listening very closely."

"So what then?" she asked as the anger returned in a flash. "You're going to break up with me because I want you to try to reach for your potential?"

"My *potential*?" he asked with a snort. "Is that why you're marrying me? For my potential?"

"Well, yeah," she said, taken aback by the question. "Isn't that why everyone gets married?"

He thought about that statement for a long moment. "Well, I guess I can't speak for everyone, but for me that answer is, 'No.' I want to get married because I'm in love with who the person is now—not because of who they might be in the future."

"But I do love you."

"No, you don't. You don't love me. You love the me you've created." He turned to her. "And that's not all your fault. I don't think you ever really knew the real me."

She started to contradict that statement.

But his explanation was rolling, and nothing was going to stop it. "I did everything I could to twist myself into the shape you wanted me to be. I never even gave you a chance to decide."

"But we're so good together."

"Because I didn't give the real us a chance to be bad." Gently he reached across the dark expanse between them and laid his hand on hers. "Trust me on this, Nicole, I'm not what you're looking for. I've known that for a long time now, and getting married isn't going to change that."

"We can work on it. We can get through this."

One-by-one the arguments against that suggestion lined up in his head creating a queue that stretched far beyond what he could even see. "No."

"Why not?"

"Because you're not the person I'm looking for either."

As he drove away from her apartment, Jaylon's hand reached up and unfastened the bow tie at his throat. Tiredly he flipped it into the other seat and then set about unfastening the top button of the overly tight white shirt. It, along with a thousand other things, was choking him to death.

Breaking up—it was the right move. He knew it was. However, somehow he hadn't been prepared for the hurt and the despair in Nicole's voice. Anger he was ready for, but she had looked so sad, and he had never done sad very well.

His mind traced back to a small boy, standing reverently next to a pair of black pants. He was too young to remember much of the funeral, mostly bits and pieces. People coming up and hugging him. That was one thing he remembered. That, and his dad's sad but stoic face. Jaylon tried to remember, but there wasn't one image of his father with tears.

No. Tears were too far beneath his father. Too human. As he drove, Jaylon couldn't really tell what the tears stinging the backs of his eyes were about—his mother, his grandmother, Nicole, Camille, his father... Loss after loss until there was nothing left but him.

Him and a little, dark country road. His whole world had been reduced as it always had been to him—alone. In disgust at his rotten life choices, he shook his head. It seemed that anyone he wanted to hang onto, he somehow managed to lose, and anyone he was better off without latched on with no intention of letting go.

He thought about Nicole. She would be all right. Her father would make sure of that. She would go on without him, find someone new, get married, and her life would go on. Just as Camille's had.

At the thought of the light brown hair and the soft smile, his heart fell further. When he had let her go, he knew she was better off without him. She had to have the space to chase her dreams—to grow into the person she was meant to be. It was clear, to him at least, that she had done just that.

When he pulled under his carport and shut off the car, he rolled his neck around on his shoulders twice, hearing it crack and pop with each move. For a second he thought about tomorrow. Calling everybody, explaining the unexplainable a hundred times over seemed overwhelming. So, rather than deal with that, he pushed it to the back of his mind, pushed out of the car, and went inside.

In the darkness, he trekked to his room where he shed the remainder of the formal attire. It felt good to simply put on some sweats and crawl into bed. His hands formed a pillow for his head as he stared up at the ceiling. How could one day hold so many different emotions? How could one day change a life so drastically?

'Why' floated through his mind, and for the first time in hours, he smiled. "Okay, God, if this is what you had in mind, I'm listening."

Chapter 17

"I know," Jaylon said for what seemed like the millionth time Sunday afternoon. "We just decided it wasn't going to work, so there was no point in going through with the ceremony...Yeah...well thank you. Okay, I will, you too. 'Bye."

The receiver clanged down—only 70 more calls to make.

All day Sunday and well into the meeting with Isaac Monday morning, Camille thought about Jaylon. He had looked so sad, so beaten down. Her mind kept saying that's not how love should be, but then it would strike that thought back. It was his life to live—not hers. If he wanted to marry Nicole, so be it.

However, in her heart of hearts she couldn't deny that she knew exactly what he was doing—trying to make someone else love him by being what they wanted him to be. She had done that more than once in her life, and it always led to disaster. Time after time, her heart was a casualty in that wreck, and she would vow never to put herself in that position again.

Nonetheless, somehow, she always managed to find her way back there. Her father was the first to walk out even as she tried to do everything she could to make herself be enough to keep him. Friends along the way had followed him out the door. The sadness in her heart traced over her mother. She had wanted to leave for all of 18 years. Remarkably she had stuck it out, but the second Daria was out the door, she too had disappeared from Camille's life.

It was probably for the best. In fact, it was often what she had wished for. Much like Ben, when they were around, it seemed like life would just be easier if they left her alone. However, that never eased the pain when they actually left. It had been three days since she'd talked to Ben, and barring some bizarre coincidence or another NightViper meeting, her chances of seeing him again were slim.

As she listened to Isaac praise the team for their presentation on Friday, her mind knocked the idea of Ben around in her brain. Why did it seem so dangerous to have him in her life and then when he left, why did life feel so empty? She made a note to herself to call Keane when the meeting was over.

It wasn't much, but it was at least something she could do to keep her whole world from disintegrating around her. The meeting broke up, and she stood only vaguely aware that she was moving.

"Camille," Isaac said when she had all of her things in her hands, "could I talk to you a minute?"

"Oh, sure." She dragged her things to the front of the room and hoped he wasn't going to ask her anything specific. In the state her mind was in, specifics were hard to come by.

"Please." Isaac waved at the chair next to his at the head of the table.

Dutifully she sat and pushed a stray strand of hair out of her face.

"I just wanted to tell you how impressed I am with your leadership of this project. I'm not going to lie to you, I was afraid we wouldn't be able to carry this off when it first came across my desk. But I didn't count on the extra hours you put in. I know you've been working night and day on this thing since it fell in your lap, and I appreciate that."

"It's no big deal," she said as if it really weren't. "I'm just glad it all came together."

"Well, that's what I wanted to talk to you about."

"Oh?"

"We'll be moving from concept models to the real thing now, and I'm not exactly comfortable with letting Lansford just run with this. He seems to find a way to take our ideas and modify them just enough so they won't work. He's done that to me twice now. Then we have to go back to the drawing board—investing more money and time and man hours when what we had to begin with was fine."

"And they won't go with another company?" she asked.

Isaac shook his head. "Lansford has a lock on the construction of this contract, but we have the right to send someone in to oversee it." He paused as he looked at her. "I want you to go."

Terror grabbed Camille's throat. "Me?"

"You know more about this plane than anybody else on this planet."

"I don't know..."

"You'll get paid as a consultant from Lansford's firm, a percentage of the final tally."

Air jammed into the top of her chest. "The money isn't it."

"What then?" Isaac asked with concern.

"I'm not...supervisor material." The hair wouldn't stay behind her ear, and she pushed it there again. "I can't go around telling people what to do."

Isaac laughed. "Then who's been running this project?"

Not me. "I don't know. I'm not sure I'm ready for this."

The ensuing pause lasted a little too long for Camille's comfort.

"There is one other thing I should tell you," Isaac finally said as he rested his wrists on the edge of the table. He looked at her as though his next statement would be the ultimate deal breaker. "Accepting this position will require a move."

"A move?" Her mind went instantly to her apartment. She didn't like it, true, but she didn't want to move either.

"To Buffalo."

"Buffalo." She sat back in her chair as the news hit her.

"New York is your home state, isn't it?"

"Well, yeah." Her mind traced over the map scrawled on her memory. Buffalo, just an hour's drive from Ridgecrest. No. She snapped that thought off. That was ludicrous. Insane. "Umm, do you need an answer right now?"

"No, not until the first of June," Isaac said slowly, "although Lansford and I would both feel better if we knew something before then."

Camille nodded, wholly overwhelmed. Mechanically she pushed up the edges of her glasses.

"You can meet with Lansford's team before you decide. They've got a meeting set for Thursday. We can fly you in for the afternoon or for the weekend, whatever would be better for you."

The air in Camille's chest escaped with one long whoosh. "This isn't what I was expecting."

"It's a move up for you. I'm sure you can see that."

But was it a move she wanted to make? "I'll think about it."

Isaac nodded as he followed her up out of the chairs. "I don't want to send anyone else, Camille."

She nodded in a haze. "I'll think about it."

"Well, just in case, I'll go ahead and have Liz make the reservations."

Again she nodded although she was becoming less and less sure what she was agreeing to. For a single second rational came back to her and she extended her hand to Isaac. "I appreciate this."

"I just hope you'll accept," he said, grasping her outstretched hand.

She smiled. "I would say, 'I'll think about it,' but I think you know that already."

He laughed. "You can think about it all you want as long as in the end you say yes."

By the time Jaylon got home Monday night, he had a splitting headache. Popping open the bottle of aspirin, he dumped three into his hand and filled a glass of water. Saying it, explaining it over and over again wasn't his idea of a great way to spend hours on end.

The kids were bad, but the teachers were worse. He had heard the hush when he'd walked into the cafeteria like the tide washing away from shore. Gazes followed him everywhere, and the whispers were never far behind.

"Trouble in paradise?" Kandice had asked as her intro when she sat down at the teacher's table that afternoon.

"I don't really want to talk about it," Jaylon had answered. But it seemed that there wasn't a single person who wanted to talk about anything else. Six bites of inedible food, and he had abandoned the cafeteria for the warmth of the springtime sunshine outside.

However, there was really no escape. They all knew, and he knew they all knew. Even when they said nothing, it didn't matter, their looks of pity said it all.

When he was back at home, with a reluctant hand he pulled the list Nicole had emailed him Sunday morning from the cabinet. The sooner he made these calls, the sooner he could get on with his life—or what was left of it anyway.

Tuesday and Wednesday passed in a haze for Camille. She had taken the unimaginable step of accepting the offer to meet with

Lansford although she couldn't imagine any good that could come from it. Thursday morning, she spirited Max over to the Hathingtons', grateful for the few stable places in her life.

She had considered calling Lexie but had decided against it when she realized she would have a hard time squelching Lexie's excitement if the deal fell through. More than that, though, something in her gut said, "Don't get excited. This is probably a terrible mistake."

One part of her wanted it to work almost more than she had ever wanted anything in her life, but another part, a much bigger part, said she was crazy for even considering it. Lansford? It wasn't where she'd ever seen herself. More than that, she knew the minefield she would be stepping into by accepting this job. Lansford didn't want her, and she knew enough about him to know he would spend every waking moment undermining every move she made.

Briefcase in hand and her best black and navy silk suit gracing her body, Camille hailed a cab at the Buffalo airport and instructed the driver to her hotel. She would only have a few minutes to get her key and stow her bags in her room, but something told her that showing up with suitcases in hand was not a good way to make a great first impression.

Luck seemed to be on her side as she was able to deposit her belongings and find another cab with time to spare. When it pulled up in front of the offices of Lansford, Incorporated, Camille's fear machine threatened to completely overtake her sanity.

Standing, looking up at the structure looming over her, made her feel to the square inch how small she was in the grand scheme of things. Pushing that thought to the back of her mind, she stepped up the concrete stairs and yanked the front door open.

"Just like in your kitchen," she said to herself softly, and completely beyond sanity, a smile came to her face. "Just you and me in your kitchen."

The receptionist at the front looked up from her computer. "May I help you?"

"Yes, I'm here to see Mr. Lansford."

"Is he expecting you?"

"Yes. I'm Camille Wright from Baker and Marsden."

"One moment."

The lobby itself was the size of one story of her apartment building. As Jaylon's calming words floated through her, she was grateful, for without them her feet would've easily won the battle with her head.

"27th floor," the receptionist said as Camille's attention traced over the collection of plants and artwork gracing the lobby.

"27th?" she asked.

The receptionist nodded and smiled. "They're waiting for you."

That was a little more than Camille's nerves needed to know, but she smiled and nodded anyway. At the elevator she punched the up button and looked at her watch. She was fifteen minutes early. They were certainly prompt around here. The elevator doors slid open, and she stepped inside with a sigh. "Here goes nothing."

"Bad news," Lucas said as he set his sack lunch on the table and swung his ample frame into the space between the table and the seat.

"What's that?" Jaylon asked, not really caring about anyone's problems other than his own.

"Career Day is going to be a bust."

"Kids aren't interested?" Jaylon asked, feeling his own interest wane.

"Kids aren't the problem," Lucas said. "I had six people lined up on Monday. Now, they're dropping like flies."

"Stomach flu?" Jaylon asked jokingly. "I hear that's been going around."

"Some kind of stomach problems but I don't think it's the flu." Lucas looked at Jaylon as though he was going to add to that statement; however, at the last minute, he dropped that idea and ripped into his bag of potato chips. "I'd better find somebody to cover, or those other four are going to run screaming from the exits too."

Jaylon shrugged. "You've got two weeks. I'm sure you can find somebody."

"I hope so, or this could be the permanent death of Career Day."

As Camille sat in the conference chair on one end of the enormous room, looking at Lawrence Lansford who was surrounded by his henchmen and women, the fear lurking in all corners of the room threatened to slash her to ribbons. How in the world had Isaac talked her into this?

"You and me in your kitchen," her brain repeated over and over again. "Just like in your kitchen."

Then in the second before Lansford pinned his beady gaze on her, the signals in her brain stumbled across another thought. *People aren't structured, Camille. People are complicated...but the people who really love you—love you no matter how many wonderful things you do. They love you not because of your accomplishments but because of you.*

The illusion of importance hanging over the meeting lifted from her mind. In the end, it didn't matter. Her performance today, her getting this job or not getting it didn't matter to the people who mattered most to her. To them, she was already worthy of love— they needed no more.

"I suppose I should let you explain why you're here, Ms. Wright." Mr. Lansford swept his hand across the table. "I'm sure we would all like to hear what you have to say about the role you are expecting to play here at Lansford."

For one second her spirit cringed under the menacing tone in his voice. He was here to crush her—to verify her insignificance in this project to the world. The pressure descended on her. So many people were counting on her. She was here not as herself but representing Isaac, and Ben, and Liz, and Kali, and Rai...

"Pressure creates diamonds, you know?" Jaylon whispered in the back recesses of her mind, and a tiny piece of her smiled. Today she would find out what she was really made of.

"Mr. Lansford," she began slowly with a nod of greeting to him, "Ladies and gentlemen, I'd like to say, I really appreciate this chance to bridge the gap between Lansford and Baker/Marsden. As you know we've been working on these designs for several years now—perfecting them so that they would further the capabilities of our men and women serving in the armed forces.

"Today I represent not only myself, but all those who have gone before me—people who have put their hearts and souls into the design of this one airplane, people who've wanted nothing more than to see it succeed beyond even their own expectations."

She stopped, and her gaze drifted from one face to another. "Men and women just like you who have lent their skills and talents to a job that they considered worthy of those abilities. That's who I represent.

"I am not here to critique and criticize. I am here to ensure that what we have designed comes to fruition as quickly and effectively as possible." With courage she didn't know she even possessed, she looked at Lansford's bloated face and hard, cold, distrusting eyes, and she smiled serenely. "I come as a colleague not as an adversary. I come as someone who wants to see this project succeed as much as you do because in its success, we all win. I hope and trust that you all have the same goal for this project, that you all want it to succeed. That you yourselves want this project to be an overwhelming success—for what that would mean for yourselves and for your company. I appreciate the opportunity to help you do just that."

When her impromptu speech wound to a halt, she sat, the nerves gone. They could throw her out of the offices right now, and she knew beyond a doubt she would be all right. It wouldn't crush her, and she wouldn't have failed. Their decision, ultimately, had no bearing on who she was or how worthy she was. It was an illusion on the surface, and underneath it had no bearing on anything truly important.

Mr. Lansford's gaze dropped from hers, and then he looked to his colleagues. "We are interested in the success of this project, too, Ms. Wright. However, I for one am not sure how your presence here will further that goal."

"Well, for one thing, you won't have to go through seventeen secretaries to get an answer to a question. If there's a question, I can answer it, or I know the name and number of someone who can. If we run into something the designers hadn't anticipated, I'm here to work with your people to find the quickest most cost effective way to fix it."

He thought for a moment and once again looked to his colleagues, clearly hoping someone could come up with an argument to her staying that he wasn't seeing.

"I'll be happy to work with your people even now as we make the transfer so that the project moves smoothly from one company to the other."

Slowly he folded his hands and laid his wrists on the table. "When can you meet with them?"

She looked at him, feeling the peak of her most insurmountable mountain within her grasp. "Whenever you want."

"I canceled the caterer," Nicole said, sounding more depressed than he had ever heard her over the phone Thursday night. "The florist knows, the minister...I haven't called the organist yet. Could you do that?"

Jaylon's heart felt resignation with each word she spoke—so many plans, so many dreams—trampled. "Yeah, I can get that."

"We've lost our deposit on the hall," she said, the business-like tone in her voice barely covering the emotion just underneath it. "Dad wants to know how we're going to split all the losses."

"Fifty-fifty I guess," Jaylon said, praying she would agree to that. After all the fact that they were losing deposits at all was his fault.

"I'll tell Dad you offered." Her side of the line went quiet. "Have you called everyone?"

"Everybody on my list," he confirmed.

"Well, I guess I'll start sending the gifts back tomorrow," she said sullenly. "I don't feel right keeping them."

"Good plan."

She waited a second and then another. "Anything else?"

He knew what he wanted to say, but his mouth was having a hard time with the words. "I'm sorry, Nicole. I never meant for it to be like this."

"I know," she said softly. "I just wish we could've made it work."

"Yeah."

"So, I guess that's it then?"

"I guess so." A half-carat ring crossed his mind, but that decision had already been made. He had given it to her as a gift, and a gift given with strings wasn't a gift. "Good luck with everything."

"You, too."

He heard the sniff on the other end of the line. "And take care of yourself."

"Maybe I'll see you sometime."

"Yeah, maybe," he said, knowing that neither of them really wanted that to happen. "I'll see you later, Nicole."

"Yeah, later." The sniffing had intensified, dragging his heart right along with it. "Bye, Jaylon."

"Bye." When he laid the phone on the holder, his head fell back against the wall. So many plans, so many dreams—gone. And the strangest thing of all was that although he had wanted nothing more than to be free of her, now that he was, a dull ache for the hurt he had caused her had replaced everything else in his heart.

"I'm supposed to meet with their team Monday morning," Camille said as she sat on her rock hard hotel room bed.

"So are you coming back for the weekend or just staying there?" Isaac asked.

"I figured I'd hang out here tomorrow, maybe get to talk to some of the team one on one before I have to face them all."

"Sounds like a plan." Isaac paused. "Did Lansford rip you to shreds?"

"No," she said with a small laugh. "I don't think he was too keen on the idea to begin with, but...well, let's just say he didn't throw me out."

"Glad to hear it." And by his tone, she knew he meant that.

"I'm planning to be back in the office Tuesday or Wednesday depending how things go from here."

"Take your time. Whatever you think you need to do."

Camille nodded. "I'll keep you informed."

"I'd appreciate that."

With a few quick good-byes, they hung up, and Camille looked around the room wondering what she was going to do with her coming hours. Tonight shouldn't be too much of a problem. After a flight and the pressure of the meeting, she wanted nothing more than to take a shower and fall into bed. However, tomorrow night lurked just around the corner, and although she didn't want to think about it, she knew what the day after that—Saturday, May 3rd —meant.

Yanking that date from her consciousness, she pushed off the bed. Jaylon Quinn was out of her life, and the sooner she accepted that, the better off she would be.

Chapter 18

Although overcast and raining would've fit her mood better, Camille was disappointed to see Saturday morning dawn bright and sunny. She should be happy for them, for him, but her heart just wasn't in it.

If she was back in Pittsburgh, she would've gone in to the office and lost herself in a mountain of blueprints, but here... She shook her head at the reflection in the bathroom mirror. Friday had gone better than she could've hoped. She had gotten one-on-one time with at least three people in the new team. It wasn't such a bad start. But today, she was on her own.

Showing up at Lansford on a Saturday might label her pushy and nosy. That wasn't the impression she wanted to convey. Like it or not, she was on her own for the rest of the day. Only problem was the answer to that question was, "Not."

Nothing Jaylon did Saturday morning felt right. His gaze kept sliding to the calendar, and his mind continued to trace over what he would be doing today if things had been different. He took his coffee and half bagel to the table to sort through the week's mail, but even that couldn't hold his attention. With only two bites taken out of the bagel and six sips of the coffee gone from the cup, he stood from the table and left everything there.

A deep, dark, black hole began creeping stealthily over his heart. He thought about calling Nicole, but that seemed like rubbing salt in an open wound. Rejecting that idea outright, he went into his bedroom and surveyed it, looking for something to do.

The clock on the table caught his eye. 11:21. By now he would already be headed for the church or at least be running around knowing he should be headed for the church. A sinking feeling engulfed him as he thought about Nicole, in a dress he was sure was gorgeous, standing on the top step next to the altar.

"Don't," he said out loud. "Don't even go there."

He sat on the bed and pulled his briefcase up to his lap. Grading papers. That would be something to take his mind off of her.

Like a ghost wholly invisible to the outside world, Camille walked out of the hotel and ambled down the sidewalk. There wasn't a crush of people today, and instead of suits and cell phones, the sidewalk was filled with people walking dogs and holding hands.

She tried not to look at those people as her feet kicked down the sidewalk, not knowing where they were taking her, and not really caring.

The papers did a passable job of holding his attention until his gaze caught on the clock at 12:56. One o'clock. He would be taking pictures by now. "Turn a little more...Smile... Good." Click.

The scene was right there behind his eyelids, and for all the efforts of his brain, it was going nowhere. Thinking was going to drive him crazy, and sitting here, there was nothing to do but think.

He pushed off the bed and went over to his closet where he pulled out some jeans and a blue, button down shirt. He had to get out of this house or risk a total loss of sanity. With a yank, he pulled the old leather jacket out of the closet.

It had always been so much a part of him, until Nicole said it made him look like he was part of a street gang. After that, he hadn't worn it much. However, as he slipped it onto his arms, he felt not only its warmth but a piece of his soul slide back into place. With a nod of satisfaction, he crossed out of the room, through the kitchen, and out the door. Today was about starting over—on his own terms.

How far Camille had walked, she didn't know, but after a lonely breakfast at IHOP and stopping to look at every newspaper rack on the sidewalk, she found herself turning down a side street and coming abreast of a little theatre. The marquee read, "My Fair Lady—matinee Saturday May 3rd, 2:00."

Strange how life always brought up memories from the past. She looked at her watch and decided that with nothing better to do, a matinee sounded like a good way to kill some time. Even if it was "My Fair Lady."

The Camaro went through Brickhaven in a blink, and although Jaylon wasn't sure why he felt a pull to Syracuse, he forced himself not to think about it and just drive. A flick of the radio, and the car was filled with a pounding drumbeat. He bobbed his head to the beat, trying to get lost in it.

Just get lost in it and forget everything else. It sounded like a wonderful idea.

In the darkened theatre Camille sat back in her seat, thankful for a way to spend the next few hours during which Jaylon would move forever out of her grasp. The curtain came up, and she shifted ever so slightly.

She hadn't seen "My Fair Lady" in years—since high school really. Her thoughts drifted back to that time. It was always what she had considered their first date although they had shown up separately and gone home separately.

As the first act began on stage, she smiled at the thought of his elbow on the armrest next to hers. Thoughts of that night or any night they had been together always brought a smile to her heart, and even as she sat there, she had the suspicion that they always would.

When the Z28 pulled up to the curb in front of the huge church, Jaylon wondered what had possessed him to come here. The clock on his radio said, "2:15." He looked at the brown-bricked building in frustration.

He wasn't supposed to be here—not like this anyway. Slowly he shook his head as his foot prepared to drive on past, but something tugged at his soul. Just once he wanted to see what that church looked like on this day. For no logical reason, he just wanted to see.

Berating himself even as he did it, he swung the car around into the empty parking lot and shoved the gearshift into park.

"This is crazy," he said to himself even as he climbed out of the car and mounted the side steps to the door. If the door was locked, he would just turn around and leave. But one yank and the door pulled out of its frame. "Great."

There was something about Eliza, something Camille couldn't quite fit into place. She looked so familiar, like someone Camille had seen before. Somewhere. Carefully Camille went through the Rolodex in her head. Co-workers were on the top of that list, but she couldn't get a single one of them to fit with that voice, that face.

Her mind shifted to college, but too many of those faces were shrouded in a hazy blurriness. She only remembered a few of them clearly, her roommate, a next-door neighbor, a few girls down the hall her first year. But none of them fit either.

By now it was a game, and she was determined to get that face to fit somewhere. But where? High school?

High school. Something in her said, "Yeah. That's it. High school."

Up and down the Ridgecrest halls she looked, but the search turned up nothing. Then just as her mind said she must be imagining things, it tripped over drama class. In the next breath Camille's gaze snapped to the stage. Ariana.

The black hair, pulled up but not quite perfect. The face, not quite as perfect as Camille remembered it, older but exquisite just the same. Her attention riveted to the stage as she watched the flower girl fighting to make herself become more than the world believed her to be.

In exasperation, Higgins circled her, instructing her, trying to bring her up, and yet forever saying in a thousand ways that she was beneath him and always would be.

"I can't hear no difference," Ariana wailed, "cep it sounds more genteel like when you say it!"

The pang in Camille's heart struck so suddenly that it took her breath away. She could hear the frustration and alienation in Ariana's voice, but she couldn't decide if that was just an act or something more—something deeper, something Ariana now understood about being at the bottom with no way to get to the top.

And for all the assurances that this was just an actress playing a role, Camille's heart said differently. Something had changed about Ariana, something fundamental to who she was—something so fundamental that it erased every last tatter of Camille's remaining hatred for her high school nemesis.

"Hi, God," Jaylon said to the empty church surrounding him, "Umm, I'm not real sure what I'm doing here." He sighed. "I guess You know what happened...course You do." He shook his head in annoyance with himself and the whole situation. "We were supposed to be here today...getting married, You know?" His head sank on the words, and his gaze followed it all the way to the floor at his feet. "I thought I loved her. I did. I honestly thought I loved her, but I'm beginning to wonder if I even know what love means."

One edge of his heart twanged with the words. They were honest, but still he felt strange saying them.

"Worst thing is I'm not even sure where to go from here, You know? It's like my future's been yanked out from under me, and I can't really see tomorrow anymore. That's scary because tomorrow has never really been a problem for me. I mean I've always known where I was going, what I wanted, what I was working for, where I was headed, but now..."

His gaze lifted only a little to the thin bookrack in front of him as fatigue and despair crowded in around him. With nothing else to say, and not knowing what to do next, he picked up one of the books and opened it. The only light filtered in from the stained glass windows, and until his eyes adjusted, he had to squint to read the small type.

One page, turn. Another page, turn. Then a word caught his eye, and he stopped. "I will instruct you in the way you should go; I will counsel you and watch over you, says the Lord."

That would certainly be nice, Jaylon thought although his heart really didn't feel like it was being guided at all. It felt like it was wandering around in the dark, cut loose from all ties to the world and even from his own soul. Disconnected and floating. With a shake of his head, he turned the page, feeling the moments pass him by, and that, in and of itself, was comforting—something to do other than to think.

"For I am convinced that neither death nor life, neither angels nor demons, neither the present nor the future, nor any powers, neither height nor depth, nor anything else in all creation, will be able to separate us from the love of God that is in Christ Jesus our Lord."

Nice words, he thought sullenly. "Neither death nor life...neither the present nor the future..." But if they were true, then why did he feel so utterly hopeless—like tomorrow and all the tomorrows to come would bring nothing but sorrow, nothing but pain and regret? Why did he feel like God had so completely forgotten about him?

Why...?

There was that word again. The far reaches of his mind whispered, "Your Holy Will." However, those too were nice words, but what did they mean when you were separated from your very soul? How could they hope to bring peace when it felt like God Himself had turned His back on you and walked away?

Follow His will? Believe? Trust? That would be easy if His led you down straight, understandable paths, but God's will always seemed to lead him into nothing other than brick walls that really hurt when he hit them.

His gaze dropped to the book again as his head fought to make him believe that he had come to the wrong place for the answers he was seeking. The answers weren't here. As far as he could tell, the answers weren't anywhere, and for all he knew, there might not be any answers at all.

Turning the page he found another passage. "Now faith is being sure of what we hope for and certain of what we do not see."

Huh, easy for them to say. His mind traced back through his life, but faith seemed a subject devoid from his vocabulary. Faith meant trusting what he could not see, and that seemed as close to insanity as he had ever stepped. He looked back down.

"We walk by faith, not by sight."

Funny, how that little book seemed to answer questions he couldn't even put into words. But even then, it seemed ludicrous to have faith in his present situation—when nothing in his life was working out. Still there was that thought, lurking just below anything he would be willing to admit, "What if it's true? What if believing could make a difference somehow?"

"Fine, God," he finally said with a tired sigh, "what's up with this faith thing? I guess I'm as ready to listen as I've ever been."

"Jaylon?" a voice behind him asked.

Instantly his focus snapped off the book in his hands and up to the freckled, pudgy face of a long ago friend. "Seth?" On wobbly legs Jaylon stood from the bench and extended a shaky hand in all-out confusion.

"Am I early?" Seth asked, grasping Jaylon's hand even as he looked around the vacant church.

Jaylon was still lost in his conversation with God, and his mind couldn't quite find the answer to Seth's sudden appearance. "What are you doing here?"

"The wedding?" Seth asked, glancing up to the altar in bewilderment.

"Oh, my gosh. I forgot to call you." Jaylon's gaze swung down to Seth's attire—church clothes if he'd ever seen them. "Oh, man, sorry about that." Then he glanced behind Seth as his mind rejoined reality. "Where's Julie?"

"Her mom got sick yesterday. I wasn't even going to come, but she said I shouldn't miss it."

Softly Jaylon laughed. "Well, looks like you're going to miss it after all."

"Yeah," Seth said, nodding but looking as perplexed as ever, "I think I missed something."

"Lucky you," Jaylon said, and his legs could no longer hold him. Heavily he sat down on the bench as the pain crashed back over him.

With another puzzled look, Seth joined him, folded his hands, and looked at Jaylon with concern. "Mind filling me in?"

A breath and then another escaped Jaylon's lungs before he could gather enough strength to say the words. "We called it off."

"Yeah, that much I kind of surmised. Mind telling me why?"

"Why?" Jaylon asked with an exasperated laugh as he glanced at his friend. "If I said, 'Your Holy Will,' would you laugh at me?"

Seth surveyed his friend's profile for an interminable pause. "No. Why would I laugh?"

"Because, that's about as close as I can come to explaining any of it, and at the moment getting a better answer out of my brain might make it explode."

His friend's gaze fell. "Oh, okay." He looked back at Jaylon. "So what's up with the book then?"

Jaylon shook his head in disgust. "Trying to find a reason that all this happened."

"Oh, yeah?" Seth asked with interest. "What'd you come up with?"

"Mostly a bunch of words I don't understand. I guess to someone who's been to church in the last twenty years maybe they make some sense, but to me, they're just words."

Seth opened his palm. "Mind if I take a look?"

With a shrug, Jaylon turned the book over to his friend's hands. Seth accepted it and flipped intermittently to a page. "Which one were you reading?"

"I don't know something about death and life and present and future. Something like that."

Slowly Seth nodded and fingered through the book. "This one? Neither death nor life, neither angels nor demons, neither the present nor the future, nor any powers, neither height nor depth, nor anything else in all creation, will be able to separate us from the love of God that is in Christ Jesus our Lord."

Jaylon nodded, and even that simple movement sent pain shooting through him. For some reason Seth's reading of the passage had wound its way further into his soul than his had, and his heart twanged at the words. "I don't get that, you know? I mean it can't be true. It can't. Because if that's true, then why do I feel so bad? I mean if nothing can separate us from God, then why do I feel like I'm in this sinking boat all alone with no bucket?"

A smile Jaylon failed to notice crossed Seth's face as he cleared his throat. "Well, J.P., did you happen to notice the one thing they didn't mention about what could separate you from God?"

The question ran through Jaylon's head a second time, and his head moved back and forth. "No."

"You," Seth said simply. "It means that nothing in the outside world, nothing out there can take you away from God. That circumstances are just that—circumstances. It's only when you choose to turn your back on God that you stop feeling close to Him. You are the only thing that can separate yourself from His love."

Jaylon wanted to argue, but it felt too much like the truth to mount anything resembling a logical case against it.

Seth studied his friend's profile. "The question then is when did you turn away? And why?"

As Jaylon thought about that, he wondered if there had ever been a time in his life when he hadn't turned away—hadn't been angry with God for all the havoc that had been wreaked on his life. Anger at every loss he had endured flashed through his veins. "So it's my fault then that all of these bad things are happening?"

"No, I didn't say it was your fault—not in the way you mean anyway. What I'm saying is that everybody has challenges in their lives—things that force them to make decisions about whether to have faith and trust, or whether they're just going to get bitter and angry."

Jaylon looked at his friend in annoyance.

"What?" Seth asked evenly. "You think you're the only one who's ever doubted God's love and mercy?" He laughed softly. "Trust me, you're not."

"Oh, yeah? Well, what terrible thing has happened to you?" That question was as acerbic as the bile rising in Jaylon's throat. However, the second Seth's face fell along with his head, Jaylon was sorry for even asking the question. "I'm sorry...I shouldn't have..."

"We've been trying to have kids for almost four years now," Seth said quietly, and the sorrow in his friend's voice jerked Jaylon's self-pity train to an instant halt. "It's been one long string of getting our hopes up and then being disappointed, getting our hopes up and being disappointed." Back and forth Seth's head moved. "She's gotten pregnant twice now, but we lost both of them."

The anguish in Seth's voice pulled the sadness to Jaylon's eyes. He wished there was something he could do to assuage the hurt coursing through the words, but try as he might, there were simply no words.

"Basically, we've tried everything, but so far..."

"Oh, man. I'm sorry. I bet that's been tough on Julie," Jaylon said in a far away voice, thinking he never would've guessed it by her behavior at the party.

"It's been tough on everybody. We've had really bad fights over it... and sometimes it seems easier to give up."

"But you haven't...yet?"

"No. We're still praying for our miracle."

Jaylon's face scrunched in exasperation at that phrase. "But how do you do that? How do you keep trusting—keep believing—even when things aren't working out like you want them to?"

"Because as hard as this is, I know God has a plan for us."

The words, "That's easy for you to say" formed in Jaylon's head instantly, but he knew the lie behind those words now. It wasn't easy. Easy would've been to get angry and resentful and bitter. To give up. To stop hoping and trusting. However, when he looked at Seth's face, although his head was still bowed, Jaylon saw no trace of any of that.

Then, looking at Seth, a new understanding enveloped Jaylon. Whatever his friend had—faith, hope, trust, belief, whatever it was called—he wanted some of it. "I don't know how to trust like that...I don't know how to have faith."

Seth laughed quietly and sniffed. "It's not a matter of *having* faith. We all have faith. It's a matter of *using* the faith you have."

That didn't seem exactly possible, but Jaylon didn't argue. "Okay, then, how do you *use* your faith?"

For a long moment Seth considered that question, then with peaceful eyes he looked at Jaylon. "When Julie got pregnant the first time, she started having trouble a few weeks later." The look didn't last. Seth's gaze fell back to his feet, but it had been enough. "I remember standing by her side while the doctor confirmed we'd lost that baby...Man, I thought I was going to die right there.

"After the doctor left, we just held each other and cried. There was nothing else we could do. For several months or so after that we were like at each other's throats the whole time. I think it was easier to be mad at each other than to really admit how hurt we both were. Then one night I went home, and I decided I had to find another path. I'd had it with that road, and I was bound and determined to find another one.

"So, that night after Julie went to bed, I went and got out our Bible—it was the only thing I hadn't really tried. But there was this one verse my mom used to quote all the time, 'Faith is being sure of what we hope for and certain of what we do not see.'"

Recognition surged through Jaylon.

"I knew what I was hoping for, but it was being certain of what I couldn't see that was giving me fits."

"So, how do you do that? How can you ever be certain of what you can't see?"

"You just have to remember that God *can* see it."

Those words stopped Jaylon cold. For as long as he could remember, he had felt completely alone in the world—like he was the only one who really cared about Jaylon. But if what Seth said was true, if God could see what was coming, somehow that made the future less scary even if he couldn't actually see it himself.

"When I didn't see any cars here today, I almost turned around and went home," Seth said with a slightly amused laugh. "I thought I must've had the wrong church or something, but I decided I'd drive around the block one time before I went home. That's when I saw your car..."

"My car?"

"Yeah, man. How many neon blue Camaros could there possibly be in the world?" Seth asked. "Besides, that's a body-style encasing an engine I won't soon forget."

Jaylon laughed. "I wouldn't know."

"This is true, but I did. And I think there's a reason for that."

Slowly Jaylon nodded. "Could be."

The silence of the church descended on them as Jaylon's soul soaked it all in. There was no force from Seth's side of the pew, not even so much as a single move as Jaylon's heart sorted through their conversation.

"One more question," he finally asked.

"What's that?"

"How come we never talked like this before?"

"Well, there's a time and place for everything. I guess this was it."

His heart smiled ahead of his face. "I guess so."

Even after the final curtain fell and the audience had begun to disperse, Camille still sat, staring at that curtain. Several small pieces of her said she had to be crazy to even think about going back stage, but one large piece centered somewhere just over her heart said she would live to regret it if she just walked out now.

With a sigh of resignation, the decision was made. Slowly she pushed up out of the theatre seat and slid through the row to the aisle. She didn't look back at the exit, knowing even that much consideration of the alternative might be enough to stop her from going to that stage. At the edge of the stage, she pushed through a small black door on the side and immediately came to a set of stairs that led into something she couldn't see above her.

"This is ludicrous," one piece of her insides screamed while another equally determined voice kept saying, "I have to do this."

At the top of the stairs, she pushed through the first opening in the curtain that she found. On the hardwood, the stagehands were already busy resetting for the next show.

"Excuse me," Camille said so softly she hardly heard herself. In annoyance she cleared her throat. "Umm, excuse me."

The two stagehands stopped instantly and turned to look at her.

"Can I help you?" the taller, muscled one asked.

"I hope so. Umm, I was looking for Ariana."

Neither man moved.

"You know, the girl...the lady...umm, the woman who played Eliza."

The short one jerked his head back quickly. "She's back in the dressing rooms."

"Back there?" Camille asked, knowing her questions were slowing them down and sensing she had only a precious few left before her invisible allotment ran out.

"Yeah, through that curtain and to the right," the muscled one said.

"Oh, okay. Thanks."

There was no reply beyond the nod she wasn't quite sure either of them even gave her. When they went back to their work, she slipped around the side curtains until she came to the general direction the short one had indicated. Pausing only long enough to search the curtains for the opening, she slipped through them to the darkness of backstage.

She had to re-gather her scattered courage to make her feet step over to the opening leading to a hallway that was devoid of any movement. One step, two, she took down the hallway that was stacked on both sides with boxes—stage props she imagined although her mind really couldn't contemplate that at the moment.

Right? He said, right. Right? Or did he say, left?

Her head spun on the questions as she stepped around the boxes, but just before her fear won out and turned her around to run, she heard the voices. Relief that she was even in the remote vicinity of the dressing rooms pulled her feet forward six more steps. However, when she was only a couple feet from the door, the underlying anger in the voices beyond stopped her approach.

"I'm trying," an emotion-strangled voice wailed.

"No you're not!" a stern male voice practically shouted, causing Camille to jump backward. Searching for any available protection, Camille shrunk next to the wall, cowering in the boxes, lest she be seen.

"Now, I'm going to tell you this one more time," the male voice said. "Just because your husband happens to be a friend of mine, does not mean that I'm going to let you run this whole production into the ground. Do you understand me?"

Absolute silence to which Camille added not even a breath.

"I said, 'Do you understand me?'" the voice boomed across the hallway.

"Yes," a voice barely the size of a child's thumbnail said.

"Good. Now, get out of that gown before you ruin it," the male voice said, and the revulsion cut through the statement.

Camille heard footsteps approach the door, and instinctively she pressed herself closer to the wall, all but evaporating into the darkness between the boxes.

"We go on at seven," the voice said from just across the box top that hid Camille. "Don't be late."

The door closed and as the figure of an obese, middle-aged, balding paunchy man swept past her, Camille smelled the rank odor he exuded. It turned her stomach even as her eyes closed and she fought to will it and the whole situation away from her.

Long after the man's footsteps receded in the opposite direction, she stood there, frozen against the wall. She listened without moving until her spirit said he was gone. A long, slow but utterly silent breath escaped from her lungs. She wondered who he was and why he had thought Ariana's performance was so abominable.

Actually Camille thought it was quite good. Far better than most of the other performances, and for the first time since she'd left her seat, she knew she had made the right decision in coming. Quietly so as not tip off Odor-Man, she stepped around the boxes to the completely black door with a slightly skewed three and knocked softly. No answer.

Once more she knocked, and without her really realizing it, her other hand reached down and spun the knob. The door gave way with barely a push, and Camille stepped into the dressing room. At one time that room had probably passed for livable, but now it just looked desolate, bleak, and steeped in misery.

A small single bulb suspended on a swinging chain hung in the center of the room illuminating so little that Camille had to squint into the darkness to even see the crumpled figure lying in a heap on the floor. Immediately her heart went out to the broken, sobbing creature.

"Ari?" Camille asked as she closed the door softly behind her—lest Odor-Man hear her and come back for seconds. "Are you okay?"

"Go away," the small, fragile voice said.

Going away wasn't even an option anymore. Carefully Camille stepped over to the prostrate figure and knelt. Never in every thought she'd ever have about Ariana had she ever imagined that she could find it in herself to make her next move. However, the thought of not reaching out never occurred to her as her arm encircled the small shoulders.

"I said, 'Go away!'" Ariana pushed Camille's arm off of her. "You're not supposed to be here. Nobody's allowed backstage."

"Well, I'm here, and I'm not going anywhere," Camille said as she replaced her arm, which Ariana didn't try to shrug out of this time. "I came back here to tell you I thought you gave a great performance."

Ariana looked up and swiped at her tears. "Yeah, right." An inch at a time she sat up.

"I'm serious," Camille said as she sat on her heels. "I really enjoyed the play."

Mascara and caked-on makeup mixed across Ariana's face making it look like some kind of surreal Halloween mask, but even under the mask, Camille could see the beauty she had always been so envious of in high school. That envy stung her heart now.

"You want to talk about it?"

"About what?" Ariana asked, regaining some defiance in spite of the sobs that still wrenched her. "About the fact that I'm a loser who doesn't even deserve existence."

Camille's gaze narrowed. "Don't even say that."

"Why not?" With a bit of her old flounce, Ariana slid up to the little vanity chair with one wobbly leg that threatened to dump her in the floor again. "It's the truth."

"No, it's not."

Annoyance and hatred drain across Ariana's face. "How would you know? I don't even know you."

Camille smiled as she looked up from the floor. "Well, you may not know me now, but we used to know each other pretty well."

That stopped Ariana, and her eyebrows furrowed as she gazed down at Camille, obviously searching the same way Camille had hours earlier. "I'm sorry. You must be mistaken. I don't remember you."

Her heart pulling her up, Camille knelt. "Ridgecrest High. Camille Wright."

The scowl of deep distrust and puzzlement on Ariana's face grew. "Camille? I don't remember any Camille."

Slowly Camille stood. "Then maybe you remember Lauren Waterford, your sister." With the last word Camille found herself standing as she looked down at the form outlined by a halo of unruly black hair.

"Sister...?" Ariana started as she looked up with a gulp. Her eyes widened. "Camille? Why...? What...?" Fear sprang into Ariana's eyes as she looked over at the door. "How did you get here?"

"Here's a better question," Camille said as compassion flooded her heart. "How did you?"

Immediately all the haughtiness and arrogance left Ariana's face as her gaze dropped to the floor. "I..." Her hand went to her hair, smoothing and trying to fix it, but making absolutely no difference for all of her effort. "I didn't know you were coming."

Camille laughed softly. "Neither did I."

In a breath Ariana whirled around to the mirror, which barely registered any reflection at all. She grabbed for a brush and nearly dropped it from the shaking of her hand. "I wish you would've told me you were coming."

"I didn't even know I was coming, but I'm glad I did."

With trembling hands Ariana fought to get the pins wedged in her hair out, and Camille's heart went out to her. She looked like a hummingbird with an injured wing. Gently she stepped up behind the wounded spirit that was trying so hard to regain its footing.

"Here, let me help."

Through the distorted reflection in the mirror, Camille saw the suspicion and fear run through Ariana's eyes. However, before Ariana could put those emotions into words, Camille reached up and unfastened the first pin. Carefully, gently, her fingers searched for the others. One-by-one the pins came out, and slowly the distrust in Ariana's gaze faded.

When the last pin released the black tresses, Camille reached down for the brush but met Ariana's hand on the way up with it. With no hesitation at all the brush transferred hands.

"We missed you at the reunion," Camille said, and for each piece of her soul saying that was a lie, there were a thousand more saying it was the absolute truth.

"Oh, I'm sure," Ariana said, and the sarcasm had more to do with her than them.

"It was a nice night." The brush moved through the hair gracefully. When it hit a snag, Camille pulled a handful of hair up and detangled it without yanking the hair in the least. It was the same way she had done Daria's hair when she was little. The thought of Daria brought tears to Camille's eyes and a catch to her voice. "I was really surprised at the turnout. I got to talk to people I hadn't seen since graduation."

"I'm sure it was great."

"It was. Nick was there. Remember him? Nick McGee from drama."

"Tall, blond-headed guy," Ariana said in a voice growing softer with each passing moment.

"That's the one."

"How's he doing?"

"Good. He got married to Lexie Everson, one of our classmates. They still live in Ridgecrest."

"Lexie Everson? Hmm. I don't remember her."

I'm not surprised sprang to Camille's mind, but she pushed that away. "It's hard to remember everybody."

The brush snagged unexpectedly, and Ariana yelped.

"Sorry."

"It's okay," Ariana said. "So, who else was there?"

"Umm, Matt Caruthers."

"No kidding? What's he up to these days?"

"Flying helicopters in North Carolina."

"Helicopters." Ariana nodded. "Fits him. Did Keane come?"

"Dinsmore?"

Ariana nodded.

"Yeah, he was there." Camille's soul surveyed an expanse of land that was suddenly spread before her. "He's in real estate now."

"No kidding?"

"In Ridgecrest of all places."

The laugh from Ariana floated out like bubbles. "How much real estate can there possibly be to sell in Ridgecrest?"

"Well, according to him, you'd be surprised."

Nostalgia draped over Ariana's face as her fingers played with the make-up spread across her table. "You didn't happen to see...I mean... Did Jaylon Quinn come?"

"Yeah," Camille said even as the brush moved through the black hair. "He was there."

"How's he doing?"

"He's getting married." The brush snagged, and Camille pulled once to free it. "In fact, he's probably already married by now."

"Oh? Who's he marrying?"

"Some model-type from New York or Syracuse or something. Real gorgeous blonde." Camille exhaled slowly. "Just his type."

For a long moment silence descended on the room.

"I always thought you were his type," Ariana said, and when she looked up, her gaze caught Camille's in the mirror.

"Me?"

Ariana shook her head. "I was so jealous of you, I couldn't see straight."

"Jealous of me? Why?"

"You were so smart, and you had it all together."

Camille shook her head, deflecting the compliments. "I think you're talking about you."

But Ariana's head moved back and forth. "I had this whole fantasy all built up in my mind about me and Jaylon going to Julliard together and how great that was going to be. Just us away from everything else. I guess it was so perfect in my mind, I never really bothered to look at how awful it was for real.

"When we broke up, it was like the beginning of the end for me, and I blamed you for it and for every horrible thing that happened after that. But, now, I think back and I don't think it was ever even about you. It was about me. It was about how I thought I could walk all over everybody and that would make them respect me." Her hand rubbed across the soft satin of her sleeve. "Truth is, I didn't even respect me. I hated me...still do."

"But why?" Camille asked as the brush went still.

"Look at me. I'm in a two-bit production so far off-Broadway, they probably have never even heard of Broadway from here. I'm married to a jerk who pimps me around to casting directors whose whole mission in life is to run me into the ground. I've got bills to pay, and no money to speak of. I play for fifty people a day if I'm really, really lucky, I don't even make minimum wage, and that's on a good day. I go home every night to an apartment that's falling down around me and a marriage that's killing me..."

"So, why don't you get out?"

"Get out? Out where?"

"Out of here. Leave. Find something better."

Ariana shrugged. "Where would I go?"

"Anywhere you want to."

"That's easy for you to say. I'm sure you've got a great job, and money, and options."

"The only part of that that makes any difference is the options part, and you have those too."

"Yeah, that would be nice, but you just don't understand how it is."

"Well, what do you say you let me buy you lunch and you can tell me how it is."

The dark eyes looked up from the mirror. "Why?"

Camille shrugged. "I'm free, you're free. Why not?"

"So, tell me about Julliard," Camille said as she sipped her cherry limeade in the little café two blocks from the theatre.

From her side, Ariana exhaled. "I was so naïve. I thought I was such a synch. That was a joke. I mean I'd been in everything back in Ridgecrest, you know? But I was no match for those girls from New York. They could do it all—dance, act, sing. I was so out of my league, I shouldn't have even gone to the auditions."

"But you did—go to the auditions I mean."

"Oh, yeah. I went, but I knew even before I got up there that it was over. When Julliard fell through, I really couldn't see any other dream worth pursuing, so I moved here and hooked up with the first casting director that would take me."

"You didn't go to school?"

"Couldn't afford it for one thing, but more than that, I thought I didn't need school. By the time I figured out otherwise, it was too late to go back."

Camille looked at Ariana, and although her cheeks were sallow and she looked like she hadn't slept in months, it was clear that her beauty was still there, just waiting to be uncovered. "It's never too late."

Ariana's head dropped farther. "I wouldn't even know where to start anymore. They'd laugh if I walked in there now."

"And what if they didn't? What if they wondered where you'd been hiding for so long? What then?"

She considered but only for a moment. "No, my turn came and went. They aren't interested anymore."

"They're always interested in someone who's going to knock them off their feet."

Ariana laughed. "Well, that's definitely not me."

Why it seemed so important, Camille couldn't figure out, but she wasn't about to let Ariana wallow any longer. "It used to be."

A bitter sigh slid from the raven-haired actress. "That Ariana's dead, and the Ariana here doesn't have what it takes anymore."

"I think you're wrong. This Ariana is older, wiser. She's got more to offer than just beauty and a talent for acting. She's got real life behind her now. Have you ever thought about taking the best of the two Ariana's and putting them together?"

In the next breath Ariana looked down at her watch and slid out of the booth. "I'd better get back. Hal's going to have a fit."

Camille smiled with serene eyes. "You take care. Okay? And think about what I said."

For a long moment Ariana stood with her gaze on the blue and white squares of the floor. Then slowly she looked right into Camille's eyes. "Thanks for today. I really needed a friend."

Slowly Camille nodded. "I'm glad I could help."

A light of pure happiness shot through Ariana's eyes. "You did."

Chapter 19

All the next week Jaylon worked on turning his life back toward God. When the kids in drama threatened mutiny, he asked for guidance, and a vision of sitting on the stage with his fellow students flashed through his mind. Wink Murder. He hadn't thought of that game in years, but it had been just the thing to bring Spring Fever down to manageable levels.

On Wednesday when Kandice started her normal tease session, Jaylon prayed for something to get him out of her sights, and immediately a food fight had started on the tables behind him. Although he would've preferred something a little less messy, he had to acknowledge that God came through swiftly.

He even laughed out loud Thursday afternoon when he asked for a break from the tedium of diagramming sentences, and in seconds Michael snuck in with news that the Fire Department had come to do their first fire drill since Jaylon had been at Ridgecrest.

Yes, the more he asked, the more he could see God's work in his life. The only prayer that seemed to have gone unanswered was the one he prayed in the dark of the night—the one that he had never told anyone. The one in which he simply asked for someone to share his life with. Sure, there were kids and fellow teachers to fill his days, but at night the loneliness wrapped around him like an unbreakable coil, threatening to squeeze the life right out of him.

However, with that request, God seemed to be taking His own sweet time, and had it not hurt so badly, Jaylon might have laughed at the irony. The prayer he most wanted an answer to was the very one God seemed to be the least anxious to fulfill.

By Wednesday morning, Camille was back at her Baker and Marsden desk. Lansford and his team were thinking over the proposition, and her heart really couldn't decide which side of the fence it wanted them to land on. Pittsburgh was safe. It was what she had known for four years, and yet, even the minute she walked back into her office, it had felt different.

Strange how out-of-place she suddenly felt in the only place she had ever really fit. She sat at her desk, fielding transition questions in rapid fire from her telephone and computer, but it all seemed to be happening outside of her body. Time and again, her brain would chance on the question of "Why?" And time and again, she would answer with a "Your Holy Will" and a smile.

"Nobody. I've called every single person I can think of in a three city range, and nobody can make it," Lucas said in exasperation.

"Can't, won't, or don't want to?" Kandice asked.

"What do you think?" Lucas retorted as he stabbed a fork in the mystery meat on his plastic tray.

"Problems?" Jaylon asked, sitting down at the table.

"One week to go, and I'm down to two people for Career Day."

Jaylon shrugged as he folded his frame into the foldout table. "So cancel it."

"Can't. That's one of the stipulations of that grant we got last year. The students must be offered 'Options Training.'"

"Options Training," Jaylon said with an eyebrow raise. "So that's what they call sticking 35 kids in a room with an unsuspecting adult for a hour of 'Welcome to My Life.' Sounds like a euphemism if I've ever heard one."

"Come on, guys," Lucas said, sounding like he'd just taken 52 years off his age. "I'm at the bottom of my barrel here. Can't you guys think of someone? A friend, a spouse, a sibling. Anybody with a job that won't put a room full of kids to sleep."

"That should be an easy order to fill," Jaylon said, looking at the mystery meat but choosing the powdered mash potatoes instead.

"Please. Think. I'm on my knees begging here."

Kandice looked at him wickedly. "You get on your knees, and I'll see what I can do."

The milk in Jaylon's mouth sucked right into his nose when he laughed, and suddenly he was choking and inhaling the sweet substance at the same time.

"It's not that funny," Lucas said harshly as Jaylon fought to stop laughing so he could breathe. "So I guess this means I'm on my own then?"

"I guess so," Kandice said, laughing right along with Jaylon.

For all she could tell, Max was glad to see Camille when she picked him up late Wednesday night. In her apartment, she grabbed her sparse mail and reentered her sparse life. Funny, as she looked around her place, she thought of Ariana. A turn here, a missed opportunity there—it was so easy to travel down a path without really questioning why until you wound up in a place you never thought you would be.

She heated a TV dinner and sat at her little table. When had her life become so small? Was that by choice? Or by design? Or had she simply not bothered to choose otherwise? She thought about Lexie and Nick. They were probably sitting down to supper right now, three little faces arrayed around them.

Camille smiled at the thought of the noise around that table as the silence around hers enveloped her. Austin and Samantha would be fighting over the last of the Jell-o while Ryann cooed softly as she spit her peas back at Nick.

What turn had led her here instead of there?

Her mind chanced over Jaylon, but she pushed that thought away. They simply weren't meant to be. God's will said that their moment was over, and that was all there was to it. She wanted that to be okay, to accept it and go on, but the truth was it hurt, and she had the sinking feeling that it always would.

The little light blinking twice caught Jaylon's attention before he was halfway into the door. Puzzled, he walked over, threw his briefcase to the table, and punched the button.

"This is Cazenovia Community College," the bored voice said. "We wanted to tell you that the drama position has been filled."

With a sigh Jaylon nodded. It was as much as he'd expected. The answering machine beeped to the next message.

"Hey, Jaylon," Keane's voice filled the room. "I was wondering if you'd made a decision on that land yet. Call me."

With a relieved smile, Jaylon picked up the phone and dialed the number he had transcribed onto his corkboard by the phone. It rang once, twice.

"Hello?"

"Keane," Jaylon said, feeling a giant weight lift off his heart. "This is Jaylon."

"Hey, I was hoping you'd call. What's up?"

"Listen, I know I should've called you earlier, but I've decided not to sell that land after all."

"Oh, no. Why not?"

"Well, we called off the wedding for one thing, and after that, plans kind of changed around here rather quickly."

For a moment Keane said nothing. "I'm sorry."

"Yeah, well, something's just aren't meant to be I guess." Peace flooded through Jaylon at that statement. He now knew the truth of it all the way down to the bottom of his soul. "I really appreciate all the work you put into this, but I'm not interested in selling anymore."

Keane exhaled. "Well, I can't say I'm not disappointed, but I don't think I'm near as disappointed as Camille's going to be."

The name exploded with a flash right in front of Jaylon's eyes with no warning. "Camille?"

"Yeah, she was the one who wanted to buy it. Although I don't really know why she'd want it—seeing as how she lives in Pittsburgh and all. But, hey, who am I to question it. You know?"

Jaylon's heart thudded against his ribcage. "You don't happen to have her number, do you?"

"Camille's? No, I'm at home right now. I could give it to you tomorrow if you want."

But Jaylon knew waiting that long might send him right over the edge. "You don't happen to have Nick's number, do you?"

"I bet it's in the phone book. Just a second."

When Keane left, Jaylon leaned against the wall lest his knees completely give out. The fact that she wanted that land jumped back and forth in his brain like an out-of-control pogo stick.

"I got it. You ready?" Keane asked, and Jaylon grabbed a pen and wrote down the number.

"Thanks, Keane. I appreciate everything."

"No problem."

Jaylon barely waited until Keane signed off before he hit the reset button. He dialed the number with one thumb and lifted the phone back to his ear—praying like he had never prayed before.

"Hello?" Nick's voice jumped over the lines.

"Nick?"

"Yeah."

"This is Jaylon."

"Oh...hi." The "hi" dropped an entire octave.

"Listen, I know this is going to sound weird, but do you have Camille's number?"

"Camille's?" Nick's voice faded on the name. "Why?"

Jaylon took a long breath. He stood in front of the guard to the golden palace, pleading his case, and praying that the drawbridge would be lowered. "Umm, well, Nicole and I broke up. We didn't get married."

Only slightly more enthusiastically Nick's voice stumbled over the wire. "So what does that have to do with Camille?"

He felt his chance slip from his fingers as his gaze dropped to his briefcase. "Umm, well, we've kind of lost some of our people who were supposed to speak for Career Day. I thought she might be interested."

"Camille?"

"Well, she's got a really cool job, and she used to be really good with kids. I just thought..."

Nick didn't sound convinced. "Pittsburgh is a little far to drive for Career Day."

"I know it's a total shot in the dark, but the counselor is desperate." *Not to mention how desperate I am*, his mind said, but he pushed that away. "Please, Nick. I'm asking."

"Okay. Just a second." The other side of the line went silent, and Jaylon breathed a sigh of relief. At least Nick hadn't said no. "All I have is her e-mail. Lexie's not here, and I don't know where her address book is."

"That's fine." Jaylon clutched the pen. "I'll take whatever you can give me."

For a full two hours, Jaylon had sat in front of his computer. Every draft he concocted got sent to the scrap heap just as soon as it was finished. Nothing that came out of his head sounded right. Worse, everything that came out of his heart sounded too right but so honest he nixed the idea of sending those too.

Finally he resorted to an innocuous: "Camille, This is Jaylon. Please write back. We need to talk." However, the second he sent it, he wanted to take it back. She was going to think he had totally lost his mind. He clicked three clicks on his computer, but the missive was gone. Sent into the void. Unretrievable no matter how much he wanted to take it back.

With a sigh he sat back in the chair. "Please, God, let her write back."

Camille was sitting at her home computer pouring over the transition plans when the bell jingled indicating a message had been received. She smiled immediately. Lexie or Daria. Either one would be a blessed diversion. She clicked over to the mailbox but stopped cold when she saw the From Column: JQuinn.

The breath on its way out of her lungs lodged in her throat, and thoughts of anything other than his eyes ceased. Hesitantly her finger clicked on the message, and her heart stumbled when it read what he had sent.

Soul-confusing concern twisted through her. We need to talk? About what? Why was he writing her now? He was married. Married. To Nicole. As those words stamped across the screen in front of her eyes, she clicked the mailbox off button and went back to her work.

Friday morning, Jaylon sent another one. It was obvious from his conversation with Nick that getting the e-mail address was pushing his luck. Lexie, he knew instinctively, would likely hang up on him. He had tried the Pittsburgh directory and even with a good amount of creative thinking, he hadn't been able to come up with her number. Unlisted. It fit her.

At every chance he got during the day, he checked his messages, but still: No New Mail. He'd even clicked through, praying there might be something there that the box had failed to read, but still nothing. He had even sent her more messages, but either she wasn't getting them or she just didn't want to answer them—either of which were not good news.

It was Monday morning before he finally came to his senses and called Keane. Actually that was just too easy, for within minutes he had her work number. Baker and Marsden. Yes, that was just too easy.

Camille's new office at Lansford was twice the size of her old office in Pittsburgh, which was a definite surprise. Somehow she had thought they would stick her in some broom closet somewhere. However, with the small exception that she had no place to live, life seemed to be very good.

It was with that thought in mind, that she reached for the phone Monday morning to call Keane. The idea still seemed a little silly, but with five messages staring back at her from JQuinn, she knew the direction God was pushing her in whether it seemed logical or not. However, just as her hand reached for the phone to make the call, it rang.

Shifting back into engineer role, she lifted the receiver. "Lansford Incorporated. Camille Wright speaking." Silence. "Hello?"

"Camille?" a definitely male but very soft voice asked.

"Yes?"

"I...hi. Umm, this is Jaylon."

Her hand suddenly felt too weak to hold the phone.

"Umm, Jaylon Quinn," he continued. "From Ridgecrest."

In spite of the screaming in her brain, she laughed. "Yeah, I think I remember you."

"Oh, well, I wasn't sure. I thought maybe you were going to hang up on me."

"I thought about it," she said teasing, but with a hint of seriousness all the same. "What's up?"

He cleared his throat once and then again. "Listen, I'm sure you're really super busy and everything, but we're looking for somebody to speak for our Career Day on Friday."

"Career Day?" she asked, and her heart fell. Somehow that wasn't what she had thought he was going to say.

"Yeah. Lucas, our math teacher and counselor's in charge of it, and he's had all these people drop out, and he asked if I knew anyone with a really cool job who might be willing to come speak."

"Oh, well. I don't know. I mean...Friday..." She scrambled through the papers on her desk. Unfortunately the office hadn't come with a built-in secretary, and until she found the courage to ask for one, she was on her own. "I've got..." Her hand yanked the daily planner from the center of the paper avalanche on her desk. "...meetings all week."

Truth be told, her planner was mostly empty, but she didn't want to tell him that. "In fact I might be going back to Pittsburgh for the weekend. I'm trying to keep up with two jobs right now, and..."

"Oh, well, I understand," Jaylon said quickly. "I knew it was a shot in the dark. I just thought maybe..."

"I'd really like to say, 'Yes,' but right now I've just got too much going on."

"Okay. Well, thanks anyway."

"Yeah, thanks for thinking about me."

The wires hummed between them.

"I'd better get back to work," Camille finally said as her hand rested on the empty planner. "Take care."

"Yeah, you too."

Like a whisper they signed off and hung up, but Camille's gaze stayed on the phone. Career Day? A pang traced across her heart at the very thought. Tears stung the backs of her eyes, but she wouldn't let them fall. No, she was going on with her life. With that determination in her head, she picked up the phone and punched in Keane's number.

"Superior Real Estate, Keane speaking."

"Keane, hey. This is Camille. I was wondering when that land's going up for sale."

"Oh, I'm sorry. I should've called you. Umm, it's not going up for sale."

Disappointment plummeted through her spirit. "It's not? Why not?"

"Jaylon decided to keep it."

Her heart dropped. "Why?"

"Well, apparently when he decided not to get married, the land thing fell through too."

"Not to..." Camille's head spun even as she fought to keep it on track. "So it's not for sale then?"

"Nope, sorry about that, but if you're interested in looking at something else..."

"Oh, no, no thanks. Not right now anyway."

When Keane was gone, Camille sat at her desk as her pencil made small marks on her paper every time it turned over. They didn't get married. He wasn't selling the land. Somehow that was supposed to be good news. Somehow, and yet... Even without Nicole all he wanted was a speaker for Career Day?

The ache reached up from her gut and crammed into her chest. With a shove she pushed away from her desk and went to find anybody available to talk. Anybody to get her mind off of him.

Stupid. Stupid. Stupid. There were boneheaded moves, and then there was that one, Jaylon berated himself as the Camaro rounded the corner for home. First of all, the fact that she hadn't replied to a single one of his e-mails should've tipped him off to the fact that she didn't want to talk to him. On top of that cold calling her when she was at a new job seemed the height of desperation.

Then like a cherry on top of his Stupid Sundae, he'd led with the lame, "We need someone for Career Day" thing. Oh, yeah. That should've really swept her right off her feet. When he wasn't on the phone with her, it all sounded so easy. Just tell her how you feel, tell her that you want to see her, tell her that you'll do whatever it takes to make that happen. But the second her voice came over those phone lines, his hold on even speaking seemed to disintegrate.

If he could just go back and start over...What? his brain asked viciously. Would it be any different? Slowly his mind searched through its files but knew the whole time that even starting over probably wouldn't help. He would find a way to mess that up too. It was a special gift he had.

All day Tuesday, she stared at the messages in her Inbox, and every time Camille saw them, her mind considered the ramifications of simply sending a reply. Her head said that even contemplating it was ludicrous, and yet her heart stopped every time JQuinn flashed onto her screen.

At five minutes to five on Wednesday afternoon, she sat staring at her computer screen. Career Day. It wasn't glamorous. It wasn't what she wanted. But the truth was that all she wanted was to see him again. Once more, and then although she should've known better, she convinced herself she could move on to her new life in Buffalo.

Trying not to think about the action, she typed in her message, clicked the send message button, and released her heart into the ether.

For no real rational reason at all, Jaylon pulled his e-mail up on Thursday morning. It was pointless he knew. In fact, it had probably been pointless when he had sent that first message.

"You have NEW Mail" blinked at him on the screen. Probably spam. He clicked it, and the box slid up onto his screen. One click and then two, and WRIGHTC Career Day slipped into the Inbox. His heart filled his chest, and he had to force his hand to stop shaking long enough to get the mouse clicked again.

"J. Sorry about the other night. If you're serious, give me a call. I'd love to come do Career Day for you."

He read it over again, then again. Soaking each word into his consciousness. It was Career Day. No big deal in the whole scheme of life. As innocuous and boring as days go. But his heart wasn't listening. It was already trying to come up with best way to accept her offer.

For the millionth time Thursday, Camille looked at the clock. 4:45, and still nothing in her Inbox. She looked at the phone, but shook her head, knowing that Jaylon had either not gotten the message or that he had found someone else for the mission. That was fine, she told herself as she went over the latest project cost figures. She didn't need that headache anyway. She didn't need to see him. It was for the best. If she could just find a way to convince herself of that, maybe life could get back on some kind of rational track.

A soft knock at her open door pulled her gaze up from the papers, and in the next breath, the report slid back to the desk like a trickling waterfall as she found herself staring into the most stunning bouquet of red roses she had ever seen. But far surpassing their beauty were the stunning blue eyes gazing down at her from just beyond them.

"Jaylon?" She sat back in shock. "What in the world...?"

A mix of vulnerability and hope spread through his smile and into his eyes. "I hoped I might find you here."

"You...hoped?"

"Well, I wasn't sure where you'd be today. Here or Pittsburgh. So I took a shot." He looked down into the roses. "I guess I got lucky."

Her brain stuck on the word 'lucky.'

Slowly he extended the bouquet to her. "Here, these are for you."

She took them, stunned into utter speechlessness. "You... I... what're you doing here?"

His bottom lip rolled through his teeth. "Well, I thought you might need a ride."

"A...ride?"

"To Brickhaven." The carefully constructed wall of confidence seemed to crack around him as he shifted nervously in front of her desk. "You did say you would do Career Day. Didn't you?"

"I...well, yeah. But you didn't write back or call, so I thought..." Her gaze snagged on the apprehension scrawled across his face as he still stood six inches from the edge of her desk like a befuddled secretary. "I'm sorry. Why don't you sit down?"

He looked at the chair and then back at the door—clearly rethinking his impromptu appearance.

"Please," she said as her tone softened with the word.

Uneasily, he took the seat, folded his hands in front of him, and looked around. "Nice office."

"I don't think you came here to discuss my office." She leaned back in her chair and surveyed him. "Why are you really here?"

"I, umm, Career Day. I wasn't sure if you were really coming or not."

"Well, I have to say I was a little surprised by the invitation, but I think I was more surprised about you not getting married."

His gaze snapped up to hers.

"Keane told me." For a long moment she sat watching him. "I was wondering why you didn't."

Instantly his gaze fled to the window behind her chair. "I wasn't sure how to tell you. I mean I didn't want to sound like I was..."

"Desperate?"

He smiled slightly. "Something like that. I wanted to tell you, but I thought you might think I was trying to drown my sorrows with you."

"And you weren't?"

"No." It took only a glance at her to send his gaze fleeing again. "At least I didn't want to do that. I didn't want that to be how... I mean... I don't know. I just... I don't want to mess anything we've got up by acting like I want more if more isn't in the cards."

Camille smiled, hearing her own reluctance in the depths of his voice. "Okay. So, tell me about Career Day. Is it as awful as it was back at Ridgecrest?"

"Worse," he said, and the nervousness slipped away from him. "Although I probably shouldn't tell you that."

"No, probably not." She looked down into the roses. "Do you give a bouquet to everyone who takes this challenge?"

His smile slipped into her spirit. "No. Only the special ones."

They stopped at her hotel room to collect a change of clothes and a few other overnight essentials, and before she had time to really think twice, they were in his car, flying east as the setting sun draped the sky in color behind them. It was strange how the seat felt so familiar as though the ensuing years had never interrupted her time in this car.

The silence between them felt more comfortable than frightening, and she didn't feel the need to fill it. The trees flashed by her window as she laid her chin in her hand and got lost in their blur.

"So what's up with the musical offices anyway?" Jaylon asked just as the scene outside faded in the twilight.

"Well, I'm now officially the Transition Specialist for the NightViper project."

"Transition Specialist? What does that entail?"

"Getting flamed from both companies probably." She laughed softly. "No, I'm supposed to help Lansford with the plans we designed, answer their questions, fill in the holes. That kind of thing."

"Why you?"

"I was the lead designer on the project at Baker for one thing, but mostly I think I was the easiest one to uproot—a cat, a computer, and three suitcases. Can't get much easier than that."

He glanced at her, and she felt it. "You're moving then?"

She pulled her foot up to the seat with her. "When I find a place. My part in this thing will probably take a year or two. Then who knows? I'm kind of in the middle of a long stretch of road, and I don't really know where it's going."

"One step at a time?"

"That's what I'm living on." She looked out at the growing darkness. "How about you? Things have changed pretty quickly for you, too, since the last time I saw you."

"There's an understatement." He drove without saying more.

"What happened anyway?"

Tentatively his gaze swung over to hers. "I think I was looking for a dream and trying to jam anyone who came close into it."

"How's Nicole?"

He shrugged. "Okay, I guess, but I haven't seen her since we broke up. We were never exactly in the same circles."

Camille nodded as her gaze fled out the window again. "But it is over?"

"Oh, yeah. It's over."

"So, how many people do you have lined up for Career Day?"

"Four."

"And how many kids do you have?"

"110."

"That's like 30 kids per speaker."

He smiled at her. "Why do you think I came and got you?"

"Smart move."

One smart move at a time, Jaylon thought as they stepped into the darkness of his house. One at a time, and he just might have a shot at making this work. He flipped the light on as he carried her suitcase to his bedroom door.

"These plates are great," Camille said, fingering the delicate China graced with small cherubs that lined the hallway wall. "Where'd you get them?"

"They were Grandma Lani's."

Camille smiled, remembering the old woman with the blank stare sitting in a wheelchair. She hadn't allowed herself that memory in many years. The love for Jaylon she had come to have during that visit flooded her heart, and it took no small amount of pounding to beat it back when she looked at him. "They're gorgeous."

"Thanks." He led her back down the hall to the kitchen. "I'm going to let you have my room tonight."

"Your room?" she asked with instant concern as he walked into the kitchen.

"The only other bed's the couch, and I hate to think what's growing in there."

Still. "What about you?"

"I'll just crash in the living room chair. It's not too bad. I fall asleep there most nights anyway."

"Oh?"

He shrugged. "It's one of the hazards of bachelorhood." His gaze chanced on the clock. "Dinner. You haven't eaten dinner yet."

"Oh, don't worry. I'm not..."

But he was already digging through his refrigerator. "How about day-old lasagna? It's not too bad."

She smiled. "Sounds great."

With the ding of the microwave, Jaylon set the dish on the table. "Here's some garlic toast if you want it."

Camille dug into the lasagna and took two bites, which were much too hot to eat, but her stomach didn't give her tongue a chance to say that. "This is incredible."

"My roommates in college were hopeless cooks. I finally had to learn how so we didn't all starve."

"No, I mean this is really great."

He laughed in embarrassment. "I'm sure it's not anything compared with what you're used to."

"What? Burnt TV dinners? Yeah, it's a stretch to get better than that."

That stopped him. "TV dinners? You don't cook?"

"It's just me." She shrugged as she took a bite of the toast. "I did to begin with, but I got to eat whatever I cooked for like two weeks straight. After awhile it was easier just to throw something in the microwave."

"But you used to cook."

Her eating slowed. "That was about Daria not starving."

Memories seemed to drift over him. "How's she doing these days?"

"Good. She'll probably graduate from North Carolina next December."

"Cool. What's she studying?"

Camille laughed softly. "Computers."

"So, she still likes them?"

"Loves them. She set up my system in Pittsburgh, and I'm sure I'll eventually have to get her to come to Buffalo to set up my new one. I can design planes, but give me a monitor and six gajillion cords, and there's no telling what might happen."

"Well, we can't be great at everything."

She pushed her hair over her ear as she cut a small piece of lasagna. "I guess not—although sometimes that would be really nice."

"I don't know. It might get lonely being able to do everything yourself. No excuse to get someone else to help you."

"You've got a point there."

He looked at her nearly empty plate. "You want some more?"

She scrunched her face skeptically. "Will I look like a pig if I say, 'Yes'?"

"No." He laughed. "I'd take a 'Yes' as a compliment."

"In that case, yes, I'd love more."

The tiny light on the table served only to cast shadows on the surrounding walls as Camille sat on the couch, letting the peacefulness of the place wrap around her. It was just so perfectly Jaylon. He stepped in from the kitchen and snapped off the light.

"It looks like you've got a lot of reading to do," Camille said, indicating the stack of books on the end table.

He sat down in the chair. "I got those from Mrs. Allen right after the reunion, but I haven't really had much time to go through them."

"Can you believe she's retiring?"

"I know, it's like the end of an era."

Her spirit slipped into remembering. "It was so weird to see everybody and how much they've changed."

"And in some cases how little," he said with a laugh.

"That's no lie." She looked at him through the dimness, and his gaze was fixed solidly on hers. "What?"

"You," he said softly. His head fell back against the chair as he looked at her. "Some of you is so different, and some is so the same it's scary."

She tilted her head inquisitively. "What's different?"

He smiled. "Your clothes for one thing. You look like you just stepped off Professional Woman's magazine or something, but underneath that shiny new exterior, same Camille."

"And that's bad?"

"No, that's very, very good."

When she finally crawled into his bed, it was well past two o'clock in the morning. His scent, his presence wrapped around her, and in two heartbeats she was asleep.

Chapter 20

"There'll be four sessions," Jaylon said as they drove to the school the next morning. "An hour each. We'll do three and then break for lunch. Then do one more."

"Sounds like boot camp."

"Well, we were supposed to have six presenters, and they were going to alternate sessions. That was the original plan."

Camille clutched the portfolio at her feet, feeling absurdly like she was about to step in front of Lansford and his henchmen again. Just before the nerves threatened to overwhelm her, his voice drifted through her head. "Don't panic. It's just you and me in your kitchen."

Her gaze went over to him, and all the nerves vanished. It was something about having his presence right next to her—it dissolved all the doubt and fear from her soul. It always had, and something now told her it always would.

"As Mr. Quinn said, my name's Camille Wright, and I'm a lead designer for the engineering firm, Baker and Marsden," Camille said in full command of every single piece of attention in the room, including and especially Jaylon's.

He smiled, recalling his statement from the night before. Yes, she was still Camille in every way, but much, much more so now.

"We just completed plans on a top-secret project for the military which will take up where the F-19 Eagle Jet Fighter left off. The project has taken the majority of the last three years to design and model-out, not including several years of planning before that. We are now moving into the actual construction phase and hope to have it in the air within two years."

Not a sound from any one of the 28 students. It was completely remarkable to Jaylon who normally struggled just trying not to lose all of them.

"I thought I'd take you through some of the processes we went through in designing the plane, and then I'll tell you a little bit about my educational background and how I got into this field."

"Will we get to see the plane?" Michael asked from a side desk.

Jaylon's first thought was that he wanted to throttle the kid. The question sounded extremely sarcastic as though Michael didn't believe a single thing she had just said. However, just before Jaylon stepped in to explain that they could ask questions after the presentation, she chopped that statement in two.

"I'm glad you asked that—what was your name again?"

Michael squirmed visibly in his seat. "Michael."

She smiled directly at him. "I'll tell you, Michael, I'd really like to show you the plane." Her eyes, teasing and serious at the same time, gazed on the cocky senior. "But being that it's classified, I guess you'll either have to get a job as my assistant, or I'll have to kill you two seconds after I show them to you."

"Hey, it might be worth it," Michael said with a shrug as he tried to regain the upper hand.

"It might be," Camille said with a smirk. "But before you make that decision, maybe you should listen to the rest of what I have to say, you never know, I could be making all this up."

Snickers crossed the room.

"I do have some of the very early concepts for the plane." She set one on the chalkboard, but it rolled off instantly. Her face fell in concentration. "Hey, Michael, why don't you get a head start on that assistantship?"

He looked at her fearfully. "Huh?"

"Come up here and hold this."

Dutifully even as catcalls sounded across the room, Michael stepped up to the front. Camille turned him around to face the class and then handed him the plans, which had seemed rather light when she held them, but the second Michael lifted them, Jaylon knew how heavy they actually were.

"No, keep them up," Camille instructed as Michael's arms dropped under the weight. With a good amount of struggle, he lifted them to shoulder height. Expertly she started through the design piece by piece as the fascinated students and their equally fascinated teacher looked on.

"It's official. You were a hit, Ms. Wright," Lucas said, extending his hand to her when the other three presenters had vacated the building just after two o'clock. "Everyone's talking about you. I snuck in on one of your presentations, and I have to say I was impressed."

"Well, thank you," she said, shaking the older man's hand. "It was fun."

"Fun?" Lucas asked incredulously. Then he pinned his gaze on Jaylon who was leaning against the sign-in counter gazing at Camille in open admiration. "Where did you find this one, Jaylon?"

Heaven, crossed his mind, but he said, "In a darkened theatre many, many years ago."

"Well, if you're smart you'll hang onto her," Lucas said just as the principal strode through the room. "Excuse me." He walked off calling to the principal.

Embarrassed by the adulation and completely at a loss for what to do next, Camille looked at Jaylon. "So, what now?"

He glanced at his watch and then smoothed his tie. "I've got drama in 30 minutes if you want to hang around for that."

"Sounds like fun."

Fun would've been nice, Jaylon thought as he stood in the cafeteria with 17 all-but uncontrollable students racing around. This wasn't exactly the impression of his teaching skills he wanted to leave her with. "Hey! Settle down! That's the bell! I said, 'That's enough!' Hey!"

Chaos ran in screaming streams around him. "If you want to play Wink Murder, you've got five seconds to get on the stage and quiet. One! Two! Three!"

Bodies flashed past him for the stage, and by the time he got to five, the whole room was silent. He looked at Camille who was obviously having trouble not laughing. Thinking better of that move as his face flamed to life, he indicated the steps with a slight motion of his hand. Then trying not to be obvious, he climbed the steps behind her, struggling not to see the gentle curves of her business suit.

Once on stage, the gazes turned toward them, and he wasn't sure if it was the stage lights or something else that had sent palpable heat scorching through his body. "You all remember Ms. Wright from this morning. She'll be observing today."

Several of the students smiled at her, and she looked at him with those eyes that melted his heart. "Ah, you mean I can't play?"

Instantly his carefully constructed thought-pattern scattered in a million directions. "You want to play?"

"Hey, I never turn down a good game of Wink Murder."

"Oh, well. Then by all means," he said, sweeping a hand in front of himself dramatically, "be our guest."

He watched her fold herself onto the stage floor, and his amazement at her grace knew no bounds. Quickly he retrieved the cards from his briefcase. "Now, you all know the rules. Spade Ace is the murderer. Everybody else's job is to catch that person, that is if you don't get killed by a wink first. If anyone can defy detection and win, I will give you a candy bar after class."

Around the circle he walked, passing out the cards as if this was some hallowed ceremony. When there was only his card left, he carefully chose a spot on the opposite side of the stage as her. He didn't want to be too obvious. But when he looked over at her, her confidence and the exquisiteness of her grace surrounded her like an aura. He knew that paying attention to the game was going to take more concentration than he possessed. "Go."

Five games had come and gone. Five murderers unmasked. Only Michael had managed to outsmart the law long enough to kill more than ten people. But the present murderer was a wily one. Students around Jaylon were dropping like flies. Unbelievably two had died nearly simultaneously on opposite sides of the room, and for the life of him, he couldn't figure out how one person could accomplish something like that.

On the stage only he, Michael, Camille, Clay, and Karen remained, and his card was the three of clubs. He looked over at Michael, then to Karen who sat three deceased students over. At that moment Clay let out a cry and slumped onto the stage. And then there were four.

He glanced at Karen who was looking at him with immense trepidation in her eyes. She looked like she was actually being stalked. His gaze left her face for a split-second just before she gasped and collapsed to the floor. He looked back at her in shock, and then across the stage where he was caught by the serendipitous wink and smile of Camille.

His mind took a full cycle to realize he had just been hit, not by her beauty, but by a killer wink if ever there was one. Just as Michael shrieked on the stage ten feet away from him, Jaylon clutched his own heart and fell to the stage. And then there was one.

"I cannot believe you won!" Jaylon said as Camille followed him into his little office after the bell had rung.

"What can I say? I'm good."

"I'm not arguing." He stepped past the boxes to his desk as he sorted through the weekend's worth of work. When he looked up, she had perched herself on the top of three boxes which looked like they could collapse at any moment. "You look dangerous."

Camille laughed. "Now, that's one I've never heard before."

"No, I mean sitting on those boxes. That doesn't look very safe."

"Oh, well." She looked down at the boxes. "It wouldn't be the first time I fell on my face."

The tips of his ears flamed as he thought of the first time he had noticed her, crashing face down onto a stage. Never in all his life would he have dreamed this moment at that one. Busily his hands sorted through the papers in his briefcase. "I think the kids like you."

"Well, the feeling's mutual. They're neat kids."

The juxtaposition between her attitude about the school and Nicole's was startling. "You're just being kind."

"No, I'm being truthful. I haven't had this much fun since— well, since the reunion I guess, but even that was different. Too many opinions already formed. Too many alliances already forged in stone. Today I could be whoever I wanted to be."

As he sat at his tiny desk, Jaylon's hands stopped and he gazed at her wholly mesmerized. "And who did you want to be today?"

She thought for a long moment and then smiled. "Camille."

As they drove away from the school and headed back in the direction of Buffalo, Camille reached over and punched his shoulder. "Hey, I thought you said I was going to get a candy bar."

He looked over at her in utter bewilderment. "Huh?"

"The winner was supposed to get a candy bar, remember?"

It was hard to remember anything with her so close.

"How about I do you one better?" he asked.

"What do you have in mind?"

The blue Camaro pulled up to the Crystal Barn just off the Interstate ten minutes later. They were halfway to Buffalo, and all he wanted was to stop time.

"Why are we stopping?" Camille asked in confusion.

"I owe you a candy bar, don't I?"

Seated at the little table, the dinner dishes cleared away and the lights softly illuminating their crystallized surroundings, Jaylon leaned onto the table, his body fighting not to close the distance between them. "So, how's Buffalo?"

"Good, I guess." She took a sip of her burgundy wine. "You'll never guess who I ran into the other day."

"Who's that?"

"Ariana."

"Vandivere?" he asked, the name instantly threatening to attack him.

"Yeah, she was performing 'My Fair Lady' of all things."

As much as he wanted to know about Camille's life, he wanted no part of hearing this story. "No kidding."

Camille's gaze dropped to the table, and her spirit seemed to sink with it. "She's having a really rough time of it these days. It was kind of sad to see her like that."

"Oh, you know Ariana," he said with an off-handed laugh and wave, "she can make the best situation sound dramatically awful."

"No," Camille said softly, and the sorrow and concern in her voice drew his gaze to her. "I mean it was like she had completely given up on all of her dreams—like she didn't even want to try anymore—like she didn't want to live."

Jaylon shifted in his seat uncomfortably. Feeling sorry for Ariana had never entered his consciousness, and as he looked at

Camille, he couldn't believe it had entered hers either. "Well, it's not like she didn't deserve to get stepped on by someone—look how many people she stepped on. You included."

However, the deep unease on Camille's face never faded. "You know, at the time I thought that was the worst thing in the world—getting picked on, being made fun of. But I'm not so sure about that anymore."

Despite his utter disbelief, he was intrigued. "How do you mean?"

"It made me tough. It made me determined to make my life work no matter what anybody said. I know that's not always what happens, but that's what happened for me. I decided I was going to prove to all of them that they were wrong—Ariana included."

"And you did that. You should be proud."

But Camille shook her head again. "It was a sham. The one I really wanted to impress was myself, and until recently I was failing at that miserably, too."

"But how can you say that? Look at everything you've accomplished. Look at how far you've come. I mean, come on, you've designed a Navy fighter plane for Pete sake."

Like a blade of grass on the wind, her voice drifted out into the air between them. "I was trying so hard to impress everybody else, I never really owned up to the fact that I didn't really want them to be proud of me. All I really wanted was for them to love me—for somebody—anybody to take notice that I was even around."

He opened his mouth to say, "Of course they knew you were around," but before he could say anything, she nailed him with her gaze.

"That's all Ariana wanted too—someone to love her, someone to be impressed with her, someone to notice she was alive and trying—but I was so busy hating her, I totally missed that fact...until the other day."

Her words slammed him backward in the chair like a punch.

"I think that's what we're all looking for," she said wistfully. "Someone to notice we're here, someone to be impressed with us—not because of what we do or because of what we accomplish—but because of who we are. We think it's about the play, about the grand performance, about what we accomplish, but that's all on the surface, it's making the connections to be able to play our parts that are the real stories. I just wish I had learned that a long time ago."

His mind traced through the kids at school, and through them, he could see exactly what she was saying. He now understood the mesmerizing quality she exuded in front of that classroom. She wasn't there just to give a presentation. She was there to make a connection, and that made all the difference.

Now letting her go back to her world was completely out of the question. "What do you say, you up for a little detour?"

When she looked at him, the softness in her eyes melted the bitterness in his heart. He hadn't made many real connections in his lifetime, but he vowed at that moment, he was going to hold onto every one he had.

"You got something in mind?"

"Yeah."

"You going to tell me what it is?"

"Say, 'Yes,' and you'll see."

Her smile lit his heart. "Yes."

The headlights swung across the tall blades of grass, and despite every rational thought in her brain, Camille's heart knew this was exactly the detour she had in mind as well. Wordlessly he killed the engine, got out, came around the car, and helped her out. High heels and a business suit seemed wholly out of place here, but that didn't seem to matter to him at all.

He took her hand in the warmth of his and led her toward the tree, which spread its new growth up to the heavens. A blanket of stars stretched above them as they strolled slowly beneath them.

"Keane told me something interesting the other day," Jaylon said as they walked.

"Oh, yeah? What's that?"

"That I knew my prospective buyer better than I thought I did."

She smiled as embarrassment heated her cheeks, but she said nothing.

His gaze drifted across her. "So, it was true then? You were going to buy this place?"

The explanations sounded lame and desperate. "I didn't want to see it go."

He shook his head. "That's quite an impulse buy."

"Well, it wasn't impulsive to my heart—it had been right here ever since I walked away the last time—headed for Princeton with my hair on fire." His gaze swung over to her face again, and she felt its heat inch up her ears. "You know. There are moments in my life that I'd really like to go back and relive. That was one of them."

The tree supported his weight as he leaned into it and then pulled her through the leather jacket next to his chest. "Oh, yeah? What would you have changed?"

Slowly her head moved back and forth as she looked out to the stars far beyond the horizon. "Not one moment."

"Even the one when you stood on that curb that last day when I drove away?" He exhaled. "That one I would've changed. That car would never have driven so far away from you."

With peace soaring through her spirit, all the struggles in her heart and soul ceased. Slowly Camille turned under his jacket until her soul was staring into his. "It's strange in a way, but I always knew deep down that whatever happened with us, it would be for the best. You drove out of my life that day, but you never really left. You've been with me every step of the way for ten years now. I've tried to convince myself you were gone, and that I should move on, but that never really worked. You were always right there, holding me up, making me stronger, believing in me...loving me. The distance between us was only on the surface—like some magician's illusion."

His gaze stayed locked with hers. "Unbelievable."

"What?"

"I don't think I could've said it better myself. Everywhere I went, every audition, every stage, every classroom, everywhere— you were always right there. 'All that I can do is all that I must,'" he said softly, and the quotation from a paper she had long since forgotten wafted over her heart again on the wings of his voice. "For my dreams have been inscribed on my heart so deeply that they and me are now inseparable. I could no more set aside my dreams and walk away than a rose could set aside its scent and bloom without it. As the stars are interwoven into the night sky, inextricably entwined, so my dreams are a part of me—no, they are me for they and me are one."

Mesmerized, she stood for several moments. "How do you remember that?"

"I don't have to. It's a part of me—just like you are." Gently he reached between them, enfolded her hands in his, pulled them to his lips, and kissed them. "I know this is going to sound completely crazy, but I let you go once, and I almost lived to regret that. I don't want to make that mistake again."

Her heart surged forward in her chest, and she couldn't have looked away had she wanted to. His smile flooded all of her senses as he exhaled slowly.

"I don't have a ring for you, and I know that asking right now makes no sense, but Camille Wright, I want to spend the rest of my life with you. Will you marry me?"

Shock engulfed her as she looked into his eyes. "What about taking it slow?"

He laughed. "Ten years is slow enough. It took me that long to get it through my thick skull that this is right, that you are what I want in my life, that it's only when you're here with me that everything else makes any sense." The intensity in his eyes softened then. "But if you want to take it slow, I'm willing to do that, too. Whatever you want, as long as I don't have to drive away from you again because I've got to tell you, that might kill me for good."

Her smile brightened with each passing second. "Yes."

"Yes?" he asked blown away by the word. His eyes searched hers to make sure he had heard right. "What yes?"

There was no hesitation, only confidence. "Yes, I'll marry you."

One moment and then two he stood there as her answer flooded over his face. "Are you serious?"

"How does it go? 'I could no more set aside my dreams and walk away than a rose could set aside its scent and bloom without it.' Well, you, Jaylon Quinn, are my dream. You're the dream that I've held onto through every storm in my life, so yes, I would be honored to stand by your side for every moment God sees fit to grant us from now until forever."

With the next breath she was spinning under the same stars she had dreamt about for what seemed like her whole life. And even when she slid back to the earth, it had no hold on her as he gazed at her. "I love you, Camille."

She shook her head slowly. "Not half as much as I love you, J."

Then under the protective canopy of the stars, he pulled her lips to his, and in one second every star in the universe fell into perfect alignment.

Chapter 21

They worked all summer, setting the foundation under their ultimate dream. Together they decided on relocating their soon-to-be-union to Ridgecrest. Then they spent every available waking hour razing the old house and rebuilding its identical twin in its place.

When school was over, Jaylon sold the little house and left Brickhaven behind, and it wasn't until one late June Saturday afternoon as he pounded in the nails on the new roof that his replacement job came into view. A little yellow car pulled up next to the house, and a small lady slid out. With one hand shielding her eyes from the blinding sun, she walked over to the porch where he was working.

"I thought I heard you were back," she said.

The pounding ceased instantly, and he nearly fell off the roof when he twisted to see her. "Mrs. Allen? What are you doing here?"

"Looking for you."

"Well, you found me." He finished the nail he was working on and then strode to the ladder and down it. Then with a jump from the second rung, he was standing next to her.

"So, Seth was right then?" she asked.

Jaylon wiped his forehead with the bottom edge of his T-shirt. "Seth?"

"He was working on my car the other day, and he told me you were back and looking for work."

With a bend, Jaylon picked up the water jug and took a long drink. "Well, he's half right. I am back, but I've been working so hard to get this place ready, I hadn't really thought too much about work."

"Well, how about you think about taking my job?"

That slammed him to a stop. "Your job? Are you serious?"

"The school board's interviewed four candidates so far, and not one of them has your passion or your talent. I just suggested that before they settle on one of them, they give you a chance, and they agreed."

He looked at her, stunned by the thought. He wiped the top of his mouth with the back of his wrist. "But I haven't even applied."

Mrs. Allen smiled slyly. "Say, 'Yes,' and you just did."

A smile broke out across his face. "Yes."

Camille's new home-away-from-home was Lexie and Nick's place. Excitement had never been a problem for either of them, but since the announcement, they had gone overboard—insisting that she stay every weekend that she came, which was every one almost no matter what else was going on.

"I thought we could have a little picnic out back tonight," Lexie said as she brushed sweat-soaked hair off her forehead. "At least that way we can have a little breeze."

"That's the best idea I've heard in forever," Nick said. "What time's J supposed to be here anyway?"

"He said six, but if I know him, he'll work 'til the sun's been down for an hour," Camille said.

"Well, then you must not know him at all," Lexie said, glancing at the door where a dust-caked, sweaty, smiling like an idiot Jaylon suddenly appeared.

Camille glanced at Lexie in confusion and then followed her gaze to the door. She stumbled out of the chair, concern washing over her. "Jaylon? What's wrong?"

"I've got news."

"What kind of news?" Camille asked in trepidation.

"I've got a job interview."

"That's great," Nick said. "With who?"

"Ridgecrest I.S.D."

All three listeners stopped and stared at Jaylon.

"Mrs. Allen's job?" Nick finally asked.

"Yep." Jaylon looked down at Camille who shook her head slowly. "What do you think of that?"

"This," she said and pulled his lips to hers.

Buffalo was where she was scheduled to stay Thursday night, but Buffalo couldn't hold Camille. Some pieces of news you want to hear in person, and this was one of them. She pulled up to the little place that he was renting until the house was finished, and she smiled at the warp-speed it seemed her life had entered.

Her key slid into the lock, and she flipped on the light. "Max, baby?"

The cat purred against the doorframe, and she sat down to pet him. Hotels and cats didn't mix very well, so she had convinced Jaylon to keep the cat until they would all be together. She looked at the calendar where July 19th circled in purple and pink shone back at her.

This whole thing was completely mind-boggling, but completely marvelous at the same time. She stood and went over to the cabinets where she pulled out dinner ingredients and started what she knew in her heart would be a celebration meal.

When she saw the headlights an hour later, her heart carried her to the door where she stopped halfway down the outside steps as he got out of his car. "How'd it go?"

He held his hands out to the sides. "You're looking at the new Ridgecrest Drama teacher."

On wings she flew down the last two steps and into his arms. "Oh, J. Congratulations!"

In bright bursts of color, the fireworks exploded above them. The Ridgecrest Fireworks Show had always been impressive, but this year they had really outdone themselves. However, Camille couldn't quite be sure how much of her awe was the fireworks in the sky and how much was the fireworks in her heart.

Her head rested in the crook of Jaylon's arm as they lay on the blanket in the darkness punctuated by the reds, blues, and greens above them. Boom! A shot cracked through the night sky, and a burst of blue fanned out.

"Gorgeous," she said admiringly.

"Always," he said softly as he looked down at her. Gently he traced one finger down the side of her face that was suddenly illuminated by another gold burst. "Man, I'm glad I didn't miss this."

She smiled at him and snuggled closer. "I told you the house could wait."

Intensity flashed through his eyes like a laser. "That's not what I meant."

His arm tightened around her as she closed her eyes and let her heart fill with the incredible feeling of just being with him. She, too, was glad they hadn't missed this.

Chapter 22

The wind caressed the soft white of Camille's dress as she took the last three steps to where Jaylon stood, waiting for her under the tree, the gash in the earth clearly visible from the spot where he stood. Simple. It had always been so simple—their love was real, all the complications and challenges were just detours. Still it had taken God's grace for them to find their way back here into the folds of His everlasting love—in this, the most perfect place on earth.

Jaylon's heart reached out to her even as his hand did. Then, as the day relinquished its hold to the purple, pink, and blue sunset beyond, they came together. The small white ribbons in Camille's hair swirled on the breeze, and with the edge of her bouquet, she brushed them out of her eyes.

"Friends," the minister intoned, "we are gathered here today to witness the joining of these two souls. Marriage is a sacred mystery, not to be entered into lightly or without serious consideration. And so I ask you, Jaylon, Camille, have you come here freely and without reservation to pledge yourselves to each other this day?"

"We have," they said simultaneously, and their gazes and smiles caught for a second.

"In this moment anointed by God Himself, we are reminded of the Apostle Paul's words to the Romans: 'We know that to those who love God, who are called according to His plan, everything that happens fits into a pattern for good.' There will be times in your marriage when tragedy will seem to overtake all the joy you feel at this moment, but even in those times, God has a plan for you and for your marriage—if you are willing to follow Him. Always put His will at the head of your family, and everything that happens will fit into the pattern of good.

"If you are now ready to pledge your lives to one another, please turn to each other and make that pledge."

Jaylon's heart turned him toward her, and although her outer beauty was impossible to miss, it was her inner beauty that brought the smile to his face and heart.

"There are times in this life," he said slowly, "when holding onto the fact that God has a plan seems really hard, but His gift of first bringing us together and then letting us find each other again shows me the depth of that reality. So today, in the company of our friends and family..." He looked past her to Seth and Julie, and in them he could see the marriage he wanted—one strong enough to withstand heartache and tragedy with grace and love. "...I pledge to you, Camille Wright, my love and my support in the good times and in the bad. In happiness and tragedy. In days of health and in days of sickness. In days of riches and in days of poverty. For all the days of this life until death itself parts us, I pledge to you my love and my life."

His words shone back at him in her eyes as she prepared herself to make her pledge. She took a deep breath as tears of joy shimmered on her lashes.

"Being with you," she said softly, "has shown me how precious every, single moment is with someone you love. And how you have to cherish each one because you may never get the next one. So today in the presence of our family and friends, I pledge to you, Jaylon Quinn, that I will never take a moment we share together for granted. I will love you and honor you, in our moments of joy and in our moments of sadness, in our moments of health and in our moments of illness, in our moments of prosperity and in our moments of want until all of our moments together on this earth have past, and even then you have my love."

Only the wind rustling in the summer leaves answered the pledges as though God wanted to speak His pledge as well. The minister waited until God's peace seemed to settle right over them.

"The rings," he finally said softly.

Daria, her hair graced with the same small ribbons as her sister's save that they were pink, stepped forward and held out the rings.

"Two unbroken golden circles." The minister took them from her and held up the two simple golden rings. "Symbols of unending love—the love God gives to us, and the love you now give to one another. May God bless these rings and those who wear them."

He handed one to Jaylon who gently took Camille's hand and slipped the ring onto her finger. "Camille, take and wear my ring as a sign of my love and faithfulness."

The second ring passed to Camille, and she slipped it onto Jaylon's finger. "Jaylon, take and wear my ring as a sign of my love and faithfulness."

The ring that he had always thought would feel like a noose, felt only like the piece of himself he had been searching for forever.

"And now, by the grace of God and through the state of New York, I pronounce you man and wife. Jaylon, you may kiss your bride."

Then with one sweep Camille was exactly where she had always wanted to be—in his arms, in his heart, and in his life—forever.

Epilogue

Children ran across the yard and under the tree in no discernable patterns. Samantha, now a teenager, provided the top step, and with the exception of two steps of identical height, they formed a perfect staircase all the way down to the bulge under Camille's sundress.

"Seth says we need more potato salad," Lexie said, setting the bowl on Camille's counter.

"Seth always needs more potato salad," Camille said with a laugh.

"Isn't that the truth?" Lexie slid closer to Camille. "Julie told me something interesting."

"Oh, yeah? What's that?"

"They're adopting again."

"You're kidding." As Max rubbed between her leg and the cabinet, tears sprang to Camille's eyes. That was one of the hazards of pregnancy as she had learned three years before with Patrick Russell. "Have they told the twins yet?"

"Actually Eva's the one who told me, Julie just confirmed it," Lexie said.

Camille laughed as she pulled a new bowl of potato salad out of the refrigerator and handed it to Lexie. "I'll have to tell them congratulations later."

At that moment Ryann raced through the room to the front door. "Daddy's here! Daddy's here! Daddy's here!"

With a shake of her head, Camille looked at Lexie. "How's that for an introduction?"

Lexie sighed. "Once. Just once, I'd like to hear them be that excited about me coming home."

"Well, you have to actually leave long enough for them to notice that you're gone before you come back," Camille said teasingly.

"Good point."

Nick strode in from the front porch with Ryann perched on one arm. "Am I late?"

"Yeah, you missed setting up and cooking," Camille said as he stepped over and kissed Lexie.

"Cool, then I'm right on time."

The day ceded to night as the six of them, still seated around the table, watched the laughing children play tag and enjoyed simply being together again.

"Another great meal, Camille," Seth said happily. "You never let us down."

"Yeah, well, somebody else is going to have to take the next one," she said, settling back into the chair where Jaylon's arm was draped. "I think we're going to be plenty busy in the next two months."

"What? J.P. doesn't cook?" Seth asked.

"Not anything you'd want to eat," Nick said from his corner of the table.

"Hey! I'm a good cook," Jaylon said defensively. "Isn't that right, Sweetheart?"

"He used to be," Camille said as she laid a hand on his stomach. "Then he got married."

"What is it with guys?" Lexie asked. "They get married, and suddenly it's like all concept of housework just leaves their brain."

"Well, you have to have something to lose it, don't you?" Julie asked, gazing at Seth with a wicked grin.

"Hey! Now what did I do to deserve that?" he asked.

"Nothing, Darling, you're as perfect as the day I married you." She patted him on the thigh and then made a face at the other couples that said he hadn't been perfect then and he still wasn't. The others laughed.

"So, how's the consulting business these days?" Seth asked Camille, obviously trying to steer the conversation in a safer direction for himself.

Camille looked over at Jaylon cautiously and then ducked her head. "I'm quitting at the end of the month."

"Quitting?" three people asked simultaneously.

She looked at Jaylon again and ran a tender hand across his shirt buttons. "I've only got two more years with Patrick and with the new baby, I don't know. I think I just want to be a mom for awhile."

"That's so great," Lexie said with a light in her eyes.

"Good for you," Nick said approvingly.

"So, J.P.'s on his own in the providing department then?" Seth asked. "Better schedule a few more of them Spring Productions. Don't you think?"

"Actually I've already talked to the Youth Center about going full time over the summer," Jaylon said, throwing the words into the conversation pool. "Then during school I'll run their Saturday Arts Program."

"Oh, boy, Sam will be ecstatic about that," Lexie said with a laugh. "That's all she can talk about is how in two years she'll be in Drama and get to be in your real class."

Camille reached for her glass and took a drink. "A budding thespian right under our noses. Wonder where she gets that."

"Nick," Nick said solidly. "She gets that from Nick."

"Must be Lexie's doing," Camille said with a shake of her head and a teasing grin.

"I never get any credit around here," Nick said, folding his arms in front of himself.

"Ah, poor, baby." Lexie snuggled up to him. "I'll give you some credit."

"Hey, you two, you better watch out or it could be three for three in the baby department," Seth said in warning.

"Three for three?" Jaylon asked in confusion.

"Yep," Seth said, a smile of pride and joy covering his face. "We signed the papers yesterday. Chase Taylor will be joining us in by the end of the summer."

"Oh, Seth, that's great." Jaylon extended his hand to his friend, and then he reached over and hugged Julie. "Congratulations. I'm so happy for you both."

"Yeah, well, all we need now is those two to get busy," Seth said, pointing at Lexie and Nick who were still snuggling in the chair.

"Hey, we did our part. You guys are playing catch-up," Nick said. "Besides at the rate we're going, Jaylon's going to have a whole drama department before long."

"I wouldn't mind," Jaylon said happily. "Maybe one star will come out of that place. Lord knows none of us went very far."

"Oh, hey, saying that," Julie said, puzzled, "do any of you know an Ariana Van...Van..."

"Vandivere?" Jaylon and Camille asked simultaneously.

"Yeah, that's it. Do you know her?"

"Yeah, why?" Camille asked.

"Well, my mom sent me this clipping from New York the other day asking if I'd ever heard of her. She just started this Broadway show that everybody's just going crazy about. The article said she was from Ridgecrest, New York, but I kept forgetting to ask who she was."

Camille's smile spread all the way through her body. "Way to go, Ari." Nick and Lexie looked at her in surprise even as she turned to Jaylon. "You think we could get tickets?"

He smiled at the light in her eyes. "I'll call tomorrow."

Peace draped over her like a long, warm blanket as she settled in next to Jaylon again. Just then, a small boy with feathery brown hair ran up to her. "Mommy, can we swing?"

"Only if Daddy will help you," Camille said as she looked at Jaylon who smiled at his son.

"You got it, Kiddo. Let's go." He untangled himself from Camille as the other fathers followed suit. Mist was in her eyes as Jaylon leaned down and kissed her, and despite the tugging hand of the child, he looked into her eyes solidly. "You take care of yourself. I'll be right back. Okay?"

"I'll miss you the whole time you're gone."

The child's pulls finally won out, and with one quick wink, Jaylon turned to follow him to the swing suspended on the new rope which hung from the old tree limb. Then as the stars overtook the darkness, Camille leaned back and watched as the dream she had held only in her heart materialized before her eyes. Her child, her friends, her husband, and her spirit all combined seamlessly to form God's most perfect pattern for good—the very one He had been leading her to her whole life.

"Thank you, God," she whispered for only Him to hear. "I couldn't have done it without You."

~ The Courage Series ~
The Adventure Begins
2009

Houston's finest have just accepted Jeff Taylor, a recent academy graduate, who's destined to become a "fireman's fireman." However, although Jeff can fight any fire and face any danger, his shy and unassuming personality coupled with the secrets he's holding make connecting with any woman impossible... until strong-willed businesswoman Lisa Matheson enters the picture. Combustible has never been so dangerous to Jeff's heart...

Watch for

To Protect & Serve

From

Staci Stallings

&

Spirit Light Books
www.spiritlightbooks.com

About the Author

A stay-at-home mom with a husband, three kids and a writing addiction on the side, Staci Stallings has five previous Inspirational Romance novels *The Long Way Home, Eternity, Cowboy, Lucky,* and *Dreams by Starlight* and two collections of short stories, *Reflections on Life I and II* in print.

Stallings has also been a featured writer in the "From the Heart" series, in "Chicken Soup to Inspire the Body and Soul," "Soul Matters," "God's Way for Mothers" and in numerous inspirational, spiritual, and family-oriented ezines across the Internet. Although she lives in Amarillo, Texas, and her main career right now is her family, Staci touches many lives across the globe every week with her blog, "Spirit Light Books" at http://www.spiritlightbooks.com.

Read articles, e-books, and previews of Staci's books at:

http://www.stacistallings.com

You'll feel better for the experience!

Also Available from Staci Stallings

THE LONG WAY HOME

City-bred Jaxton Anderson thinks he knows more than the "country hicks" in Kansas ever will. However, one intriguing farm girl, Ami Martin, who is about as welcoming as the thorns on the rosebushes in her garden, and a grandfather Jaxton hasn't seen in years soon convince him that he doesn't have as much figured out as he thought. The harder Jaxton tries, the worse he makes things until a series of crises force him to reevaluate himself and the ideals he has always held to be important in this life.

Winner of the WordWeaving Award for Excellence

ETERNITY

Aaron Foster is in a bind. His fiancée has dumped him and moved out. Then to Aaron's horror, his new roommate, Drew Easton, unwittingly comes home with her. To save Drew's heart, Aaron conspires with his best friend, Harmony Jordan to break them up by setting Drew up with Harmony. Unfortunately for Aaron, the plan works better than he could ever have imagined. Now with the tables turned, Aaron struggles with regret while remaining hopeful that somehow Harmony will come to want him as much as he now realizes he wants her.

REFLECTIONS ON LIFE

Fifty-two stories to encourage you on your journey. This book will compel you to look at each challenge in life as an opportunity to observe a miracle. It will encourage you to allow God to transform your ordinary life into an extraordinary one. It will remind you to reflect on your own life experiences and learn from them.

COWBOY

Cowboy is a grace-filled story about the power of giving everything to God and how a simple act of compassion can change lives forever. Emotional, soothing, and heart-wrenching, Cowboy is infused with the message that no matter who we are and no matter what life has thrown at us, we never have to walk alone.

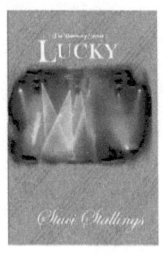